Michael Barrymore was born in Bermondsey, South London, in May 1952. Today he is one of the most popular, versatile and sought-after comedy entertainers in the United Kingdom. He is married to Cheryl, and together they live in London with their West Highland Terrier, Candy.

On television, Michael has hosted ten series of the game show *Strike It Lucky*. He has appeared in three Royal Variety Performances in front of Her Majesty the Queen, topping the bill to universal acclaim in 1993. Most recently, Michael has developed his own unique light entertainment show entitled simply *Barrymore*.

Throughout 1993 and 1994, Michael was presented with numerous awards, including three silver hearts from the Variety Club of Great Britain, and four British Comedy Awards (two of which, for *Barrymore*, were voted on by the British public). Michael is currently ITV Personality of the Year for the third time.

Now having recorded a fourth series of *Barrymore*, Michael is looking forward to the prospect of an international future.

BACK IN BUSINESS

Michael Barrymore

ARROW

Published by Arrow Books in 1995

1 3 5 7 9 10 8 6 4 2

c Michael Barrymore 1995

The right of Michael Barrymore has been asserted under the
Copyright, Designs and Patents Act, 1988 to be identified as
the author of this work

First published in the United Kingdom by Hutchinson

Arrow Books Limited
20 Vauxhall Bridge Road, London, SW1V 2SA

Random House Australia (Pty) Limited
20 Alfred Street, Milsons Point, Sydney,
New South Wales 2061, Australia

Random House New Zealand Limited
18 Poland Road, Glenfield
Auckland 10, New Zealand

Random House, South Africa (Pty) Limited
PO Box 337, Bergvlei, South Africa

Random House UK Limited Reg. No. 954009

A CIP catalogue record for this book is available from the
British Library

Papers used by Random House UK Limited are natural,
recyclable products made from wood grown in sustainable forests.
The manufacturing processes conform to the environmental
regulations of the country of origin.

ISBN 0 09 956191 3

Printed and bound in Great Britain by
BPC Paperbacks Ltd,
a member of The British Printing Company Ltd.

To Cheryl

In memory of a man who said the following:

'Look into the eyes of our dog, Candy, and you will always see me.'

Now we can see you both.

Eddie Cocklin (1918–1990)
Kitty Cocklin (1921–1995)

CONTENTS

ACKNOWLEDGEMENTS

My thanks must be recorded to:

Austin Tate, my psychiatrist, for always understanding me;

Father Martin, for giving me faith;

Tim Thompson, for taking on the strange English man;

Bill Cremin, for starting the recovery ball rolling;

Bob Beckett, for sitting with me 'till the small hours (twelfth stepping me);

Norman Murray and Anne Chudleigh, my agents, for having the same belief in *me* as in my career;

Maurice Leonard, for his encouragement;

John Davis, for his strength and humour;

My Personal Assistant, Mark Palmer, for his work beyond the call of duty;

And Paul Sidey, my publisher, for understanding my style of writing!

PROLOGUE

It seems strange to write a prologue after the text has been completed. Six months ago I had no intention of even writing a book. For the most part, this is an account of one month in my life. A month in which I did a long awaited stock take. It is a story of what happened and how I felt.

My usual trick is to observe, soak, sponge-like, and keep things locked away in my mind. It is a mind which until April 1994 had been kept in self-imposed solitary confinement, let out every now and again to be aired, to work, and then put back at my command.

Those who truly loved me, threw endless lifelines as the water deepened. My wife, Cheryl, threw her whole self. A life for a life that wasn't living.

I tried to give myself parole, but every time I put myself on trial, I found myself guilty as charged.

Although these writings are an account of a month in my life, they are actually about my whole life. A life in which at my last-chance, self-staged trial, I was given freedom to go back into myself, into my past, in order to come to terms with the present and start again. To feel how I feel now. At peace with myself, and unhurried.

I have just recorded two parts of my fourth 'Barrymore' series. They have always been a joy to make, but this time they were a pleasure.

At rehearsals we break for a sandwich. Today, cheese, tomato, raw onion and pickle on crusty bread, a packet of crisps and a coke. The frantic, hyper atmosphere of rehearsing slowly loosens up as our bodies tick down to idle, refuelled by our brunch and conversation rather than my Producer, Alan, shouting, '*Again! Concentrate! . . . No! . . .* Step, step, pick up, change, spot, front . . . Turn, and forward . . . *Now get it right!*'

As my friend he asks, mid cheese and onion, 'How are you feeling?'

'*Knackered!*'

'Good! How are you in yourself?'

'Okay.'

'You look so much better now.'

'Is it noticeable?'

'Everyone has said at the studio how well you're looking.'

'I don't remember them ever saying how bad I looked.'

Kevin, the Stage Manager, approaches, 'Alan, there's a call for you.'

'Will you be okay while I take this call?'

'I think I can manage!'

Phil, our rehearsal pianist, smiles behind his crusty bread. 'So you're better now, are you?'

'Yes, fine, Phil.'

'It sounds from what I've heard, that it was some experience.'

'I've had several. Do you mean the rehab?'

'Yeah. I understand if you don't want to talk about it.'

'No, not at all Phil, it doesn't bother me. In fact I've written a book about the whole experience.'

Phil pauses for a second. 'I bet that's interesting.'

'I don't know, Phil, you tell me!'

Alan returns from his phone call. 'Finished yer sandwich? Come on, let's get this routine right. Play it for me, Phil.'

'I was just talking to Michael about his book.'

'Sod the book, we've got a show to get right!'

Step, step, pick up, change, spot, front . . . Turn and forward . . . Again!

CHAPTER ONE

[Ashley]

Arrival

DAY ONE

Saturday, 23rd April 1994

Nurse checks my temperature and pulse in my bed at six o'clock. Says she's checking my status. My room mate's name is Dave. He says 'Hi! Welcome to detox.'

Why am I in detox? Only four hours earlier the nurse had given me a breathalyser on my arrival that had read zero. The zero made me feel good.

I didn't feel so good about being strip-searched. My whole body screened for any sign of hidden substances. My cases ransacked. Shampoo, hairsprays, confiscated. Anything that could contain alcohol. Who drinks shampoo?

Nurse said I could sleep a bit longer because of late arrival, but Dave says if I don't make breakfast by 7.15, no food. I get up, I've had four hours' sleep, so what!

I thought the rule was to be smart and tidy in here. The other 'patients' are not too bad, although it seems to me that they walk around unashamedly, but they do seem to laugh a lot – about themselves.

At 10.15 a loud hailer gives a list of names to report to the sanatarium for medical aftercare. That's very prison-like. Everyone is known by their first name, and the initial of their second name. I've just wandered through the gardens. The view is stunning. We are atop a hill, overlooking a huge river. Straight ahead of me

3

is a small fishing boat. One guy is on the boat. Knowing my luck, he's taking photos for the press. For once I don't care. I keep thinking of Cheryl. I miss her. But that's my problem. So why am I here? I am here because Cheryl has finally given up on me. It's out of her control. I am out of control.

The first, and only other time I sought help, she said, 'Don't go, we can work this thing out.'

I stared at her and said, 'I have to.'

I should have known then I would end up butter side down. I still feel I'm different to all the others.

My table this first morning is number thirty. Two guys in their thirties greet me. I like them. They take the piss out of the situation the whole time. One is leaving today. He thinks the whole thing sucks. But he's lasted the course, so God knows what he was like when he arrived.

There must be an army training ground nearby. Every now and then a loud bang goes off. I think to myself that the one thing you don't need in a rehab for alcoholics is a large shot every fifteen minutes.

Just met Skip, a Freddie Kruger lookalike. Two of his teeth need filling, another four between them would complete the effect. Everyone says 'Hi!' Skip is really high! He says he'll catch me later. He's really over the cuckoo's nest. I don't know if I'll see him later, or ever again.

Two great women, fully made up. I know they are going to be appearing on a lot of these pages. They are fascinated by me. The accent and my dress style. They know I didn't arrive cheap. One's had three marriages, wears designer glasses, and is covered in gold. Some nice black guys here, very quiet and sit at their own tables, just like in the American prison films.

The big chief, Father Martin, has asked to meet me. Classic. Just how I thought he would be. I'm sure he was in a film with Jimmy Cagney, and a load of kids. He's a little bit greyer now. It's only my first day, so I don't know if I'll see him again, unless he wants to come on my show. We'll see!

They should call this Marlboro country. I've never seen so many cigarettes.

After breakfast, we have to stand in a circle in the dining room, hold hands, say some sort of prayer, and do a funny handshake. It is the first time I've said to myself, 'Oh shit!'. At this point, I feel like putting my hand in my pocket, and giving myself a shake!

If open prison is like this, I'm going to do a bank raid. Still miss Cheryl.

One of the golden girls told me the rooms are bugged. How many times has she been here? I asked her where she gets her nails done.

'At the salon.'

'Which salon?'

'The one in town, right next door to the liquor store, honey!'

When it comes to my turn, which I'm dreading, I'm going to stand up and say, 'I'm Michael. I'm English. We've been alcoholics a lot longer than you have.'

Or if they know the song, 'I'm Michael with a "P". 'Cause Michael with a "P" gets pissed. That's the way you say Minnelli!'

The bad language is part of the communication. But you can't find offence in it.

At least if I don't get a reaction, I'll get a pill out of it.

Just seen a rowing boat pull off with four people. They're on holiday. If not, four inmates have just gone AWOL!

*

5

DAY TWO

Sunday, 24 April 1994

New room mate. Leo. Looks like a sixteen-year-old member of the Partridge Family. Completely screwed up. Now I'm getting really American. Couldn't believe, when he started to talk, how much he knows about Sixties/Seventies rock music – Credence Clearwater Revival, Eric Clapton, etc.

Leo doesn't believe my age. Not sure whether he thinks I'm younger or older. This lad has gone from no talking to singing every Sixties' and Seventies' song. The cells have gone out of his head, but the colour is back in his cheeks. Every time black Keith, who is old enough, remembers the Sixties'/Seventies' bands, Leo sings the songs. Keith reminds me of one of the wide-lapelled, lurexed backing singers. Leo sings like one. Necessity is the mother of invention.

Last night I attended my first AA. It frightened the life out of me. A room full of people from all walks of life. The evening starts with one person at a time saying their name, and their addiction:

'Hi, I'm Bob, and I'm an alcoholic.'

The room chants, 'Hi, Bob!'

'I'm Mary, and I'm an addict.'

'Hi, Mary.'

This continues around the room. I think to myself, 'I'm Michael, and I'm out of here!'

It comes to my turn. I'm shaking. I say, 'I'm Michael. I'm from England, and I'm an alcoholic.'

They all laugh.

I think the accent gave it away.

I think I need to talk to Penny. She seems to know a lot. She never stops talking, and is the self-appointed Ashley tour guide. Round face, round glasses, huge round mouth. She obviously has to keep talking to stop the endless supply of gum from setting. Rose obviously loves pink. Howard has a pit-bull terrier. Conversations about the addicts' dogs are many and often. They all miss their dogs. This is the one thing they can associate with. The speaker at the AA meet tells how he was stoned on the day he got married. He got more stoned after the ceremony, and then carried on mending his Harley Davidson. Penny tells me that the main house here at Ashley was originally owned by a senator. Senator Tydings. This was the house where J.F. Kennedy would arrive by limo; Marilyn Monroe would arrive by helicopter. Penny is staying in Room Eight, the room where they both screwed. I wonder why Marilyn didn't throw herself off the cliff here. It's a thought that crosses a lot of the inmates' minds. Penny tells me she had a lie in. How can you have a lie in when there's nothing to do at night? Iced tea is really popular.

Howard said this morning that the people in this place know more about drugs than any pharmacist. I'm sure a prescription must be printed somewhere among the mass of tattoos that cover his body. Probably between 'kill', and 'death'!

People keep breaking up into twos. Not for sex, which is strictly banned. Typical Catholics. I asked if I could fish in the river. A simple 'no'. They said it used to be allowed, but couples were found down by the river screwing. I just want to cast a rod, not dip it.

Everyone is fascinated with doing an English accent. It makes them laugh. Rose dreams . . . pink dreams?

9.40 am

Another speaker. I'm having trouble understanding what they are saying. Can't decide if it's their accents or they're all stoned. Just found out Alison is bulimic.

7

10.15 am

Subject: *Charlotte*.
Topic: *Faces of Denial*.

This is back to school. Starts with roll call. Seems quite strict. There are people to make sure we behave ourselves, called PSA's. They look like plainclothes police. 'Policeman' Geoff said no families were allowed in the rooms or parking lots, so absolutely no screwing. He reminds us that cups and glasses are being left all over the place. Father Martin is not happy, so Charlotte says. This is not a lady to like on first meeting. Time will tell. She is a reformed alcoholic. Seems very angry. She says her husband says that she was a drunk. She doesn't seem to be reading from a script. She's going on and on about a couple of drinks. She's really converted, and a complete con. I've just noticed that she *is* reading from a script. Even when she lightens up, there is no humour. God knows what she was like when she was drunk. She's talking *at* us. These people can't relate to her. She talks about 'driving the road':

'You know how twisty and turny it was when you arrived here?'

If you came in stoned, how would you know, Charlotte . . . ?

She bellows, *'You people!' 'You addicts!' 'You druggies!'*

She was different. This is like a step back in time. She tells us all drugs have the same effect. Life is a drug. Anger, anger, anger.

I haven't noticed her look at me yet. We've been listening for twenty minutes so far. Her tune is the same. But we are all listening. Maybe she works. I would have thought that she could have warmed up by now. Everything is hell to this woman.

Owen, the old man, must be ninety-three. He's sat at the back. What is he here for? Loneliness? I am only two days in. It will work, but is there another way? She's telling us what we already know. Back to childhood.

She has just turned her back. Howard keeps yawning. I think he means to do it. He's in a slumped position.

She says, 'If you bake a pie, and it tastes awful, why do you keep baking it that way?'

I say because you want to learn how to make it. I may not get sober, but I could end up with a great recipe for pie.

Leo has just run out. Seems very agitated. This is not good for a sixteen-year-old. Howard wants a fix.

Charlotte continues, 'It's eighty degrees outside. It's a great day. Where are you? 'You're in here getting treatment for addiction.'

So why don't we hold the meeting outside on the grass? The message would be the same. The grass would be different.

Todd is a news anchorman. He's concentrating like he's on air. He takes the whole thing just like a newscaster. I think this is his problem.

Dave, a big guy who wants to emigrate to England, is blowing huge bubbles with his gum.

Charlotte's best friend had to die because of addiction. So why did my best mate Eddie have to die? This may be my anger. Who knows?

She says, 'My idea of a date was to go to a bar, and have a drink, and get drunk.'

Howard, who is in front of me, turns around and says, 'So is mine.'

I smile.

In the room are thirty-two men, and fifteen women. Charlotte admits she's not a crier. She's just written on the board in chalk, which I hate. Two words: HONEST. REALISTIC.

9

I look back at the words as she says, 'These are another two things you have to do.'

I can see 'honest', but her writing reads 'honest and ballistic'!!

Geoff the Policeman is back. With a flat black hat, he'd make a great Quaker! Charlotte's been talking for thirty minutes.

Six people have to go to see the doctor. She carries on. I think they're going for their fix. I wish sometimes I was as bad as these people, because I have had nothing. Not even a sleeping tablet. And they are all being dosed up.

She just cracked a gag. It bombed. Like most of the people here. This is a designer nuthouse. I wonder what the profit margin is. Father Martin seems really happy. I ask an inmate if the blood of Christ is real red wine? Must find out.

No black women. Five black men.

A Gene Hackman lookalike has got up, and gone to the loo. I can't see his name tag. Judging by his attitude, it should read, 'Mr Angry'. This guy hates this woman. So why does he always attend? She's losing even the die-hards. Forty-five minutes into the talk, I wish I'd gone to Mass. At least there was a song in it. She doesn't like the word 'graduation'. So what? So we seem just to have her point of view.

Charlotte says, 'Alcoholics get into their cars, and drive into walls.'

What about the people who don't have cars? Do they *walk* into walls?

Mr Angry is back. I'm not sure whether Father Martin is head of all this, or, the way she talks about him, the Moonies. Now she's selling the film we've got to see. She shouts, 'This is your life!'

Howard shouts, 'Come in your old friend you haven't seen for three days . . . Mary-Juana.'

God, she is hard to listen to. I don't know what the hell I'm here for.

She ends with, 'Get realistic about why you're sitting here.'

After Charlotte

The Sunday papers have arrived. This is a major event. Your name's called, and you're given the paper you ordered. One per nutter. I've kept the receipt. I now know the name of the shop, Kleins Superthrift, the address and the telephone number.

Two days in. And I can find a way to get supplies into this stalag. Maybe it's unfair to call it stalag. Howard said he's been locked in the Penn, and, by comparison, this place is heaven. Even though he hates it. I believe him.

Midday

I feel like I've been up for three days, so it must be time for lunch, and I'm going to read the *New York Times*. Apparently you can't have them after today. Russell told me he keeps pages hidden so he can have something to read over the week. Odd, that. A place that preaches not to hide anything, but makes you do exactly that. So I'm going to hide my one and only Sunday paper. If I could get a mobile phone, I could ring and order some of the things I might find in the classified pages. Like a helicopter.

Meet Frances. Everybody else has. This is definitely from a space in time. She latches on to me. The other girls tell me she sleeps in the bath. Uh-oh! See you later, Frances . . .

Skip is really fed up. A recreation counsellor told him not to spit on the volley pitch. He's been out there for two hours, trying to retrieve it.

Video-time

Geoff the Policeman announces his arrival. 'Some of our patients are missing.' Right statement, wrong film. That's your problem, Geoff.

Howard goes to the bathroom. I think he's writing a letter. I think it reads:

> 'Dear Jim,
>> Could you fix it for me.
>>> Love Howard.'

Don, the man in the video, says he's a pig. We all laugh. Correction, they all laugh. That's all these people want to do – laugh. This place is a real experience.

The sound quality on the video is appalling. It can't cost that much to get the sound right. And why are we watching videos? This is my second. Surely we should have the personal touch. Sheep, sheep, sheep.

But we all listen to anything to distract us. So what's going to distract us when we get out of here?

Just heard that the girls 'snitched' on seriously rich Samantha this morning. When she was told off this morning, she gave a seriously rich reply, 'Ooooh raaarely? These people are sooooh gross!'

Check nails, swish hair, blink, blink.

Don's talking to the other people in the film. Asking questions. They are answering. None of us are. We are not part of it. We are ten minutes into Don's video. Attention still good. I can't see this lasting. I'll give it five–ten minutes, and then people will fidget, sleep, or talk, unless they say something that they haven't been told two thousand times.

Met Tony today. He sat down beside Dale (an unshaven John Denver), Howard and myself after lunch. Very shy. He wants to talk.

'What do you do, Tony?'

'I'm a DJ.'

This gives me a certain familiarity.

'Radio, Tony?'

'No, I like the feel of a live crowd.'

I can't believe this quiet, unassuming man likes the feel of a big crowd.

Todd the newsman is watching intently for the man on the video to hand back to him. He just can't forget he's a TV anchorman.

'*Well, a big thank you to you, Don, for that addiction report. Hope it hit home. It sure did to me. Now let's look at the weather for the rest of the day. Well, it's a great day out there for everyone.*'

Pause.

Then, under his breath, 'But for me, it's real shit!!'

Samantha has just left. I was bang on time, five minutes in!

Just noticed that Todd the anchorman is making a lot of notes. Correction, he's falling asleep. He's nodded off.

He must have been writing, 'Stay awake, you're the intelligent one here!'

Todd, we are all intelligent here!

The gossip last night was that one of the girls screwed two of the black guys, but so far no proof. The only proof I know is 70%.

Another man moves out. Don is still going, on the video. The fidgeting is starting. We are twenty minutes into the video.

Don has just got a laugh. A little light relief. He followed that by saying that some come here strong, and some weak; white, black; intelligent, unintelligent. Well, I can see the strong. The weak are obvious. White is white, and black is black. But all of us are thinking, who's the unintelligent drunk? I think we would all admit to being alcoholic before being the thicko!

There is a noise from Mr Policeman's radio. Everyone turns round. It's better than listening to Don. Even Kate (whom I need to investigate a little), is wearing down. Another laugh, thirty-five minutes into the video. And another. And another. We're on a roll here, Don, and I just said you were a bore.

One of our party shouts out, 'Heard it all before. His act gets better towards the end.'

I think that this Don could have run for President. Senator at least. But the drugs must have got him. One of the black guys is asleep. Mr Angry is enjoying this one.

The moment the act stops, and the point comes back into play, they switch off. The Evangelical Approach.

Apart from not having the one I love here, I must say I'm having the time of my life. It may be too early in the programme to work out why. I think it's just nerves, or are we all free from respectability? Is this the cop-out? How many times do you have to come back here to get straight? Or have we found a way of getting real time to ourselves? So why can't we just say to the ones we love, *I'm going away by myself. I'm just going to laugh and be on my own with all the other people on their own.*'

But no drink, and no drugs. I'm sure my wife should be sitting beside me listening to all this. We are only taking in what we want. Like Jack Daniel's. It's something I take in because I want it. The problem is, he doesn't want me. He has plenty of people who want him, and he's quite happy to love them, he just doesn't want me.

These talks and videos are too long. The only thing I know already, just from my own professional experience, is that less is more. After all, they aren't saying to us less is more, they are saying 'no more'. But they are taking too long to say it.

Less *is* more!

2.00 pm

It's family time. This is right out of the Moonies.

Evening

Vital signs. Annie the nurse is not too happy. I think it's just the photograph. Now I know why I'm in what I call 'Toxic Waste'. My pulse has gone up, and my blood pressure. I'm starting to feel shaky and very sorry for myself. Suddenly this is not so funny.

She has given me two Librium to calm me down. I've spent two days asking everyone, 'Why am I in "Toxic Waste"?'

I felt fine until now, but the other patients said, 'You're still stoned, even though you haven't had a drink for two days.'

I'm writing this chapter despite the beauty of the world outside and, believe me, this place is beautiful, and the sun has shone all day, but I don't feel sunny. Nurse Annie asks me if I'm upset because this is visitors' day. I *know* what it is, of course – the addiction – but it's day two and I'm still sorting through my cases, the two cases that Cheryl my wife packed for me, perfectly, as always, but she's not at this end to unpack them. At five-thirty on this second day I found the leather wallet with my family picture inside: Cheryl and my parents-in-law (who have become my family in life) Kitty and Eddie, and my dog Candy. I asked for that picture, to have with me . . . I feel terrible, it should have been the first thing I took out of the case, the normal me would have, this other me had to find it by accident.

I have been thinking of them for two days and they were there to see all the time – lost in my case, because of my lost mind . . . *I want to talk to them. I want to talk to Eddie so much. I do, but he doesn't answer, he isn't here in body any more.*

I've lost my family, but, like Eddie, one day it will seem like it was only a moment ago that we spoke.

Still Day 2 – Part II

Another video. I haven't listened to one part of the film. It has made me scared. If you have only been on this earth two days, find out that your name is Michael Barrymore, you're forty-one, and you're in a Baltimore Rehabilitation Centre with the cast from *The Living Dead*, in full make-up, you would be scared shitless, too.

To go back to late this afternoon, I was the life and soul of the party. These people, whatever they look like on the outside, are real people. The whole human race is here with me. And I must say that we really are a weird bunch. Everyone here is convinced that everyone else is a complete nutcase, and they have all agreed that the man from England (I think that's me), is here because of a disease of their creation called 'multiple personalities'. They have all told me about a patient called Rene, who, in their opinion, is the biggest nut they have ever had here. Until I came along. Apparently I make him look sane.

This is a worry.

Among other things, which I will endeavour to find out, he insisted on painting all the patches on the lawns green, to match the grass! And this place is sixty-five acres.

Black Keith has left the building. Jennifer the Policewoman has gone after him, and anarchy has set in. We're like a bunch of schoolkids. One of the inmates, Mary, has a sneezing fit, so we are all in fits of laughter. Not that funny. Long video.

Still Sunday Evening – Long Day

Five minutes late for meeting. Had to get Leo up. He's feeling bad. So am I. Tried to sit in my allotted seat. Howard had it already. Jennifer the Policewoman **tells** him to move to his assigned place. As is his style, he mumbled 'Stupid bitch', just for the hell of it. The prison mentality moves on apace.

Our speaker tonight is Paul, a big black guy. This is a narcotics meeting. I thought I was an alcoholic. What does it matter what I think?

Paul has apologised for his nervousness. It's like he's still on something. He started at nine, drinking his dad's beer. He says he wanted to be like everyone else, so presumably everyone is an addict. Five minutes in, one of the women starts to tell him not to drink. I think she's lost her way.

A new patient called Hattie, who's really out of it, has had to leave the room already. She's crying again. Bulimic Alison has gone to help her. As she runs to her assistance, I remember being told that Alison was screwed in the woods by her boyfriend during the family visit. And who kept a lookout while he made her feel happier? His mother. So much for the no-sex rules. But full marks for a family disease.

Owen has done something to his hand. A small thing for such an old man with an even older problem. As far as I can see it's a big enough problem just being here.

Paul, our speaker, finally saw his wife in hospital, on medication. He thought, 'How can I help her, when I'm on medication myself?' He went home and had a drink. This guy is like a black heavyweight boxer. Who could tell him to stop taking tablets and drinking, without being floored? Seems like only himself. He says he can't show feeling, his drink can. This must mean something.

Everyone seems to mention God. I don't know if that is just an expression, or if they really believe. We shall see. I suppose, we will all see. Nerves, nerves.

I bet Paul could do with a drink right now.

The two dogs have arrived.

They really must have a lot of relapses. Howard has just clicked all his fingers right back. I think a nerve has been touched. Maybe it's the black guy talking about kids being shot for no reason. Why do big black guys want to put all their energies into saving young kids? It's a nice trait.

Leo seems to have stayed awake for this one. It looks like hero worship. All kids love big tough guys telling them how it is. Again, just like the Jimmy Cagney film with the street kids.

More sneezing has started. Must be something to do with the drugs. Or the pollen is high. We must get pollen into our rehabilitation.

I feel better now. Must be the two tablets the nurse gave me. And I thought that had all finished. I must make an observation at this point. *If you have no addiction, and you were to attend and listen to these people's horrific stories, I would defy you not to cry the whole evening. If you could last the whole evening.* But you're probably not an addict, and so you wouldn't know why these people don't show emotion. Not that you can see. Weird, just weird.

More sneezing. I'm sure all those who had visitors today are the sneezers.

Too long, yet again.

These people haven't had the shit scared out of them. Their life has just gone. I feel like I'm entering the twilight zone. Who knows how long this series will last? Howard can't hear the black man. Again, all this money and a shit sound system. What is the point?

I think back to seeing Charlotte, desperate to put a cigarette in her mouth at the end of her lecture. So desperate, she turned around and smoked the chalk. Either that or she was really quick on the cocaine.

The last meeting of the day closes. Time to get to know more people. Time to work out where I fit in all this. DJ Tony from Virginia, a pharmacist's son, is very agitated. A deal is going down at this very moment, and he's not there to collect. Skip has started to speak in a language which we can all understand. His Freddie Kruger voice has receded. I'm doing time, but this is a nice prison. John, the camp ex-Benedictine monk, has spoken. I get to hear Leo string together more than five words. My God! And thank God I woke him up!

We have all given each other the compulsory hug. I get to hug Howard. This guy did nine years for shooting, and not up his arm. With a gun. Things are really hotting up.

Night

Another policeman has arrived. Gerry. He tells Kelly, a downtown table-top dancer, to take her feet off the table. Leo tells me his last trip before he came in was with a friend. They drank two bottles of vodka, smoked pot, and some heroin. His friend's parents had a full-sized chicken costume, and a full-sized rabbit outfit in their loft. Leo said that as the drugs hit, they dressed as a chicken and a rabbit. His head felt eight feet high. He repeatedly smashed the top of his rabbit's head to lower it down to normal rabbit size. They both drove down to the local 7-Eleven, the chicken driving, and the rabbit navigating. They ran around the 7-Eleven, shopping frantically, the chicken clearing all the shelves whilst squawking, followed by the rabbit, screaming at the customers, 'Naaaaaaaa, what's up with you's, Docs?'

Leo thought it was hilarious. The memory makes him convulse. It's infectious. I laugh.

Then the reality. It ain't so funny.

Lights out.

STEP ONE

———————— • ————————

*We admitted we were powerless over alcohol – that our lives had
become unmanageable.*

CHAPTER TWO

Monday, 25 April

DAY THREE

6.00 am

Geoff the Policeman has told me to go somewhere and get some books. Hope they're a good read. Leo is with me. He has to get some, too. Howard is talking about robbing the drug store. Apparently he used to do them with his wife, and a gun. Leo is much better. So am I. He is becoming normal, whatever that is. It's only day three.

7.30 am

Just been told we've got morning reflections, so the coke-takers must still have their mirrors!

Skip is better. Looks totally different. I must get his notes from his book. They make funny reading, depending on your sense of humour. Tony is about the same. Keeps himself smart, though some are really letting themselves go. Strange when you think how strict they are here. Chris, the blond prison-transfer, never says a word. He has a fresh look. Fresh from prison.

Howard goes to the local town every day, under escort. He gets his methadone down there.

Hattie has started on me. She said she was waiting in her room for me last night. Noodle soup has gone missing. We have a

Jewish guy just come in. Rose is fully made up. She has a thread hanging off her skirt.

I have been told that Patricia Denney is the Family Counsellor. Dale told me she will counsel my wife. I don't remember saying in my marriage vows, 'all my worldly goods, and a share of my counsellors.' We are now checking the list of our day's duties. It's eight o'clock. Mass is optional. Well, well. A choice in this place. I'm probably missing something.

Hattie says, 'Why am I not on the new admissions?'

Gerry says, 'Because you've been here a week.'

'Have I been asleep for a week?'

This lady came in, taking three hundred milligrams of Valium a day. I didn't think you could wake up from that. Hattie still owns the farm, which paid for her addiction.

Penny wants to know if she is in my book. I don't see why not. She has three dogs. Here's the love of dogs again. Her dogs attack her, but she loves them. She has a cockatiel too.

I may have misunderstood. I wouldn't be surprised if she had a cock or two.

Gerry the Policeman, who is God's right-hand man, freaks every time he hears a profanity. This is not the place for him.

Mr Angry woke up with yet another attitude. He tells Tammy at 8.30 am, 'I'm not into this today.'

Since I've been here, he's not been into anything. I want to talk to him. Or do I? He gives me weird looks. It may just be me. He's talking well to Tammy (Patsy Cline). She can't sing 'Crazy', she is. Maybe he would be nicer if one of the girls let him jump them. I don't know. I'll find out.

Penny had a wild experience. She told me her counsellor played the part of her addiction. They gave it a name. SEDUCER??!!**?!

8.45 am – Graduation

Bubble-gum David's graduating today. His mum and dad are here. He's nervous. No surprise. Father Martin sits alone. During the first part of his lecture, he does the two-thirty/tooth-hurty gag. Bad start.

That smile is switched on. He's always injecting humour. Good idea. I could give him some advice. But, hell (very American), I'll keep it for myself!

The parents of those who are graduating look bemused. Why are we here? Their apprehension and fear is clear for all to see. Father Martin tells everyone how the graduation will go. It will be with no razzmatazz. That must be reserved for him. Fear, fear, fear. It's every other word. He hopes it's gone. Father Martin talks well. A funny teacher, in a warm kind of way. I think we could get rid of all the crap videos, and just have this guy. It could work even better, but even a disciple of God cannot be split too many ways.

You get a medallion, he says. It's worth a dollar-and-a-half. This is the most expensive dollar I have ever bought. The exchange rate means I'm fifteen thousand dollars down, plus air fares, taxes, and the dearest part, my life. Oh, and you get a video.

Owen, the old man, is about to speak. He starts well. Six kids, Catholic, booze. He arrived at 8.15. His room mate took the big bed. He'd told everybody that he was an ice-cream salesman. He is, in fact, a lawyer. I got the age wrong, too. He's sixty-three, so the booze really did get to him.

Eric, the black guy, who's totally sold on this whole thing, likes Gerry, the butt kicker. He's started to sing. It's a number he's written himself. Howard is starting to wring his hands. Finish quick, Eric, or you're dead.

Young Jerry is up. His mum, for some reason, is on stage with him. Must know someone in the business. This is the guy I met at table thirty on my first day. He said, 'Welcome to *Groundhog*

Day.' I liked him immediately. He's a classic American college kid. His mother speaks. She is so proud. I feel a bit emotional as I am writing this. Instead of screaming, she is thanking everyone for giving her her son back. I make a note, there aren't that many tears.

Samantha gets up. She says she didn't know that she was graduating today. Surely one of her staff could have graduated for her. No speech. Best Gucci forward, she returns to her seat.

Burt is up. Nice guy. What's he doing here? His wife is beside him. He thanks her. She speaks. She's nice, too. They should succeed. They are really nice.

Russell is up. Suit and tie. Senator Russell. Very gracious. He's spoken at a lot of conventions. This is just another one. Maybe his hardest. They all thank their respective tables. He mentions going home, and his mammie. Typical Senator humour.

Father Martin speaks. He delivers a gag between every graduate. I've got to top this guy. I'm going to write down all his gags, and say them all before him!

Kurt is up. Head banger gone straight. They have all thanked the kitchen staff. I suppose I will find out that when you have no drug or booze crutch, the food is really important. Kurt's wife speaks. Shout, shout!

Bubble-gum's up last. His dad is crying already. He is standing behind his wife. She has decided to be strong. David reads from a prayer book. He speaks fast. I think it feels really slow for his dad. Mum says a word. A tear. Dad says, 'I never speak.'

Pause.

Today David has two friends with him. One of them is an ex-employee of this place.

Father Martin speaks to the first-timers. He talks about a penguin on stained glass as you leave. He tells us that the return of humour is a great thing for a drunk. As I try to work out what the hell he's talking about, I remember I already have humour.

Mae, the big cheese who put this place together, is a recovering alcoholic. From her despair, she got all this together and made a fortune. Good luck to her. Even if she didn't make as much as you're led to believe (fifteen million a year, gross), then still good luck to her. She's here. It's here. And we are all safer.

9.35 am

Nearly time for a cigarette. I've got fifteen minutes to walk across the complex and have a lemonade before Gerry the Policeman kicks my arse for being late. Here we go, into heaven or hell. Let's see.

Time for my first encounter with my counsellor, Tim. It would have been, but my lemonade and cigarette break is interrupted. Father Martin wants to see me in his office.

He shows me his pictures.

He says, 'I count certain people as special.'

I say to myself, 'Or do you treat special people for certain?'

'So, you're in television?'

'Yes, I am.'

'That's great.'

Where is this going?

'You have a great means to spread the word.'

I've only just bleedin' arrived! And Gabriel, the great white agent, has booked a tour for me!

'You're going to benefit from this. Are you a Catholic?'

'Yes.'

'Do you keep up your vows?'

'No.'

But I've got a sneaky feeling they're about to return . . .

'I've got to see my counsellor.'

'Which one?'

'Tim.'

'Oh, great, he's the best.'

Why do I have this feeling that I've been singled out? I must take advantage of this. Everyone else is. Addicts teaching addicts. What a format.

'I'll catch you later, Mikey!'

I smile. And whisper to myself, 'Missing you already!'

I check my arms for wings. None. I'll have to use my legs to get to the group meeting on time.

Gerry reprimands me for being late for my counsellor.

'I was with Father Martin.'

'Just hurry up.'

Just get off my back, Gerry.

10.15 am – Group Counselling with Tim

I try to clear my head, and work out what I am going to tell this lot. It won't be that hard, and then I'll be out of here. They will realise it's all been a mistake. They've got the wrong man. I can see Joan Crawford in one of her films, waiting for the phone to ring before she is executed. It did ring, but too late. I remind myself that this is '94. We have satellite. Poor Joan was born in a time of bad connections.

'Hi, I'm Tim Thompson.'

I do what everyone else does. I realise that this guy, who is going to save my soul, has actually been to the real hell. How can any of us have a problem, when you consider that he bears the scars of a fire? Scars that you only ever witness in a horror film. This is no make-up artist's creation. This is real. It actually makes you forget what you're here for. You wonder if this is part of the master plan to your recovery.

Then he speaks.

'I'm your counsellor. These people here will be your family

for the next four weeks. Who would like to tell Michael what happens here, and what we are all about?"

Silence.

They study me.

I've never sat so still.

'This is Sarah, Louise, Kelly, Tammy, Rene, Skip, Todd.'

The newsman begins, 'My name is Todd, and I'm an addict.'

He tells me how he got here, and the rules about group confidentiality. It is of the utmost importance that what you say here stays in this room. You are encouraged to open up, as are the others, and no cross-talking whilst anyone is speaking. No passing sweets, and wait until someone finishes before speaking. You get out what you put in. Honesty is best.

'We centre in every day by a few seconds' silence. Only go to the loo if you really have to.'

Tim tells us in his best Jimmy Stewart voice that these are the basic rules. I can't see the scars now. The person, not the tragedy, is talking.

'Tell us how you got here, a little about yourself.'

'My name is Michael. I think I'm an alcoholic. I'm not sure. I can't cope with my own time. With me. I'm fine when I work. I work in television. I present a programme.'

They are all staring at me. The room is getting smaller, and I feel like I'm giving the opening address in the trial of my life. The jury are all head cases. What chance have I got? I can't stop blinking.

'A man called Bob was talking to me on the deck which overlooks the sea in Palm Beach. He had asked to talk to me alone. It was 3.30 in the middle of the night, and he said I should come here. I was disorientated. I must have played up again. You see, I can't say much, it's different for me. No one knows I'm here. What would everyone say back home? How will the papers take it?'

My face is flooded.

No one reacts.

I must be the only one who can see the end of this tragic film. But they all have their own. This one is tailor-made for me.

Tim interjects, 'Fuck 'em!'

'What?'

'Fuck 'em! Don't say I said it. What do you think? Do you think you need to be here?'

Somebody does. And I'm here. I'll give a logical answer.

'Yes.'

'We're glad to have you.'

In turn they all welcome me to the group. Maybe this is a bad dream after all. Maybe Tim really is Jimmy Stewart, and this is a debrief for another mission over Germany in our B52 bomber. At last I am in films!

I cry.

Tammy, to my left, gives me a reassuring tap on my arm. Todd looks at the floor. Skip looks completely out of it. A tissue is passed.

Sarah tells her story. I can't recall much of the first group. I feel very numb.

At the end, we all stand, arms around each other, and look at the floor. I hope for my sake, and sanity, that 'ring-a-ring-a-roses' is not the next part of therapy. Tim says, 'Good group.'

I say to myself, 'Good God!'

Lunch.

Primary Meeting – 2.30 pm

This is a whole new ball game. I think this one knows what he's talking about.

Recovery Process: 'One drink, and you're back to square one.'

The rabbi has just walked in. He's arrived five minutes into the meeting. What's a nice Jewish boy like him doing in a place like this? We could be in for a mass barmitzvah: 'Hava Nagilla, too much tequila!' I thought he would have left.

This speaker is good. It is the best meeting so far. Kirk says that he knew he would end up here ten years ago when he was with a friend in the woods, drinking Scotch and doing coke. He laughed about it then, and still finds it comical, even now. He laughs. We just listen. He laughs.

Mr Angry likes this. He has spoken. Denial, that is the word. Leo speaks. He's getting good. He asked me when I knew I was an alky. I told him that I knew I had a problem, but I wasn't an alky until the night I said, 'My name is Michael, and I'm an alky.'

This is hard.

I am now in my new home. I hope Leo copes with his new room mate. Mine is Gary. He's going on about fifty-odd. He smokes, thank God!

For the first time, I've got my cases unpacked. If Cheryl saw the creases, she would freak! But in this place, I think an iron is the last thing I'm going to get. At least I'm getting more organised. I have been moved to a wing they call 'Animal House'. It sounds like the sort of place that is right for me. There is a notice on the bed:

> THIS BED HAS BEEN SANITISED FOR THE NEXT ADMISSION.
> PLEASE DO NOT SIT, LIE DOWN, OR PUT ANY OF YOUR PERSONAL BELONGINGS ON IT.
> YOUR COOPERATION WILL BE GREATLY APPRECIATED.
> THANK YOU.

This is 'My Kind Of Open Prison'!

It's been a bit of a tearful day. I have my family picture in place. I have just found a small diary that Cheryl put in my case. I flicked through, and my birthday is marked. May 4th, and it's going to be in here. Welcome to forty-two, schmuck!

Hattie has started to rely on me. She's Bette Midler on acid. She bought me a little sticker for my ID badge. It reads, 'Do It Sober'. Only a complete stonehead could do that. She cries and cries. It's pathetic. I try and calm her down. She says that the only man she loved abandoned her because her grandmother would not leave her an inheritance of $300,000 unless he left her.

I thought I was saying the right thing: 'You're worth more than $300,000. Screw him!'

'I did, and he still left!' she says and bursts out crying.

A policeman intervenes. They don't like one crackpot being counselled by another, let alone one from London.

Evening Meal

Time for dinner, 5.20. Believe me, this is the middle of the night here. I can hear the other guys laughing. This is not going to be easy. It's just like being back at school, only this time I'm paying attention.

The laughter has returned, but this time it's making me hyper.

Our table has changed. We now have Rabbi Stephen, Lewis (no job description), and Rene. No way out, this is the man I've been told about. It could be good luck or bad luck, depending on how you look at it. At this moment, I am finding it hard to describe him.

He wears glasses, gold-rimmed, and he's from Guatemala. Stormy blue eyes.

'Hello Rene, I'm Michael.'

'Uh . . .'

'I'm Michael.'

I turn to sanity, Dale.

'Is this *the* Rene?'

He nods, without looking at Rene. Howard, the mass murderer, has moved to my left. Lewis is shaking so much it could register 6.4 on the Richter Scale.

Howard speaks to Lewis, 'So Lewis, what do you do?'

'I load lorries. Load and unload them.'

Blockbuster

There isn't much to say at this point, but I'll try. I have time, because another of those boring films is on. A complete waste! They are just bombarding us. I suppose it gets into the brain this way, but at the moment not for me.

I have a thought. If I said maybe . . . no, not maybe . . . I really am ill.

Rene asks me where I'm from.

'London.'

'Oh, you know Marble Arch?'

'Yes, I have a flat in Knightsbridge.'

'Uh . . . ?'

'I said I have a flat in Knightbridge.'

'You know Bond Street?'

'Yes, I have shopped there.'

'The Cumberland Hotel?'

What is this, a tour of the London Underground? He mumbles something else. I can't hold on any longer, I go into a complete fit of laughter. I can't get my face out of the dinner plate for fifteen minutes. Dale goes down. Howard turns away, stifling his laughter, and Shaky Lewis marinades his chicken with iced tea. He can't hold it still to his face. I am surprised I haven't been thrown out of this place, and I am glad.

I must get some more of Rene.

Rene has walked in and walked out. Geoff the Policeman has gone after him. They are having a discussion outside the video hall. I would give anything to listen in . . .

Howard to Lewis.

'What do you load, nitroglycerine?!'

Rene returns, and speaks to me again. I think he finds me to be a similar person. Oh God, they were right, we mirror each other. My guess is that this man is beyond genius. So what is that wall in his mind for? What it is, at the moment, is insanity. This man is not drugged. Well, he is, but that's not the problem. I don't think he should be in Ashley. I really, really hope I'm wrong, but I can't see Rene returning to real life, if indeed he were ever there. As I write this, I feel guilty about my reaction, but it is what is real, and that is what these writings are about.

The video has ended, thank God.

8.00 pm – Another Meeting

Penny reads the prologue. I'm buzzing now, and there is not a drop inside me. You want to get high? Just stay up from 6.00 am until 2 the next day in one of these places. You will be high. Well, so far it works. Cheryl is up on the stage. Not my wife, but an ex-nurse who's messed up.

Hattie is up. I can't believe it, she seems really together. She's reading the twelve traditions.

Gary the stammerer is getting up. He stammers out the twelve steps. We all know how difficult each step is. Imagine what they're like for Gary.

'These are the best twenty-one days of my life.'

This is real street stuff. The food gets a mention again.

'We did it for ourselves.'

Gary is a good man, with a thick, Southern accent (stammer inclusive).

'I can't lose my wife again. I can't lose again. I might not be able to say much, but what I say is real. Men of few words can't afford errors.'

Great speech!

Messed-up Cheryl is leaving soon. She gives a speech, which is also messed up. Hattie completely understands her. Obviously, if you take three hundred milligrams of Valium a day, you comprehend the incomprehensible.

As messed-up Cheryl finishes, Hattie bursts out crying. The speaker didn't show, so we are having a round robin. Kate speaks. This is a real party, but without the booze. Half have gone off to another meeting. Kate is leaving. Found out nothing about her. She came, she saw, she conquered, she pissed off. Alice, a party freak, goes girlish. Without a speaker, this is the first time everyone speaking gets attention. It's ironic. The two labradors haven't appeared on the night a speaker failed to turn up.

I look around, and think that we should marry the women here. If it didn't work out, at least we'd have something in common.

I start to wonder why I am the only addict here from a country of 55 million people. The others must think that England only has one addict. Me.

At the end of the meeting, we all link hands, say the serenity prayer, and shake our hands up and down. Half of these people are cured, and they're still shaking!

Geoff the Policeman, an ex-addict, tells me he used to earn $45,000. Now he gets $17,000. But he's sober. And happy. Take the tax from $45,000, plus the cost of drugs. He's probably better off.

It's late.

I'm going to have thirteen steps built in a penthouse, leading to the roof of a 200-foot building. On each step, I'm going to have written the 'Twelve Steps'. Then, anyone can walk up to the top, read the twelfth step, and enjoy the view. On the thirteenth, after which you will fall to certain death, I am going to have written: 'If you can take this step, and survive without even a scratch, drink as much as you like.'

Over to Todd for a news update.

His wife has presented him with a legal contract that he has to sign before leaving Ashley. If he drinks again, she automatically leaves, and keeps everything. No signature, no marriage. Earlier he received news of his mother's death.

That was Teetotalling Todd, fighting for survival, in Ashley, Maryland, for CNN.

Lights out.

STEP TWO

———————— • ————————

Came to believe that a power greater than ourselves
could restore us to sanity.

CHAPTER THREE

Tuesday, 26 April

DAY FOUR

6.00 am

Gerry the Policeman, wakes me at 5.50 am.

'You've got to go for a blood test. Get up.'

What have I done to this man?

I get myself to the nurses' station.

'Wait in the queue,' says Nurse Devile.

Todd asked me where you get your blood tested. I showed him. He walked straight in. I was before him. Never mind, I'll go next. I return to my seat. Three people are now in front of me. I'm sure Gerry has something to do with this. I look towards the end of the corridor. I can see Leo talking to Hattie. What's going on? This distracts me, and another two jump the blood queue. I am now forty minutes behind.

Gerry says, 'Come on, you'll be late for morning reflections.'

I don't believe this place!

Leonard Dahl, the George Bush lookalike (concierge to the Godfather-Martin), reflects. Very stylised. This one has a personal microphone, and Armani-style suits. With a mixture of dramatic hand gestures, he says, 'Don't make any more of this programme than what there is. Keep it simple. It is simple. Simplistic people drive down roads dead straight. They don't turn left or right.'

Addicts look for rows, then skid.

I have dressed myself in black jeans, black shoes, black polo shirt, and a hint of white T-shirt through the collar. I rewrite my name plate 'Father Ashley'. I welcome the new inmates as Father Ashley, and tell them in my best American accent to enjoy themselves, and that we shall look after them. I can feel Gerry's eyes boring into my back. Time to move.

8.10 am

Went to Mass.

The altar has one of the best backdrops, the 'Cheap-Speak' River. Mass is worth it for the view. Jerry, the all-American boy, is to my left as Father Martin recites mass.

Jerry whispers, 'Bald eagle.'

I think that it's a cute nickname for Father Martin until I look up, and see a real bald eagle swoop past. Wow!

Father Martin says he drank from twenty-four to thirty-four. Shorts, he says.

There's quite a few new inmates. I'm now one of the old school. Policeman Gerry is winding me up. I think he's got a problem, not just with booze, but with keeping his job. Father Martin says he's been sober longer than some of us have been on this earth. I'm sure there are some here who have been stoned longer than the creation of this earth. If you came to this place, and your name was Adam, you'd have been drinking and drugging for a long time.

The new ones look confused, frightened. I must be seeing myself in these people. It's day four, and I know there is an alternative to drinking. I hope there is an alternative to drinking. I am damn sure there is an alternative to my chosen career. That's a great feeling, knowing that there is an option.

*

Father Martin says he had a boy (careful now), who, because of his drinking, got thrown out of a football stadium for being rowdy. He adds, 'That's a pretty hard thing to do.'

My God, he hasn't seen British football. He would be saving souls for years, just from one match!

The old drinking gags continue to pour out. It's still evangelism, with Catholicism, with gags, and mine's with coke!

Gerry the Policeman reads out a list of places certain people have to be at certain times. I've got two. Nine o'clock, Noble Hall, Finance. Time to pay for my sins. And two o'clock, meeting with my personal counsellor, Tim. This is going to be another first, this place is full of firsts . . . but here it can only be quenched with soda. All sugarless.

Father Martin has brought kids into the equation. That'll go straight to the heart. He says, 'Ask your kids about your drinking.'

There is the stab. Right in the heart. I know the reason he's using children. I don't have kids, but I know the reason. Guilt.

He tells them, 'You may say "my kids were too young to realise what was happening".'

He tells of a case of a five-year-old who was asked to draw a picture of a typical day in his life at home. He drew a picture of a martini.

Another woman has just arrived. Don't know her name. I introduce myself as 'Father Ashley'. 'How are you?'

In a broken voice, she says, 'I'm floating.'

In my best Jimmy Stewart, I tell her, 'You're not allowed to go down by the water. Hell, there's trouble down there.'

She says, 'Sorry, Father.'

I could get a taste for this priest business.

I was told to go to Finance at nine o'clock. It is now 9.25 am. I'm going to get in trouble, because of Father Martin. He's still going. You may have noticed that I haven't chronicled his sermon verbatim. I suggest that if you want to hear all of his lectures, you start drinking right now.

Lewis is here. The Elvis shake he had last night has settled a little. He is transfixed by Father Martin. This place should be called 'The Land of the Rising Yawn'. You can't help it. This yawn goes on all day, and all night, every day. Not particularly because it's boring, it depends on your choice of meet. Some bits are great. Some are really boring. Whatever, we all yawn. The rabbi is still here. I am amazed. He even laughed at the table last night. That was a real buzz for me. I thought he would be uncrackable. My agents, one of whom is Jewish, would be proud of me. Even prouder, knowing him, that I'm here at all.

9.35 am

Ray, my room mate, shows me the quick route to our room. He's an airline pilot. More later. Got to go somewhere.

10.25 am

Group.
    Tim.
    'Before we start today's group, any questions?'
    Rene's hand has been in the air since we started.
    'Yes, Rene.'

'I want to die.'
'Any other questions?'

Skip apologises for repeating a story that I told in group. He has broken confidentiality. It's just that he thought it was so funny. It had played on his mind. He had to get it off his chest. He dreamed he'd had a trip.

Rene shouts, 'Holidays!'

This is going to be very difficult. Everybody in the room looks everywhere, except at Rene. It's all anyone can do to stop laughing. Tim tells us the blond guy I met at my table has gone down after three days on the outside.

Shit.

I ask why God is included in everything.

Tim explains, 'He's there if you want it. Your higher power can be whatever you want. Some people use trees.'

Hum . . .

Rene's hand is still in the air. Todd tells his story. He was born in Panama. Wall-to-wall liquor is cheap in Panama.

Rene interrupts, 'Cocaine is cheap.'

Kelly tells us that she was on a binge.

Rene, 'You know what a binge is?'

We all look towards Rene. He starts singing *Lucy in the Sky with Diamonds*.

Tim is losing his patience.

Rene asks Kelly if God is helping her.

'Yes.'

'How do you know?'

Rene is trying to interview her. 'Do you know where tobacco comes from . . . ?'

Silence.

'. . . America!!'

All this money to sort my life out, and I'm a contestant on 'Jeopardy', with an insane host!

Tim asks, 'What are the reasons that you believe in what you do?'

Rene shouts, 'Hope!'

Tim tries to regain control.

Rene, 'Let Kelly speak.'

I can't work out just yet whether Rene is, as I have already said, a genius. Or whatever the complete opposite is!

Kelly tries to continue. 'I'm afraid of . . .'

Rene shouts out, '. . . relapsing!'

Kelly drops her pen. Rene moves to pick it up. She gets the pen. He reseats. He reacts to her every movement. Kelly tries again. 'I'm worried that people will turn on me.'

Rene, 'Don't worry, turn left!'

Kelly says, 'Give me my will.'

Rene, 'Willpower . . . !' He lets out an enormous yawn. He keeps pushing his legs together. I'm sure he has got a hard on, and is getting off looking at Kelly.

Sarah says to Kelly, 'Your mother should get together with my mother.'

Rene, '. . . and mine.'

Tim tells us all to take a day at a time.

Rene, '. . . a second at a time.'

I've been watching this circus, and suddenly have a fear of leaving. I feel secure. I'm only four days old. When I leave here, I'm only going to be a month old, and you wouldn't send a month-old child out into the world without the comfort of his or her own security. Would you?

I have just learned my first lesson. Do not send anything to the laundry. Two of my Armani shirts have come back ruined.

Father Martin Video

Tedious, I'm sure, is the word. Put it this way, if you are not an alcoholic, just four days of this routine would drive you to drink. That's how I feel at the moment. In fact, I feel okay ... considering that today has been a bit traumatic. We had our morning group session, which, with Rene in situ, was hysterical. I don't think I can laugh much more. I think that every day.

So far.

But sure enough, there always seems to be a point that the funny bone gets its dosage. I've just found out that the thirteenth step in this place means going with a woman. Strictly forbidden. Like the fruit. And you can't be that here, either.

But that's crap. Like all of us. Never break rules?

Lunch was fairly tame. I go to my room, and think of my father-in-law, Eddie. And how he would have dealt with this. I remember him so clearly. Telling me how he coped with being a prisoner of war for five years. How I wish he had written every day what happened. Then I would have spent my time reading that, instead of writing this. I decide to take on a prisoner-of-war mentality. Not an idea the people who run this place would be pleased with. But you always do for yourself first, then save other souls.

So, as prisoner Michael P., or my alias, 'Father Ashley', I suggest to Ray my room mate and Dale, who's in the same wing, that we make a kite. I know what you may be thinking. But read the list of things you can't do, or have, in this place. You will see why, when I suggested the kite idea, the thrill, sense of danger and anticipation came over Ray and Dale's faces.

How to Build a Kite

Forget the problem of flying it. Just how to build it. I fell on my feet yet again. And this time not on my arse. I am dry, remember. So is this place. Completely dry of kite-making equipment. How did I fall on my feet? Ray is an airline pilot. So that's the principle of flying covered. God knows what the Principal of this place will say if he sees it in the air. And Dale will help me and Ray put it together.

KITE LIST

Frame – drinking straws.
Kite Material – laundry bags.
String – dental floss.

Location – Rear of maple tree

Watches synchronised. Disguised as a common gardener, I kick leaves. Dale and Ray, disguised as two addicts, approach the tree, heads robotically checking the area. Ray whispers downwind, 'The straws of time fit tight like a socket, drinking away here in my pocket.'

Dale whispers upwind, 'This place we live in is simply a drag. Which one of us is truly the fag? Let it be known I have a laundry bag.'

I whisper, tree-ward, 'I hear you both, but I don't give a toss. Our task is complete, I have dental floss!'

How to keep your kite top secret

1. Check materials:
    (a) Drinking straws (in Ray's possession)
    (b) Laundry bags (in Dale's possession)
    (c) Dental floss (in my possession)
2. Never talk about the project ever again.
3. Remember the thought of making a kite is a buzz higher than ever a kite can reach!

AA Meeting

The tannoy just bellowed out another message.

'All community members wishing to ride to the eight o'clock AA meeting, please meet outside Bantle Hall, at this time.'

You've seen stretch limousines, well, we've got a stretch golf-buggy! So sit on that!

Geoff, the now-newly-named 'bobby' (Dale told me he hates being called a Policeman), is checking that we are in the right seats. They have just moved Howard to sit beside me. That is good news. Ann has just moved in on a stick. She's off the frame. I can't work out if she fell being drunk, or is a spastic. I'll try and find out. She is the woman I found on my first night wandering in the halls of toxic waste. I told her to shout at the ceiling, because the rooms in toxic are bugged.

The rabbi has got up, and told us he is an alcoholic. Howard points to the rabbi's kopel, and whispers to me, 'I'm going to ask him if he's got a propeller to go on top of that!'

It makes me smile.

Wayne and Cathy are the speakers tonight. She says that every time she comes up the drive to Ashley, it reminds her of another trip. I think saying that must remind a lot of people of a trip that, at the time, was much better than the one up to Ashley.

Rene has managed to make this meeting.

During the break before the meeting, he came to our table.

I said, 'Where have you been?'

'Administration.'

'What for?'

'My passport.'

'You've only been back one day. You don't want to leave, do you?'

43

'Yes.'

'Why, have you had enough?'

'Yes.'

'When do you want to go?'

'Tonight.'

'Where?' says Dale, who's sitting with me.

'Guatemala.'

'What, tonight?'

'Yes.'

'I don't think there are any flights to Guatemala tonight.'

Ray, the pilot, confirms this. 'That's right, no direct flight.'

I tell Rene that it's best to stay. So I'm a counsellor now.

'Okay, Michael,' he says.

Dale says, 'Stay and have a laugh, that's what we all do.'

Something must have dropped into the quagmire of Rene's brain. He's still here. Well, in body at least.

Another van-load have gone to an outside AA meeting. I wave them off. They all wave back. I feel sad and happy. Happy that they all waved back, and sad that I'm not going with them. I haven't been here long enough. I suppose, if I went out now, I wouldn't come back.

Every time I think of my family, I can't help but cry. God knows what it's going to be like when I see Cheryl, let alone talk to her. Since I was sent here, my emotions are so extreme. They're the happiest, and the most painful feelings I have ever had.

Rene was absent from this afternoon's group meeting. Tim could not cope with him any more. I wonder how much longer he can cope with me. I was crying about dealing with the press back home. Once again he gave me the full weight of his years of experience as a counsellor. 'Tell them to fuck off.'

*

Howard shows me one of the books that everyone signs, 'The Big Book', as it is affectionately known. As each member leaves, there is a ritual signing. He shows me a message. One part says, 'What you have done has mint so much to me.'

Howard says, 'I wonder if that is spearmint or peppermint?!'

Rene is staring at the ceiling.

The speaker isn't up there.

Wayne is speaking. He tells a story where his partner (who is sitting hostess-like to his left) kept going out every night. Her husband thought she was having an affair. He followed her to AA meetings. He saw his best mate, Wayne. He left her. Wayne married her. They look at each other and smile.

Howard mumbles, 'Pass me the sick bag,' then leans over and adds, 'I think he's speeding.'

I must say, he is speaking rather fast, and without taking a breath. And he is constantly flicking his nose, a cocaine taker's habit. If we are wrong – sorry – if we are right, this is going to be a long night.

We are here to be cured. There is a guy who is telling a terribly sad story, and he is as high as a kite.

Rene seems to like Wayne. If he is interested, he must recognise another tripper.

He is going on and on. Non-stop. And he is getting redder and redder, and to top it all, Howard is snoring. I am starting to get that giggling feeling again. I hope I can contain it. Others are starting to give the knowing look of 'we are sober, and this guy is on some trip'. I hope they laugh. I need some relief. This man is putting me through hell, trying to keep awake. We have all been up since six o'clock. It is now nine in the evening. If I feel like this, what are the more serious cases going through? I wish I had told Rene to get his passport. He's put his treatment back years. Arthur is sitting beside me. He never looks right or left. The man stares dead ahead, eyes motionless. His head bobs like a bird.

Arthur, the cuckoo, thumps the chair with his fist. I can't bear the tension. Anarchy is about to set in. I think there is going to be an AA riot! I'll let you know.

I feel sorry for the young girl who has just arrived from New York. A customs clerk. This is her first AA meet. She will do well to survive this.

They are now, thank God, nearly all asleep. Dale just turned around and confirmed that Wayne's high.

I don't believe this! Road Runner just ran past, and I'm clean as a whistle!

Leo has fallen asleep.

If someone turned off the lights now, he could just carry on talking, and we could all have an early night, sleeping right where we are . . . !

Bubble-gum David has just asked me for my tablet (my book?). He also asked me about the last speaker. I said I thought he was speeding. David said, 'Okay', and wrote down his address.

Lights out.

STEP THREE

•

Made a decision to turn our will and our lives over to the care of God, as we understood Him.

46

CHAPTER FOUR

Wednesday, 27 April

DAY FIVE
5.50 am – Wake Up

Gerry the Policeman must really have it in for me. He's given the call at 5.50 am. Ten minutes of your own time here is precious. I've got to get up anyway, so stuff him. He's done me a favour. Last night, the boys here in Animal House asked me if I would be in the picture they are going to take at sunrise on the porch. This I considered a privilege (as I've only been in the Animal House for two days), and an honour. Hope the picture comes out.

At six o'clock, Gary the stammerer reads out a message of goodbye he wrote the night before. This is heartrending stuff, as he includes my name in his goodbyes. Another honour.

Just before the picture is taken, Ray the pilot is sitting talking, drinking his morning brew. He goes to get up, and his chair slides back. He shouts, 'Hell, I didn't know this thing was on rollers!'

I say quietly to Dale that this was the last thing he said on the flightdeck of the 727 before he came in here!

Breakfast. Fried eggs and bacon. Great! Everyone seems a bit down this morning. Hattie points to my name tag, which is hanging near my crutch, and says, 'Hey everyone, look what I gave him.'

I hold my crutch and say, 'Yeah, thanks a lot!'

It amuses all who hear.

Tall Dave really has got God. Unlike George Bush, he has no microphone. He has a quiet voice. Dale has just told me he thinks Dave is a counsellor. I think he sells insurance. Just an observation.

*

Rene is still spaced out. I saw him at the nurses' station. I was there for my last shot of vitamins, from a nurse I haven't met before. She is about fifty, and a nice lady. She seems concerned with Rene: 'Did you sleep last night, Rene?'

'No.'

'I'll rock you tonight.'

I say, 'Why don't you rock *me*?'

She says, 'You don't need rocking.'

'How do you know?'

'I come in and see you every night.'

She doesn't have a name tag.

'You haven't got a name tag.'

'I'm privileged.'

'Nice to meet you, Privileged!'

I leave.

Judy, a swarthy, sultry, sit-on-my-face-if-you-dare type of a woman, is talking to Rene. Just found out from Dale that she is also from Guatemala: Hmmmm!

8.10 am

Went to Mass. Got to do a deal. One with God, and one with Father Martin. My cell mates reckon I can get a radio. So I've got to trade the fishing for the radio. Also, I was going to say some heroin, not for me, but Howard asked if I could put the stuff in the deal for him. I think that could be a hard bargain to bring off in here. Impossible. But God believes nothing is impossible. Wanna bet? I must find out if the blood of Christ is real red wine, because I could do with getting a trustee job in the small church here.

President Nixon was blessed in the mass, so it was worth going to, to get an update. Whatever day this is, I know that the shamed Nixon was buried. They all seem to like him here, but somehow, as time goes on, you seem to like everyone – 'Never met

A Man I Didn't Like' – the last song I sang on my TV show before I came to Ashley. There *is* someone looking after me.

My Eddie must have got a job as God's accountant and has just done his tax returns. God must be pleased, and asked Eddie what he would like as a bonus – Eddie must have said, 'My son back'.

Praise to the accountant almighty!

8.45 am

Another sermon. Oh, by the way, the bald eagle didn't fly past today. Maybe he's gone to see Nixon off. This is the time to catch up with writing. Howard is upset. His room mate has snitched on him. Apparently, Howard has been doing the godly thing after lights out, making sure that the girls are neatly tucked up in their beds. What a sweet man! Obviously, his room mate is not aware that he is sharing with Charles Manson. He may leave here dry and alive, but he will need more than the twelve steps to keep Howard from hunting him down.

Father Martin gets my attention once again. Deal time. I tell him that I have always put my career before money. Now I'm making a decision. To put myself before my career, and tell everyone, when I get home, where I have been.

Rene is here. He seems much better. I hope he stays. He fascinates me. I turn around. He is right behind me.

In a whisper, I ask him, 'Are you all right?'

He nods.

Dale told me that Rene comes from a wealthy family. I must say I could have guessed. For someone so spaced out, he's always well dressed. His family own a coffee plantation. The lumber rights for the whole of Guatemala. And he sells cars. In fact, the only car sales franchise for the whole of Guatemala. I think it would be an understatement to say that this man is seriously rich . . . and seriously ill.

Tony the DJ seems to be struggling. Every day he works out at the gym, and every day he gets fatter. I think it's depressing him. It depresses half the world. And they're not in here.

I almost wrote, 'I wish you could get stoned out of your brains, just to experience this place. You don't know what you're missing.' But when you realise what you miss outside . . .

Father Martin is just finishing up, and referring to 'you folks at the back'. I think the Russians have arrived.

I've just noticed that two people are fishing in a small boat at the end of the jetty. I say to Ray, 'I thought there was no fishing.'

'Oh, they're real people, it's okay for them.'

Ray has a sinus problem. I ask, 'Do you have an allergy?'

'Yes, the United States.'

9.30 am

At last, for a few minutes, I'm totally alone. I'm sitting on the sun deck. It's early morning, watching the men fishing. Birds are singing. They sound great when you take time to listen. The gardeners are making the place even nicer than it already looks. My mind is empty for the first time. I'm going to leave a space on this page, to have a moment to myself. Why don't you?

10.15 am.

Here we go again. That space is over. I wrote a card to Cheryl. It read:

Noone knows the pain of living with a name. Except you.
Love, M

She will know what it means.

I have to go to something. I think I'll wait till I'm called. I'm getting the hang of this now, which is always a dangerous thing. Also, I have managed to get an iron and an ironing board. That took some sweet talk. Sweet being a Snickers bar. Now I can get smart. Maybe that's one of my problems?

A blue heron has just flown past.

Dale said, 'It's a blue heroin!'

He dreams of it flying right on top of his head, and pecking him with its needle-like beak. What a trip.

A black cat has just passed by me. Things are about to change.

Large Group Meeting

I am late. Thanks, black cat. It's my counsellor, Tim. There are twenty-eight people in attendance. Now I am back at school for real. I hated school, but at least I like this teacher. Great, Rene is here. He is in his forward, interested position. Bud, the old farmer-guy, is sitting to my left, and Chris, the young prison-transfer, to my right. Strange guardian angels.

The rabbi and Rene are sitting together. Israel goes Guatemalan!

Tim says, 'For the first five days here, you are incarcerated.'

Five days, and that's the first time it's been explained. All my other, usual, small group are here. Elvis, Mr Shaky is here. He's cleaned himself up. He's definitely *Wayne's World* – not. Mr Angry is here (Randy). Sorry, twenty-nine people. Alison just came in, fifteen minutes late. That cat must have passed her twice!

Define Your Addictive Self

Todd the newsman gives smart answers. Mr Angry says that these things make him annoyed. Kelly (she's nice), has still got a problem. We have two students sitting in. If they get through this, they're going to need a drink. And when Rene speaks, another one. Skip really speaks well today. I'm proud of him.

Rene speaks. He looks confused. At least he's consistent. He says his name's 'Hell'. Where are we going with this one, Rene? He says he hears voices. Tim smiles at him politely. End of consultation. The rabbi speaks very concisely. Arthur, the cuckoo who has made me feel uneasy from the first day, speaks. Now I know his problem. He tells us all. He has a book that should have been published, which is still sitting on the shelf. And I sit by him every night, writing.

Rene suggested I buy a book, *One Hundred Years of Solitude*, by Gabriel Hesum Marcus (Gabriel Garcia Marquez – I told you Rene was confused!).

'Is it a good book?'

'Yes, very.'

'I'll get it.'

'Are you going to get it?'

'Yes.'

'Could you get me a packet of razors, and a decent bar of soap?'

'What's that got to do with the book?'

'What book?'

'Do you need razors and some soap?'

'Yes, please.'

'I'll get them for you.'

'Okay, Michael.'

His eyes wander into the distance. I wander off to get his toiletries.

Ashley Calling

Tim has just told me that I can speak to Cheryl on the phone, after the group meeting. They all leave the counsellors' office, and I am given the telephone number of the house in Palm Beach, where Cheryl is. My hand is shaking as I press nine-one-four-zero-seven- - - - -.

I hear her voice for the first time, and cry like a lost child in a supermarket. She says, 'Thank God. Are you all right? I love you. Do you know that I love you?'

She breaks my heart, and this is now breaking my heart as I write. But for the first time in my life, after being married for eighteen years, via this thing that has happened to me, I know the reason I married her. I love her beyond the greatest and happiest thing you could singularly think of. And some. So for that alone, I think I know that there is a God. I can't remember feeling so happy and contented as I did on the walk back from the phone call to my room. By the way, after the loving bit, I asked her for shorts, T-shirts, white socks, and pumps. And a bar of chocolate if she could smuggle it inside the clothes parcel. 'Don't worry, they won't find it.' And a cassette player, which is also forbidden.

She said, 'Shouldn't you ask?'

I said, 'I think I play them up enough.'

She said, 'I know.'

'How?'

'They have told me. But you are a model patient, and the inmates there are very fond of you.'

'I have been writing all the time. I have laughed like I never have before. And I have cried like never before.'

'That's what you needed.'

'Leo and Hattie have been thrown out for screwing.'

'I hope you don't.'

'You must be joking. Have you seen Hattie?'

Tim opens the door.

'Come on, get off the phone.'

I said 'I love you' as many times as I could.

'And don't forget my Red Cross parcel!'

One of the happiest moments of my life.

A huge storm wells up. This delights everyone in Animal House. We all stand at the porch like it's firework night. What a thrill. And what a surprise. And surprise number two, the rabbi is still here! And he's loosening up. Burt (nice guy), is leaving soon. He's asking about the Leo/Hattie situation. Apparently due to first-hand news not being reliable, Leo did not screw her. She gave him head. Burt shudders, and says, 'I'd rather fuck pâté. But not the smooth.'

I must buy the book Rene suggested. Somewhere it may explain the complexity of Rene. Or it may be just another book.

I missed telling you much about the afternoon group meeting. Skip wasn't there, but Rene was. One nut in, and a bolt out! Skip has gone missing. Upset that Leo had been held responsible, at sixteen, for letting Hattie suck him. He's not the only one who got upset. It's spread like wildfire.

Evening Meal

Power cut. For a treat we get real coke . . . a . . . cola, and pizzas brought in. And real lemon meringue. We all dive for the coke. Have you ever had the real thing?

Rene sits with us at table thirty. He's happy. He's singing *Lucy in the Sky With Diamonds*, and various Beatles hits at the top of his voice. Encouraged by me.

With the power out, there is a real club atmosphere. I think the people who have just arrived think AA meetings are done in the dark, so that no one can see the other addicts.

Dale lights up.

Shaky Lewis whispers, 'You can't smoke in here.'

Rene screams out, 'Fuck 'em.'

On the way to Bantle Hall there is commotion, Howard seems to be practising Step Twelve of the Kama Sutra. He has his legs entwined snake-like round a tree. It's a great impression of the three-foot-long blue razor snake which is staring straight at him. This is nice for a boy like me, who has never seen a worm longer than an inch, and who is now witnessing a scene from *The Good, The Bad and The Alky*. It's the fang fight at the OK Corral!

Dale whispers to me, 'This is the snake season. They've been crossing the grass for two weeks.'

My heart rate rises. Where the fuck is Tonto when you need him? Cue music.

'Ah-ah-ah-ah-ah . . . Ah Ah Ah!'

The snake blinks. Howard doesn't. Triumphantly, he holds up the blue razor for me to see. This one is not made by Bic; it's nature's own. I look heavenward. Why me, why me?

The power is still down. We have been moved into the dining room. We sit wherever we want and I am beside Rene. Next comes the rabbi, then the now-newly-named Reverend Ray 727.

Big Black Joe has sat himself down to my left.

Rene is really tripping. He thinks, because of the disco-like atmosphere, we are having a party. The rabbi is really coming out of his shell, and tells me he's worried about losing his job.

How do you tell a man of the Jewish faith that he must worry about losing himself before his job?

Rene takes his shoes off. Bare feet. A second later he puts the shoes back on again. He did this earlier on. He must be getting quite well – he now knows where his feet are . . . I've just looked down. He has them on the wrong way round . . . I know it's dark with the power cut, but come on Rene, you can do better than that.

He is listening to our speaker. Tonight it's Marlene, a well-spoken lady, and he's started the swaying leg movement, another orgasm about to arrive. I wonder who's got the right idea!

There is a new guy, a 'Baywatch'-type character, but without the money. I'm prejudging, but he sat down behind me tonight, and said, 'Hi, I'm Mitch.'

I respond with a nod.

'Are you writing a movie?'

Oh my God, my reputation is preceding me! I know this lot, they will make up any story. My writing relieves some of the boring moments, which can come in waves. But I'm here. I'm still here.

Baywatch Mitch follows his movie question with, 'Do you know The Cure?'

For peace, I say, 'Yes.'

Stupid Baywatch screams out, 'Oh, really, far out!'

He's only just arrived. He's euphoric. He shouts out, 'Hi, everybody, I'm new here. And my name is Mitch.'

Wrong!! He thinks he's on a Universal Studio tour; he's in a movie I'm writing; he's met someone who knows The Cure; and he's cured. He's going to come down with a big bump very soon.

Tim tells of a patient he had. She was eighty-four years old. It was a hard case for him. He wondered if she was worth saving, until her family told him everyone in the family usually made it to ninety-four.

Marlene tells a story of spinning the chamber of a gun, and holding the barrel to her mouth, rather than take another drink. I wonder how long you can last if you carry an addiction and that happens to you. Betty, who has a deep Southern accent, could be the best speaker so far. If she doesn't go on too long. She likes working in the dark. Does she only come to meetings after there is a power cut? Frances has asked to see me. If it's a shag she wants, forget it. I hate withdrawals. And at the moment, I don't want to be withdrawn from this place.

The lights have just come back on. And Reverend Ray shouts out, 'Praise the Lord!'

It's a light relief.

Because the lights have come on, Rene sees the woman clearer. Oh, God, not another handless masturbation! He's got a new trick now. Cracking his fingers. I must get him to stop that. It's eerie. I feel sorry for Betty, the addict (who's speaking). Yes, because of her problem. But mainly because when the lights come back on she is faced with Rene, no more than eight feet straight in front of her. This bothers her. Stephen King would love this scene. Betty talks of a thing called 'The Hollywood Death'. I must check this. She is also doing what a lot do, bringing in family deaths. How do I put this after losing Eddie? I have been here only five days, a mere baby in this sad and sometimes (believe it or not) happy world of the addict. But, as with the drink, you become anaesthetised, immune to hearing about death. Even Rose, who cried at everyone's story for the first few days, has the look we all have that says, 'I have heard so much death. Not seen it, *heard* so much. Plus, day after day of crying for myself, and my own family, means that the only thing I – and everyone else here –want, is humour.' There is something that is in the addict, and if it is not the drug, it has to be another high, that quenches that craving. And believe me, from first-hand experience, this is laughter. Is that sad, or is that life? Until you've tried it, I don't think anybody knows.

Even Benedictine John, the Mr Magoo on speed, has lost attention, and he could be interested in paint drying. Far too serious. Betty's dream was to go on a cruise. It was an AA meeting. Alcoholics Aboard! That's a new one.

She comes out with another. She tells us her nickname in this field is 'mother –'

I thought, 'Surely this fine lady isn't going to say . . .'

She's beaten me to it.

Thank the Lord, it was 'mother superior'!

Thank you, Betty!

Reverend Ray turns to me, and whispers, 'Father Ashley?'

I acknowledge, 'Reverend Ray.'

I've decided I like airline pilots. Very dry. Well, most of the time!

It's all too long again. She is now preaching, and we are over time. Everyone, yet again, is really pissed off. She says, 'I have been sober now for nineteen years.'

We all give a look which says, 'We wish you had been pissed for nineteen years, and we could have had a night off.'

I'm off.

Lights out.

STEP FOUR

•

Made a searching and fearless moral inventory of ourselves.

CHAPTER FIVE

Thursday, 28 April

DAY SIX

6.20 am – Status: Me, Awake. Ray, Asleep.

My first sunrise on my own. Wow! No wonder they made me co-pilot with Reverend Ray Captain 727. It is stunning. You would get up just for this alone. Like screwing, in this place you do it alone!

Captain's log, stardate 6.20 – 28.4.94.

'Sorry, Captain.'

'What is it, Snotty?'

'Something's gone down on our starboard side.'

'Oh shit, man, is Hattie back?!'

As Rastafarian, 'Illogical, Captain.'

'Thank you, Spock, Spick, spack, smack, crack, cocaine.'

Here comes the prison mentality again. You learn more than what you came in with about drugs and how to use them. Howard told me that one of the problems of coming off heroin is that your dick remains permanently hard!

Tony, the DJ, tells me how to mix substances to obtain the perfect high. I'm not sure I want to know.

The books he's read on the subject, means he can now mix the perfect speedball. Methinks a little knowledge . . . !

Penny tells me she hates America. Everybody is stupid. 'They're so stupid here.'

She tells me her car's been in the car park for two weeks, full of cocaine. Who's stupid, Penny?

7.00 am – Breakfast. And Morning Erections!

Nursery rhymes are now brought into play. Jerry, the college kid, whose entire family I have now met, recites a whole batch of bawdy rhymes. Rene joins us. I tell him as a joke that I have three hours' sleep per night. It's actually three-and-a-half.

He doesn't joke. He says, 'I have one-and-a-half.'

'What do you do for the rest of the time, Rene?'

'I just think.'

I refrain from the next question. This is all too sad.

George Bush is back for morning reflections. A lecture, actually. He's pacing to-and-fro. He continues. He tells us that the Russians will be here by ten o'clock tonight. And then, if that isn't frightening enough, he says, 'We are finishing off the making of a video of "Ashley". So if you see any cameras around here in the dining hall, around the grounds, or in any of the group therapy rooms, don't be bothered by this.'

Thanks a lot, George. I've got top security and secrecy surrounding me. Unknown to all. And the only people, apart from all at Ashley, who know I'm here are my family and my agents.

D-Day. I've got to have a word with the big boss, and tell him the idea is *not* to publicise my attendance here!!!

Seems to be quite relaxed this morning, so time to catch up with some chores (and chores in a place like this are a delight) after Cheryl's call, during which she asked me to return the traveller's cheques that I have with me. I must have been a novice to bring three thousand dollars' worth of traveller's cheques to this place. She wants them sent back to the house in Palm Beach. I'm sure she hasn't been cured of her shopping addiction in such a short time!

How to Get Back Large Amounts of Money that Belong to You!

1. Go to the Admissions hall, where you were first admitted (logical, Captain).

   'No, you go to the nursing station.'

   'Thank you.'

2. Walk to nursing station.

   'Have you got my traveller's cheques?'

   'No, not here. They must be over in Admissions.'

   'They said come here.'

   'Oh well, the walk will do you good!'

   That is not what I need. You walk miles in this place.

3. Return to Admissions.

   'Nursing said the traveller's cheques are here.'

   'Oh, really?'

   The lassie with the expensive chassis lowers her glasses.

   'Are you trying to make sure my physical and mental states are in order?'

   The chassis replies, 'No, we're testing your patience, and tolerance.'

   I lower my glasses, 'Oh, I've got plenty of that.'

   A battle of wits could be starting, but I'll do my usual trick in these situations. I'll kill her with kindness. 'I have a mile of patience,' I say with a broad smile. 'Nursing said that my traveller's cheques are here.'

   'Okay. The finance lady isn't here at the moment. It's her day off. Sarah has taken over, but she isn't here at the moment. Come back at 9.45 am, and she'll be here.'

   'I have a meeting in Hallas Hall at 9.45 am.' (You are never, repeat never, late for your meetings. This is the only prison you can get thrown out of for unpunctuality). 'I'll go to the meeting, and come back later. Will that be a solution?'

'That would be just dandy!'
I leave to go and iron my creased shirt.

Hallas Hall, 9.45 am. Meet the Flintstones

Fred Flintstone is giving the lecture today. This guy is fat! And he's a toucher. He tells his story, his experience, and his hand never stops wandering. I'm surprised there's any skin left on his palm. All his examples include women. I suppose, if you're deaf, you can understand his problem.

'You see, my wife,' (rubs woman's shoulder), 'had no life with me,' (rubs back of woman's neck). 'It was hell,' (strokes young girl's leg). 'I wasn't aware,' (wanders down chest), 'that I,' (caresses hair), 'was being,' (smiles at all girls), 'an arsehole.'

All the men, including myself, give a 'we know what your game is' look. I just hope, for his sake, he doesn't go through this routine when Cheryl arrives. Wilma will be Fredless!

Jack (Fred) hates the word 'cute'. I bet he likes cute ass. Cute Jack says he doesn't like foul language. Get real, Jack. He says that after one meeting he told a man that in his speech, when he said the 'f' word, he lost all the women, and half of the men. I know what he means but as I have said at the very beginning of my scribbling, this is an account of the reality of here. The reality from a patient's point of view, not the preacher's!

You can easily cure bad language. You ask them nicely if they would refrain. If not, you smack them in the mouth. I think you've got an idea of what I'm saying. I'll say no more. I'm starting to preach.

I hate preaching.

I perform shows in front of millions of people, every week. I don't use foul language. Some at the very extreme may disagree. We must learn – and I have learnt this even more from this place – to be tolerant of our fellow human beings. But back to the real world.

If you are brought up in the street, you speak street language. If you are brought up in quite a nice place, you speak in quite a nice way. People from a very nice place speak a very nice language. If you come from a really nice wealthy place, you can say what the fuck you like, you should care.

Lewis just got up for the first time. He says, 'Hi, I'm,' he looks at his name tag, 'Lewis!'

A laughter release.

Rene has been taken out of the meet. Hope he's not going.

Do you know what makes all these people equal? Addiction.

11.08 am – Round Three, the Lawyer

Joseph. Alcoholic. Grey hair, sixtyish. American, casual/smart. Light-coloured tan/beige jacket. Mauve/pink shirt. Thin Walter Matthau. He's from the bible belt. Father a coal miner, from a town of three hundred and fifty people. Very religious background.

Still dry. 3.2% beer. Didn't like the taste. This man doesn't swear. He liked what booze did to him. Married at nineteen, she was eighteen. His wife was his backbone. Two kids, going to lawyer's school. Went into business young, started having a few drinks. His turning point was 1975. Wife always knew when he had had enough, and told him. This annoyed him. To stop the nagging he would go to his daughter's house, and have a drink there, before going home.

'You always hurt the one you love.'

Joseph started to become another man. They would just ignore him, he would make business excuses to have a drink. No drink before five, then four, and so on. Until 1985, when he took his young son's sports car, his boy's pride and joy. Off he drove, a fifty-five-year-old man, reliving his young years. He got hit, he was pissed, he got a ticket for going through a red light and he wrecked the car. He didn't have the courage to tell his son. He told his other son.

'What did Peter say when you told him?'

He just said, 'Is Dad okay?'

This reaction filled him with remorse, he took off for three weeks, his family meant everything to him, but booze was between them.

On Thanksgiving Joseph went to the Islands. More drinking. On his return to Miami his wife went cold on him.

At 6.15 am, his daughter-in-law called. 'You are needed at the house.'

He had to go there at nine o'clock. His family and kids are sitting there, and he thought he was going to help someone. His daughter said, 'We are here to help you.'

Joseph gave in, but not without a fight. He was argumentative with her. He thought she was a witch, he was taken off to a rehab (or nuthouse as they were perceived then). The doors were locked to his room (cell). At this point, instead of shame, he got his respect back. After two weeks the doctor told him he had acute alcoholism. He listened. The doctor let him know he wanted Joseph to go to Alcoholics Anonymous. He said, 'Why?'

The doctor told him it was the only answer.

Joseph was nervous, he was still in denial. He said, 'I AM AN ALCOHOLIC.'

He just said it, he didn't admit it. Emotionally he came out broken down. He returned to his life, business as usual. In restaurants he would now say when the drinking question came up, 'I don't think I'll have any today.'

After all, he couldn't tell anyone too important. 'Who am I kidding? They all knew!'

This is the first man I have completely related to. I like him. He's not unlike Eddie's brother, Kenny. The sort of lawyer you would like to have on your side. Joseph had tried a case for a man who spent fourteen months on death row. There because he couldn't remember where he was on the night of the murder, because of booze.

Joseph proved he wasn't guilty, and two weeks later they got the guy who really did it. Now this is 'My Kind of Lawyer', straight out of a film.

I asked him if he would have told his community that he was an alcoholic.

He paused, 'Yes.'

Thank you, it will help me with a decision I have to make.

Midday – Lunch

As I walk to the dining room, Rene is sitting with Gerry the Policeman. Gerry calls me over. Maybe he needs an interpreter. He apologises for an earlier incident. I thought he singled me out at a lecture.

'I wasn't pointing to you, I was looking in your direction.'

He must know through the grapevine that I am the new concierge to the Godfather Martin. Now I have the police in my pocket!

He is now very wary of me.

I have a terrible feeling, I ask tentatively . . . 'Is Rene leaving?'

'Yes.'

Rene looks at me, lost as always. His eyelids flicker for the first time in four days. I now know what sadness is. It's very different from the words you use to describe the loss of a loved one, that's almost indescribable.

Rene strings together a sentence. 'I'm going to miss you, Mike.'

'I'll write to you, Rene. Gerry, can I have the address of where to send Rene a letter?'

'Yes.'

Rene gets up, puts his arms around me and says, 'Thank you, Mike, thank you for making me happy.'

I can't bear this, the full gamut of emotions run in this place. I turn to leave, and sing to myself to stop myself crying . . .

> *'DON'T WALK AWAY, RENE . . .*
> *You won't see me follow you back home . . .'*

1.30 pm

Before group starts, I've managed to catch up with a few chores. The traveller's cheques saga is over, I located them three miles from their original base. A parcel has arrived. It won't be long before this conflict is over if the Red Cross are starting to get through.

The police, who are now playing the part of customs officers, have ripped my parcel to shreds. They found eight Hershey bars. Geoff the bobby says, 'You can't have 'em, Mike. Would you like me to keep them until you leave? Or can I give them to the nurses.'

'Let the nurses have them.'

'That's really kind of you.'

'That's the kind of guy I am.'

He places them behind the reception. 'Do you want to take your parcel now?'

'That's okay, Geoff, I'll pick it up later.'

As I walk away, I hear him say to the receptionist, 'He's a really nice guy.'

I've got five minutes to get to group. Dale is in the hall.

'Stand guard,' I say.

Dale looks bemused.

'Just stand guard.'

I kneel down, check my parcel, turn, pick up three Hershey bars. Dale smiles. I smile. Sorry, Geoff, but needs must . . .

At the group, Kelly tells us she's pre-menstrual. She says she feels so bad she could cry over 'The Price Is Right'!

Skip tells us he's had a letter from his mother. It's very encouraging, and very short. It reads

> Dear Skip,
>   You're really in the shit now.
>   Mom

Skip laughs. Not at the message, just the fact that she's used a whole page. He holds it up pathetically.

After group, I meet George Bush. He asks me how I'm doing. He asks everybody how they're doing. He has a very reassuring manner. It's a good format. Just say everything's going to be fine. Smile. And carry on walking.

Michael the Chef is Speaking

Everyone seems to like Mike the Chef. He's a large chef, nice style, and really nice food. I suppose he's trying to make everyone here as big as he is. And he nearly always succeeds. If they have to make thin people get off the addiction of thinness, then meet the founder of Thin-Anon Michael, the AA Chef.

We are all late for this lecture. Father Martin has left, so when the cat is away . . .

Mike is from an Irish-Catholic background. He says that God created alcohol to keep Ireland from ruling the world. He drank every night with his father and his mother. He started drinking at thirteen, at school. His mate's dad worked for a booze firm. He got beer in half gallons. If Mike liked something, he wanted all of it, or nothing at all. Puts it in a nutshell somewhat. Well for me, anyway. He says he mixed a load of drinks together, made up concoctions. It didn't matter what the taste was, the high was the thing.

Something weird. His school report read exactly the same as mine: 'Michael would do really well if only he would apply himself.'

He was sent to an Italian-Catholic school. The only Irish boy. He was thrown out. Then went around with older boys. The bad older boys.

A few of the people I have talked about have left.

Rene you know.

The rabbi is sticking to it. Must be hell for him. He has my admiration.

Big Dave is off tomorrow. He'll be missed. He's asked me if I can help him get to England. I wonder now what is the land of opportunity for an alcoholic. It must be wherever he can find sobriety.

Burt is leaving. Still a nice guy. Believe me, there are such people. I didn't think they existed. God knows what Burt's like with a drink. Anyone got a mirror? He's not boring, he's not the life and soul of the party. He has a strange balance. I hope he knows that. And he has a nice wife. He loves his dog. He loves his cars. Anyone who loves his wife, his dog and his car, can't be all alcoholic.

Need to find out a bit about the new interns.

Lewis is still doing Elvis, only he decides he's going to do Elvis on milk!

'You can have too much milk, Lewis.'

'Hell, I don't even like milk! But I'm going to have it.'

Dale tells him that he had a friend who overdosed on milk. Lewis's eyes open. 'It got worse. It was one of the saddest sights he had seen. He took to eating grass in the middle of a field with a friend of his milking him all night. He was so creamed, he had to be put down!'

Lewis said, 'I didn't know that. Are you kidding me?'

Dale threw his eyes up to the ceiling. I lean across, and whisper to Dale, 'This will be a hard one to save.'

All human life passes through Ashley.

I have just remembered that Mr Bush said this morning that the Russians are coming at ten o'clock. Two hours and fifty minutes to go. Thank God I've got my loaded sweatshirt on.

There's a new guy, Bob, about fifty-odd, with a pink T-shirt on. Worries me a bit. I don't think he should be part of this. But I keep hearing myself say this. So who's paranoid? But he keeps looking at me. I'll keep you posted.

Now the turnaround is moving apace. I am becoming one of the known and privileged few. It doesn't mean you get any more; it means you get away with a bit more. I've checked my Red Cross parcel. At least Saddam Hussein didn't stop this getting through. It has been opened by the guards. Two bottles of shampoo, my own pen, three cards, two baseball caps, two jumpers, and two pairs of jeans. Where are my shorts and socks? There must be another box. I ask. Answer 'No!' And no, it's not the end of the world. But in here, a card, a letter, anything is like a golden nugget appearing at the bottom of a miner's pan. And I can't phone Cheryl until my counsellor, Tim, lets me. Oh well, it will take me enough time to put these things away. I mean, I will make it take time. *Groundhog Day* (I feel that here, every day is the same).

I wonder, when you get out of here, if you give up not only the drink but talking as well? Because that's all there is to do here. Long way to go yet. The rest of my life. The amount of people who relapse (go back to drinking) in here, almost equals the primaries (new alcoholics).

Whilst writing the last page, I am late for roll call. When my name comes round, my room mate, Reverend Ray, shouts out, 'His flight's delayed!'

Nice Burt has given me an update on Hattie. George Bush received a phone call from her. A threatening phone call. She demanded to be reinstated, saying that giving head to Leo was all a misunderstanding. Bush was not about to make a U-turn. She started to curse him, saying she had a whole bag of cocaine, a bottle of vodka, and an open razor, and that if he didn't let her back in right now, she was going to down the lot, and slit her arms straight up to her armpits. Personally, I thought this could be a vast improvement. The crisis office were listening in the whole time on another phone. They rang 911 (999). And as the police arrived at her house, she had to stick the whole bag of cocaine down the toilet. It's not working, Hattie.

8.03 pm

Another AA meeting. You are supposed to attend ninety of these after this treatment. It's enough, the way I feel at the moment, to send anyone to drink. We have, Dale thinks, two lesbians speaking, one black. I haven't a clue if they are.

For some reason I feel numb at the moment. Now there is only one hour and fifty-five minutes until the Russians arrive. I hope that if they win, we are taken prisoner. It can't be worse. Take no notice of me. My will to behave has gone. Nothing else. I just feel uneasy. Remember that, for years, I've been used to being captain of the ship.

The black woman is Sue. The other lady is Linda. Dale comes close, but Sue gives the shortest speech so far. She gets full marks from me. I don't care what she is.

I'm sure Policewoman Jennifer is on something. How can she be so enthusiastic about every single meeting? And she works here all year round.

There is a card that Cheryl has put in my Red Cross box. I can't work out why the picture is of Robert De Niro. I can't understand what it means. The card reads, '*I love you more for this than any Royal Variety, or anything that you have ever done. Be very brave for me. C.*'

I show my cell mates at the Animal House. You show everything in these conditions. Well, maybe not everything.

I say, 'I can hardly put a picture of Robert De Niro up in my room.' Well, I can. Stuff them. Which I don't want to do, thank you. As they look at it, I realise. Another delayed reaction. I'm not fully treated yet. The last film we saw together starred Robert De Niro, and Jerry Lewis. A great film, which I could do with seeing now. It's called *The King of Comedy*. Cheryl has got style. So have I. Slurp, slurp, slurp.

Despite the De Niro distraction I still feel a bit low. I'm tired, and I wish that alcoholic prat would shut up. It's not her fault; she happens to be here on the day, on the night, I feel like this. Martin Luther could be up there tonight and I wouldn't give a toss about his dreams. This is torture. Have the Russians sent these two as the advance party, to wear us down? Linda has just said something. I'm not too sure what. It sounded like, 'I was having a seizure.'

I feel like I'm dying. My head is now slumped down over my

book. But I am still writing. Please forgive me for whatever I note down in the next seventeen minutes. That's if she finishes on time. If my hand wasn't so numb from writing, I would join it to the other one, and squeeze them both round her neck. Half the room is asleep. Only the sound of the air-conditioning is muddying her monotonous voice. The rabbi has nearly pulled his entire beard out. Now he *has* to stay the course to regrow the beard. Thirteen minutes to the Russians. Please hurry up, take us over! I'm dying here. If Howard had a gun, we would all be dead, thanks to her. This is taking real willpower. God knows what Kelly feels like, with her PMT. I'll just look up from writing – she's dead – lucky girl, free from this. What a sad way to go.

Sue has just told us that her friend said, 'If you need me, just call me.'

Can someone, anyone call her? And while she's on the phone, we can all escape. Not only her, but the Russians whose arrival is only six minutes away.

9.45 pm The Russians

Back in Animal House, correction, fifteen minutes to Russians. I must have got confused. I am having a break. Time for a Howard story. This afternoon, returning from the traveller's cheques saga, Dale and Howard and I met. I think we should be called 'The Three Amigos'. Anyway, Amigo Howard showed me a letter from a friend in prison. He's killed three men. Howard's friend, that is. I haven't asked Howard how many *he's* killed. Here's a paragraph to give you some idea of the contents of the letter.

> God dammit, home dog, you ain't fuckin' with no ordinary guy here. I mean after it's all said and done, I'll be there. I can fight bare handed, or in the square ring. I can hold a tin can in the air

*with a rifle, one of the best snap shooters you've ever seen with a
shotgun. Left- or right-handed. I play poker, like Burt
Maverick. I can shoot pool better than 99.9% of the bosflees here
'bouts. I can crack safes and sell a sweater to the devil, and last
but not least, at the age forty-two, on the August of twenty-three,
I do believe my dick is getting bigger.*

So ends day six.
Lights out.

STEP FIVE

—————— • ——————

*Admitted to God, to ourselves, and to another human being, the
exact nature of our wrongs.*

CHAPTER SIX

Friday, 29 April

DAY SEVEN

5.45 am

Policeman Gerry has brought the wake-up time forward by five minutes. At this rate, in no time at all, it will be 'goodnight', and 'get up'. You slow down as each day goes by. You learn to, it's necessary for survival. One thing I remember from last night is that Frances was talking to Tony and Jim, and was asking why her boyfriend of nine years has given her up. Especially as he told her he loves her. He's only seven years younger, and the last thing he said to her as they took her away screaming was, 'Let's give ourselves eight years to work this thing out.'

I have to get Captain Reverend Ray up. We have a new wake-up system.

'Mother Fucker Two, to Mother Fucker One.'

'Yo!' as he bolts up, and grabs a cigarette, 'What's happening, Bro?'

'It's time to get up, Captain.'

Time, 6.10 am. The Reverend Captain 727, Ray, is on form this morning. He has also received a parcel from his girlfriend. It's a new blue and white sweater. 'Well,' in his Jack Benny style, 'what do you think, Bro?'

'I'm going grunge.'

'Let's both go grunge, Bro!'

We pick up the baseball hats, reverse them, fourteen-year-old street style, and slide on down to the dining hall. We pick up Benedictine John, the Magoo, on the way. He's not too sure he should be part of this. The Reverend Ray and I speak in unison. 'Yo, yo, yo, slide, slide, we talk the talk, and walk the walk.'

I'm forty-one, he's fifty-two. MEN! As we pass Admissions hall, the Rev has another idea. 'I know, let's go moon at the Russians. And welcome those sons-of-a-bitches.'

This is a great way to start the day. And gives a lasting memory to our dorm friends in Animal House, Bubblegum Dave, Kurt, and Nice Burt, as they are leaving today. We just get a good battalion together, and they go and flee the nest. Good luck to them.

Tony, the DJ, is on my left on the patio as I am writing this. I know his sniff, it's distinctive. Morning reflections has just been called. It's a grey morning. We have all reflected so much, if the sun had risen this morning, we could have burned the Russians right out of here.

Diana Ross singing *Reflections* drifts through my head. George Bush tells us the Russians are here. They are tired from flying. He says Rene is somewhere else. I already knew that. He's going to visit him. He tells us today, his dad was a mail man. It's a theme on mail. He tells us of a man who was a letter writer. His point is that phone calls can be inflammatory. The Hattie one certainly was. It probably prompted this speech. By the way, he is twelve feet away from me as I am writing this. He obviously likes me writing. He suggests we all get a piece of paper today, to write a letter to our loved ones, so that in years to come, we can always have something to look at, and a reference in time. You can't with a phone call. Mind you, Skip's mother has sent him another letter. He says, 'Look, I haven't heard from my mother in seven years, and she sends me a whole page with three sentences on it. The rest is blank.'

It reads,

Hello, Skip.
Don't think you're gonna bring your shit
arse problems back to this place.

Love, Mom

8.45 am

Gerry the Policeman is speaking, the big screen is down in Carpenter Hall. I didn't know we had one, and it's day seven. I must pay attention. There is a smart lady I haven't seen before, Miki. Hey, we got us a slide show. She is dressed in DKNY (Donna Karan New York), with a Joan Rivers face. Maybe we are going to be offered some nice products . . . why not treat yourself to this handy fold-away whisky bottle, or this bag of flour-lookalike cocaine holder!!!

Miki is hard-faced to start with. Her hair is cut like Cheryl's. That's the only similarity, I can assure you. She's talking about disease. Baywatch Mitch shouts out, 'They couldn't cure it,' to her question, 'Why do they call it a disease?'

Now we're back into 'JEOPARDY'. Next category . . .

She has just said, 'Is everyone awake?', à la Basil Fawlty. 'Could you at least sit up, and show some interest!'

Who's she kidding?

Arthur, to my right, mumbles under his breath, 'That's your problem.'

This is the very reason I hated school. If your teacher has had a bad day, they take it out on you. She tries a funny, to lighten up. I've got my head down, writing, so, like all the others she thinks I am really interested. I wonder if I will be caught out before this sentence is over.

Arthur just mumbled something else and he's chewing gum.

He doesn't like this woman at all. I think he's got a problem in that department, so this hard bitch better watch out. His words, not mine.

Simon, the apostle, looks exactly the same as he is portrayed in the picture of the Last Supper. Presumably, he is here because he never asked the Lord to change the wine back into water. He has taken to writing in his book. I am sitting behind him. Yes, he's got the idea, he's not taking notes, he's drawing cartoon pictures.

Hold on, she's just said, 'PAY ATTENTION!'

Everyone looks up, they are all now doing what I am doing, except the Pictionary version. They should counsel them with the 'Quick On The Draw' method.

Howard's late as usual. He, like the apostle Simon, is drawing pictures. He's showing them to Alison, who, I can assure you, will be on the booze tomorrow night. She is like the woman who starred in *Bewitched*, and she is well bewitched!

Eva, the German, recognises something in this woman. Eva says she was here seven years ago . . . so it's the return of the Clampets. 'Mother, vot have ve here, Hound Doggy?!!!'

Back to Joan Rivers.

In her speech, which I'm sort of listening to, she has just said as an example, 'I don't like what I am.'

Jim interjects, 'I'm sorry, I didn't quite catch what you said.' 'Pardon me?'

This verbal tennis match needs refereeing. He can't understand her, and she can't understand him, and they're fellow Americans!

Joan goes for an ace. 'I'm sorry, I don't have my glasses on.' False laugh.

What?

Simon and Arthur are struggling with this one. Simon, the apostle, has drawn a whole cartoon strip, and Arthur, who at least seems to have warmed to me, is gripping the edge of his chair. Smiling head, angry body.

She is so vain. I know that's a woman's right, but really this is her job. Every time someone answers she's having to screw up her face, which is such a waste of her face-lift. She has just said, 'PREACH TO YOU.'

Wrong.

The words 'Sports Car' get a reaction. I have noticed people attach a lot of importance to the car. It comes up in every speech so far, and very early on, eg 'I lost my family, my job, my car.' Usually third on the list and sometimes first.

Baywatch Mitch is now the blessed Baywatch Mitch. It's the high pollen season, so a lot of sneezing is going on. After every outburst he's taken to screaming out, 'BLESS YOU!'

I hope she says, 'What would you like to do to me?'

He could answer, 'FUCK YOU!' and get thrown out. He is driving me mad. He now knows what I do for a living, so he tells me he is an artist as well. Ain't that a coincidence! He carves wood. First time I've been likened to a piece of wood! He keeps clicking his fingers and leaning on the back of my chair. He never keeps still. Much more of this and I'm going to run out of pens, they will be straight between his eyes! I know I'm going to be sober, but feel like I'm turning into another person. It is what everyone wants, but a psychopath . . . really!

Black Keith has had a haircut, and shaved his beard. He looks like an ebony carving. That dick, Baywatch, has been chiselling him during the night. Doesn't he know the rules yet? No slouching, no pairing off and no chiselling the black community during the night.

Bob, the Pink Pervert, has got up to go to the loo. Thank God he hasn't looked at me again. Rabbi's here. He's okay. He keeps out of most things for obvious reasons but he's got a good sense of humour. That's the only tool you need to survive this. I said to him this morning, 'Where were you at breakfast?'

These are the only pictures I have of me as a small child. Held by my gambling, alcoholic father, both arm in arm to face the future, and the only two to face the camera!

People who have little or no money always have a picture taken in their best or only clothes. My sister Anne's confirmation. Of what, I'm not sure.

Right: The original 'Spinal Tap'. The band is a story in itself. I am wearing my crushed velvet trousers. They were green, like the guy wearing them.

Above: I actually remember having this taken at St. Joseph's School. It was the first time I felt good. I didn't know why then, but I liked looking into a camera. They don't talk back.

Right: The first time I ever had a group photo. The start of a solo career surrounded by many. *(Butlins)*

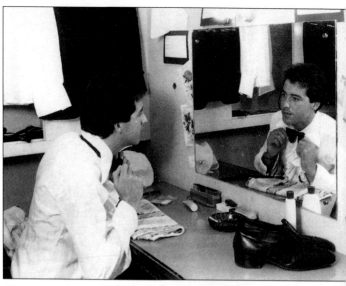

Above: A period in my life when I would do whatever the photographer asked. The frills on the shirt are very funny. They give you that 'just arrived in the business have you?' look.

Right: The worst suit ever made, and at the time, one of the worst acts in the business. A perfect match. *(Fay Horne)*

bove: Still no idea, I decide to pose as 'Marvo the Magician'. Thank God men 'ow up... eventually! *(Dezo Hoffman)*

Above: Here's a rare sight from the early days, I'm actually working! *(LWT)*

Left: As a comedian, I'd make a great cricketer. *(Martin Dawes)*

A shot of Cheryl surrendering, and admitting that a singing career wasn't for her. As good as she was, this wasn't the side of the camera she enjoyed being on.

My first front page. *Evening News* (only because of Cheryl) on the announcement of our marriage. On reflection it looks like a promo for 'Saffire and Steel'.
(Dezo Hoffman)

No work, no money, no home. Not my clothes. You can see why she just had to marry me. The man in the glasses looking over my shoulder is Cheryl's much beloved Grandad, Wal.

Eddie and Kit. All I can do is just look at the picture.

Dumb, stupid question. At least he laughs. We had scrambled eggs and bacon!

Miki has now started to cough violently. If she turns green and her head turns round, I'm off! She's got five minutes left, not of the lecture, of her life. This meeting has gone really fast. There is something I like about her – NOT –

10.15 am

Post has arrived.

It's time for Tim. He seems tense, but that's his problem. I gotta stop worrying about how other people are. His problem isn't mine . . . or is it?

Sarah is speaking. She says, 'I had my own apartment. It wasn't a shit apartment. Someone told me to get married, I can't remember who.'

I'm sure I would remember who suggested that I got married, even if I was as messed up as her.

She is obsessed with her child. The story is bearable until the child comes up. She is scared to death of losing her son. I've known this all along.

I am not feeling very well at all.

Tim, my counsellor, says (and remember this is said in group session, in front of Skip, Kelly, Tammy, and Todd), 'Michael, there has been some concern around the community that you are always writing and that, because of who you are, that you are just here writing a screenplay . . .'

Well, that's straight through the heart. I get very upset . . .

'Oh yes, of course I am.

'I started this plan twenty years ago when I began drinking in a small way. Get married. My savings all go down the pan after being married for six months, because my brother ruins the business that I started, by not paying the debts. I'm made personally bankrupt in 1976 for forty-seven thousand pounds. I don't have a penny. Just married. Everything is taken away from us. No work. Living with my in-laws because we can't afford the money for a flat. Start to do odd jobs here and there to get some cash together. The odd show for little money. Doing warm-up jobs. Struggle to get our lives together, living eventually in a council flat for seven years in not the most sought-after location in the world, but we have each other, thank God (back to religion). For eight years that goes on, my own family blown apart by all the upset. That's without what I went through as a child, which is God knows how many chapters on its own. A small break. I'm now thirty-one, still doing warm-up shows, still in a tiny flat. We have no children, but not by choice. Work, work, stop, work. Two steps forward, three back sometimes. I get the breaks eventually, Cheryl works her butt off to keep it all together. I am her life. My adopted father, Eddie, and mother Kitty support us. Things get really great. We get the breaks. Eddie starts the business side. Success, success. Money, money. Big house, etc, etc. Holidays I've never had before. It's all just great. My own family start to bleed me dry. Whatever I give, it's never the amount they *quite* had in mind. So they go to the papers. The pay's better. Then Eddie dies of cancer, after a battle for two years, in which we are all drained. Still doing the shows. Devastated isn't the word. I don't think it's been invented. We carry on, try to adjust our lives. I throw myself into my work, Cheryl likewise. Then, because of the punishing schedule, I get thinner and thinner. More drinking to keep going. Some of the press, via a rumour (allegedly from a fellow artiste), decide I have AIDS. I'm on the front page of all the tabloid papers. Editorials. Comments. News items. Debates. Everyone's opinions but mine. My family get creative and sell yet another story. The house surrounded. Press going through my dustbins for evidence. Being followed for months. Brewing scandal with no foundation. I get sicker and sicker from the pressure, and work. The topic of showbusiness dinner party conversations. Try a holiday in Key West to go fishing, which I love. No way. At Miami airport, we are besieged by reporters, followed to our holiday destination, holed up in a hotel for a month. I can't describe the lengths to which they went. I am on the verge of a breakdown. Cheryl is going demented, but somehow keeps her head. We can't even go on to the veranda of the hotel. All this is being reported back to England. This carries on, and on, and on, and on, and on. I get to the summer of '93. I'm doing a show every night, a two-and-a-half-hour one-man show, to three thousand people a night. I come off. I can't take any more, and break down, sobbing like a child, because I'm helpless. Everything I've worked for has no point. Even life. So what's a drink when that happens? I'm put into the psychiatric care of Austin Tate, who helps save my mental life at least, if not life. I have a small recovery. The press find me. My family really get into this news business, "Read all about him." The press start again. I am choked. I now have three personal security guards for protection. I've got nine months ahead making my TV show, which I love. My family continue to sell, sell, sell. I don't reply. I never do. Eddie taught me you can always stoop down and pick up nothing. I can't bear it. I come away to get a break at the house in Palm Beach. I am there one week, and two photos appear in the press at home, of me fishing, taken again without permission. I start to get that "here we go again" feeling. I take to Mr Jack Daniels when I like. It's never when he likes.

'And a couple of paranoid addicts complain that I'm not ill, because I laugh a lot.

'Why am I here? Is it because I can't handle a drink? Does that qualify me? Yes. But I have more than one qualification. Three times in my life, I've wanted to die. Three great qualifications.

'*And I've just come here to write a screenplay?*

'There really are some sick mothers here.'

Tim pauses before his reply.

'You must remember, these comments are from a few people who have paranoia. Which means the entire community, including yourself. Just ignore them, and carry on doing what you're doing.'

'Thanks, Tim.'

Break for lunch. At the next lecture, Miki explains the family programme. I'm not sure which bits apply to me. I raise my hand.

'Yes?'

'I need to ask Tim which parts apply to me.'

'Oh.'

'Can I catch Tim before he goes?'

'You will have to hurry. He's taking cocaine at four o'clock.'

Loud laughs.

Her mouth widens east and west. Her eyes head north. Her jaw drops south. 'I mean, he's taking a cocaine class at four o'clock!'

Howard comments, 'Either way, who gives a shit?!'

Jelly Beans Have Arrived

Dale is dishing out dope, or, as it's known in here, jelly beans. Dale is determined to get laid tonight. Paul, another Policeman, has just told us not to put our cigarette butts out in the planters. I also thought that they were ashtrays. Your mind can really wander in places like this.

Howard is happy. He's going wild on the beans. 'Man, these things are so addictive.'

I wonder how you come down from jelly beans? Tic tacs?

Behind me are four Russians. Three addicts, and one interpreter. I hope they turn up at our group meetings. That should be mind-blowing. Jelly beans and Ruskies. What a narcotic combination. Someone's just whispered that it is a narcotics' meeting, and that blonde Christine, the speaker, has been brought down to this place.

I'm finding it hard to describe tonight's speaker, what with the Russians behind me. She's in front. This could be a hard night. She starts by telling us she has a real attitude. She says, in her own words, that she is not very happy at all. And she doesn't mind telling an all-male audience. Tonight, the girls have been taken off to the outside AA meet. She could be my favourite so far. I've got it, Meryl Streep at her finest. One of a family of twelve German-Irish. She says, 'I'll be fine if you pay attention.'

The mumble from behind is weird. The interpreter is translating. Maybe this is what has pissed her off. This feels like a real meet now. This lady deals with cases in prison, to get them to here, Ashley. She, with her husky voice, is the only one so far who has held anybody's attention. She says at eighteen she attempted suicide three times. How is it that when the Russians are here, we get the best speaker? Permed hair, talking as if she is stoned. Just the style. Brown autumn-flowered suit. She's really been through it. When she was stoned, she wandered the streets. It was raining. It felt like bugs running over her body. She uses finger movements to demonstrate. She thought the trees were talking to her. She asked them to stop. She got married. He raped her in the first year. She had three children. She never mentioned the rape to him. In 1980, she found narcotics better than alcohol. It made a dull life into life. In 1983, a new year. No one knew she was a closet user. It's a lonely place to be. You have no one to tell, because you are ashamed. She didn't like shopping. When she had a bad time with the drugs, her excuse was to say she had the flu. She wanted help. She rang all the hospitals. Sorry. Click. Phone down. She went to Alcoholics Anonymous. She didn't know what else to do. She didn't tell anyone she was going. She did the twelve steps. She's been dry for six years. She's clean. Even to date. If she saw someone she knew, she ducked down at meetings. She was doing the right thing, but she wasn't happy. In 1989, her husband beat her up. She went to the liquor store. She bought a bottle of Grand Marnier (brandy), booked into a motel. She drank a whole bottle, but left a little bit at the bottom so that, on discovery, the maids would not think that an alcoholic had been there. She drank again. Then pills. Then drink. Then pills. But it was her husband who died.

Howard whispers, 'She probably frightened him to death.'

She never cleared the rubbish from the house, didn't answer the door, or the phone. She only dressed in the evening, so she didn't look like an addict. She got arrested outside a drug store, picking up drugs. She made up her own prescriptions. She came to Ashley. This disease makes us all grievously ill. Not just the user, but all around. She says she doesn't want to hear any jokes about AA or NA.

Hear, hear. If I weren't such a prat, I wouldn't be sat here.

She says, 'Shit!', then excuses herself to Policeman Paul, the Chief of Police. She's a great speaker, but she needs to soften a little.

I certainly can't, myself, find any of this funny, but I have laughed. You have to. It is the only other thing that is a release, when you feel that need to have a drink or drug. It doesn't matter.

Laughter is free. It's clean. It's addictive. But I don't know many people who die from it. If they have, it must be the greatest way on earth to go.

I write to find a way through all of this, to concentrate the mind, to inform, to be truthful. You can't give an account of a part of your life, and only give part of it. You must say it like it is, which is the message.

Burt's Letter

Skip is very upset that I didn't have my writing book for the earlier meeting. You may have noticed a time gap with no explanation. I let what I said earlier get to me, and let a few people's paranoia get to me. And the network here is faster than the phone. All of them, apart from the paranoids, want me to carry on and write. Skip says, 'Hey, man, where's your book?'

I am slouched over. He is upset that I was upset. And he talks to me like a caring father. He's the same age as me, and he's talking like a father. And this man, who's been to hell, had a fantastic time there, and just, only just, got back, is cheering me up. Giving me encouragement. He's a greater man than many I have met who think they are great. And some. If you read Burt's letter, and listen to Skip, Howard, Captain 727, Dale, Tammy, etc, they follow his sentiments.

> *My dear friend,*
>
> *Please take care of yourself, and your beautiful wife. Please keep up the laughter, because this is the best drug in the world. If you ever get down near the hills of Tennessee, please look us up. Take care of that Bentley, and call me anytime, if I can ever help you out about cars, or anything.*
>
> *Love Burt*

DJ Tony joins in. He says, 'The only thing that has got me through so far, has been you making me laugh.'

So, as my fellow friends would say, 'Stuff you – I'm writing'!

11.50 pm

I've been watching a film. It's a treat, once a week. Some treat. Crap! So bad, I couldn't remember its name when it finished. I came back to bed-base. Captain Ray 727 and Dale are up. Everyone else is asleep. We're all just relaxing. I'm glad this up-and-down day is over. Dale and I are talking, and Bamm! out of the shower jumps the Reverend Ray, shorts on, 'Excuse me, fellows, do you think this is serious?'

He has, around the right side of his waist, the biggest, straightest bruise I have ever seen outside of a car accident. Serious. Dale diagnoses it's a hernia. Paul has come in to check us, and calls for the nurse.

Reverend Ray is obviously worried. He keeps his humour. 'I've only had cracked ribs, in all these flying years. When my neighbour pops his head over and sees this, he'll say, "Is there something up with you?" I'll reply, "No, I just have a syphilitic testicle." Well, my cracked rib was caused by a seven-thousand-foot parachute fall, due to a failed opening. I've got to rest. Goodnight, Gentlemen.'

Lights out.

STEP SIX

We're entirely ready to have God remove all these defects of character.

CHAPTER SEVEN

Saturday, 30 April

DAY EIGHT

Last of the Series

A very grey start to the day. Very grey for Reverend Ray, who, despite the mysterious injury, wakes up cracking gags about his imminent death. For me, not so grey, except my waist is getting harder to cover.

6.50 am

Still grey. I put up the picture of Cheryl, Candy and myself. It really brightens the place up. I can't tell you what it does for me. Do you know how many face muscles you use to smile? And how many to frown? Don't try finding out, just do it.

Reverend Ray says that he would like a song dedicated to him. Benny Hill-style. It will be my pleasure.

I go to breakfast. The Reverend still hasn't seen the doc yet. There is delight as Paul asks if anyone would like to go to Aberdeen at 8.00 on Sunday, to a Protestant church.

Howard says, 'I've never been to no church, but I'll do anything to get out of this place.'

Dale signs up. Elvis too. Howard, myself, and the Reverend Ray. Dale says that if this crowd is going outside to something other than an AA or NA meeting, he's not going to miss it.

However today turns out, the thought of us lot in a new situation is mind-blowing.

Charlotte is back at nine o'clock. Return to that ever popular film, *Groundhog Day*. You soon forget those who have left. Not that I can't remember them, just that, although *Groundhog Day* means the same thing day after day, the only thing that changes, apart from learning more about yourself, is the faces. Eight new interns last night, we are informed. Haven't seen them all yet. A couple of young girls, a young lad, and an older man. No names yet. And four in 'toxic waste'.

Alice came back the other day with her husband, Lew. Very dapper man. He says, 'It's my turn. I'll be in tomorrow.'

I think he's joking, but, sure enough, he's here. I imagine the conversation between Alice and her husband.

'Well, dear, do you want to do the first session, or shall I? You go in, and I'll carry on my addiction for just one more month.'

Only in America, the land of opportunities and family rehab.

Apostle Simon is continuing his pictures. Rabbi (Steven) is still here.

Charlotte has just said, 'Your families, if they are drinkers, will be angry because you don't drink any more.'

Well, I don't know about that. I'm sure she is more qualified. Charlotte gives out a football score from last night. It's only to get the men's attention. It does. They ask for more information. She bellows, 'I don't know any more than that. Don't ask me anything about football. I ain't got no interest in things like that!'

Hey, steady on, Charlotte. Loosen up. Surely even you can't cure the world of football. It's 9.30 here. In Britain, it's 2.30. The only reason I'm thinking of home is that, in five hours' time, the last of my series 'Barrymore' goes on air. I hope everyone enjoys watching it. As I write this, I'm feeling a little sorry for myself.

The last song, 'Never Met A Man I Didn't Like', runs through my head, and I'd like to think of one man I didn't like.

There is, I've found out, one man I don't like now and again. His first name is Michael. His second, Barrymore.

People, all people, have some addiction. If not drugs or alcohol, then golf, etc. You are the one you have to like. If you like you, those who want to will like you, too.

Charlotte reminds me of an English teacher, Miss Bond. I really didn't like her. The feeling was mutual. Until I played the part of Friar Lawrence at school. I was a third former in a sixth-form play. At the end of the show, she came up and congratulated me. I learnt then how to get on the better side of people. It may happen with myself and Charlotte. Who knows? At least her suit (black) is better this week. She likes animals. She ran over a cat once. What is it with addicts and animals? It has to be the two A's. Charlotte has a real problem with men. Everyone in here has a paranoia, including me. Hers is men. Ours is her.

It's recreation day today. No counsellors. Yesterday, Tim asked me to look at a book called *Under the Influence*. I opened it just before I went to sleep last night, and a page fell out. Page 37/38. It talks about rats and mice, some being drinking mice (scientifically, C_{57} BL mice), and others non-drinking mice (the scientific reference for *them* doesn't apply!). Please remember everything I am saying is true, as I see it, and you can check page 37/38 of this book. If it's not there, I am a lost cause. Have you ever seen a stoned mouse come in really late on a Saturday night, go to the fridge, and try to eat a piece of cheese? It's hysterical. Unless you're the unfortunate relatives of the addicted mouse. I'm glad that page fell out. It reminds me of the Monty Python 'Cheese Addict' routine. It was one of my favourites. I didn't ever think, when I first watched that sketch, that I would end up here. And where is here? It's where your life starts again. If you want.

IF YOU WANT.

The Russians aren't here. What sort of routine is this? Isn't it 'all for one, and one for all'? If I ask, I wonder what the answer will be. Why don't I remember the lesson of yesterday, and say, 'That's your problem.' Don't try and change the world when you haven't changed you.

Charlotte has just said, 'I never went to bed once with my husband in twenty years, without a drink, or a pill.'

So let's take a break right there. In part two, it will be your turn. Don't go switching around now.

Cue commercials.

We take a very long commercial break for a ciggy.

. . . and cue Charlotte.

She says, 'It's your turn.'

This is all of us.

'If you don't speak, I will, and it will finish at twelve o'clock. If you do, it's eleven-thirty.'

My hand, and everyone else's, shoots up in the air.

First I called it a prison, now it's become a school, because of the fire and brimstone of Charlotte.

This, and I must give her some credit, but not all, is one of the fastest lecturers.

Benny Hill's 'Ernie the Milkman' song buzzes through my head . . .

CHAAAA–LOTTE, and she gave the fastest lectures in the West!

It gets quite heated, especially after Baywatch Mitch says that because of his addiction, he grabbed hold of his wife, threw her down a flight of thirty steps, walked down, stepped over her into the kitchen and carried on drinking, not bothering to check if she was breathing.

Charlotte turns to the other addicts, 'What is your reaction to that?'

They, I assure you, say nothing, save Frances. She shouts, 'I think he should be locked up!!!!!! . . .'

Hardly any reaction.

It may not be obvious to you, if you don't have a problem. But addicts together cannot be shocked by this. They can cry for themselves and for letting themselves become little more than untrained children again, but they are never shocked. They all have a story to tell, and Baywatch Mitch's is a mere fleabite.

Charlotte says that she doesn't go anywhere with a booze connection. And that if you work at a place where there is booze or drugs, change the situation.

Get real, Charlotte, we're not all the same monkeys. There aren't that many jobs, are there?

Dave, my first room mate, is a bartender, and has been for thirty years. And I myself work in a business that has it all over the place. So three thousand employees at the studio can't have a drink because of me?

'Barrymore's back in the studio.'

'Oh him, he's very dry, isn't he?'

Yes I am, now, but please have a drink. Don't stop because of Charlotte.

Cheryl is coming to have family counselling, and I've just found out that Charlotte is the first person she'll meet!!! It will be interesting to see how Cheryl reacts to her.

1.45 pm – Volleyball

Ever played it?

No, nor me. It's very popular with our firemen, to keep them fit. And very nice it is, too.

I played for two-and-a-half hours with Terry (head of recreation). Very absorbing, like his nappies. Haven't got his story yet. Also in the team were college boy Jerry, and Howard (yes, Manson goes Volley et al). Nothing much happened, except when a couple of cars drove past with visitors, we all played like the entire cast of *One Flew Over the Cuckoo's Nest*, shouting (in a deep southern accent), *'WELCOME TA ASHLEY YE ALL!!! YE HA YE HA.'*

No, we're not nuts, we're all learning how to play again, so we can do it, laugh, have fun, not hurt anyone, and *not* take a drink.

After a wash and brush up I have a reflection of my own. I loved the volleyball, a simple net, a ball, a piece of grass. Easy fun.

Table Thirty – New Face

Jim looks like Juan Carlos, correction, like Cheech from 'Cheech and Chong'. He's from Baltimore. Howard has latched on to him, and we fall right on our feet again. He ends up on our table. We are getting to look more like a rock band on the road than people trying to get well again. He seems quite nice. His eyes look like the bottom of beer glasses after a barmaid has jerked them in a washer. I've never seen spinning eyes before. Every blink they're a different colour. I'll let you know what he says.

I'm just thinking this now – at times it feels like the worst tragedy. I'm sharing a small, nice but small, room. I have a few clothes, a few dollars, and a picture of my family (Cheryl, Candy, Kit and Ed). At the moment it feels like they have all been wiped out, plus everyone I ever knew. As though I never existed, as though the picture is something that . . . *I don't want to think any more.*

I sing to block out thoughts. Elton John's 'Sorry' seems to be the hardest word.

Lights out.

STEP SEVEN

Humbly asked Him to remove our shortcomings.

CHAPTER EIGHT

Sunday, 1 May

DAY NINE

Woke up.

That's a good start.

Look through the window. Manson is staring out to sea. Could be the start of a holocaust. Relax. He's sitting with Dale. I don't think he sleeps. He's still high.

Reverend Ray opens his eyes.

'Hey, that was a hell of a party last night. We must have been really stoned, all of us sitting there staring at a wall for an hour.'

Last night, at Animal House we discussed Charlotte. It is unanimous that she will purge this evil from the whole of the human race. At this rate, it would take her a week. Then cigarettes. So watch out all you cigarette addicts. We all agree she must have a kitty-guilt. Sometime during her drinking days, pre-exorcism, we pictured her on an angry night drinking, full of gas (her, not the car), and singing:

> And now I'm doing a hundred and ten,
> And oh how I hate men.
> Drug, drug.
> And now I'm doing one-two-O
> And oh how I hate men.
> Drug, drug.
> And now I'm doing one-three-O
> And what is that ahead?
> A – CAT – DEAD, DEAD.

At the AA meet, Lewis shouted, 'Hi, I'm Bob and I'm an alcoholic!' Pause. 'No . . . Lewis.'

Still time, boy, still time.

Met Samantha's parents. Rich and very nice. I wonder if they were as nice when they didn't have the daughter problem. It doesn't matter, does it? They are nice. A lot of people would say that we could all be nice if we had money. Not true. I have experienced both ends of the financial spectrum. All money means is that you don't have a money problem. And that's it. The rest is in your feelings.

8.00 am

Oh, the excitement. We are going for a ride to Aberdeen. Our journey should be an experience, with free drinks in first class! This Aberdeen is in Maryland, where the church concert is on. In the end, there are only five going. Me, Dale, a new lad, Ty, Lewis (or Bob, as he knows himself), and Michael (Norman Bates), who sits up front with the driver. Michael has that 'Son of Arthur-the-cuckoo' look. I am excited and frightened. The excitement – the journey. The fear – that Michael is really Anthony Perkins, and I am in a re-run of 'The Return of Norman Bates'. I'm surprised he's coming. Who's going to look after the motel? Wes is driving. He's very easy-going. We move out of the gates. I've never had an experience like it. I feel like a kid from the inner city who has never been to the countryside. I didn't know there was such a wonderful-looking world out there. Every house, all the trees, the ever-changing scenery, like Disney would make-believe for you. I think I must have had this experience before. I went to the countryside as a kid. Yes, I did. But I didn't see anything. It frightened me. Trees, and grass, and nice houses don't frighten a growing kid. No, but it does frighten one who is scared of going back to where he came from.

When I was a kid, I was too frightened to look up.

We pull up fifteen minutes later. All too quick. Wes says we can have a cigarette. 'I'll park the van.'

As he does, I take the opportunity to run across the road and look at the shop. A laundromat. Dale runs to a payphone, quickly rings his mum. The other three cover for us.

Captain's Log, Stardate 1.5.94

Five of us have been beamed down to a strangely quiet place. There is a strange neatness about these beings. They are a smiling, friendly race, even though we are dressed in Ashley-grunge.

Wes calls us to come in. I keep his attention as Dale talks back to the Starship Mother!

Church Interior

The show is great! It starts with *Toccata*, by E. Gigout. The organ player is cooking on gas. Who is playing the part of the pastor? Jimmy Stewart. I have seen the light. The tour through the countryside, the opening number, and now Jimmy Stewart. I am cured. Dale is cured. We can leave now. It's all okay. A week is more than enough to get your act together, and be freed.

Pastor Stewart tells us of an oak tree.

'Waallee, I'll tell ya theyee sure as I'm standing here, saw the faceee of Jaesus.'

Take me home, take me home, I love this! It's going all too

quick. I have to thank the church of Aberdeen for one of the greatest mornings I have ever had.

On our return journey from Stepfordville, we ask Wes if we can have the radio on. He lets us, breaking a rule. Elton John is singing, *Sorry Seems to Be the Hardest Word*. Is someone telling me something? It can't be Eddie, he's busy looking after me. So who put the record on? Weird.

I am not upset at coming back.

Charlotte is back. Jack Nicholson flashes in front of me, 'Honey, I'm Home!'

She's in pink, the same pattern as the first time I saw her. She is telling us how not to fight when we first see our loved ones, because of little things like, 'Why did you allow this to happen to me?' I get the point. Don't listen to the messenger, listen to the message. A lot of people listened to a message, and the messenger was Hitler. That's my point, and the only thing that unites us is an addiction. When we go back to a real world, things happen for real. Hell on earth.

If you can say all that backwards, without hesitation, you should be in here.

I've just been told by Dale that Penny is a nympho. We discussed what sort of clinic you would need to cope with that addiction. Just imagine what it's like weaning them off that one. I'll let you imagine. All you need is a programme of shorter doses, and extremely tight panty hose!

I am at this moment a little anxious. It seems some of them have got relatives coming for the first time. I'm not sure. I know it seems daft, but the Brit is always the last to know. There are a lot of differences in how we Brits speak English, and how the Americans do. For example, we say, 'Bollocks'. They don't use the word. How nice that I can leave a little of my cultured upbringing with my fellows here at Ashley.

The sun is bearing down on the veranda overlooking the sea. It is to the left of Carpenter Hall, where we have most of our general meetings. Charlotte is inside with the relatives who have come for the Sunday two-hour visit. I haven't absolutely confirmed that Cheryl is coming, and somehow I can't. I'm like a child again, waiting to be picked up, and taken home from the nursery school. I sit on the edge of the teak deck, the seas and islands behind me. Is this stage-managed, or what? No, it's just the only spot I can see her before she sees me. I don't want to be standing in front for some reason. We are human beings, and not one of us has worked out exactly what we are, what we do, and why, when in basic human terms, we are born the same. The person who works that one out – well, they won't. So we try to deal with our life pattern. We do what we can to do it right, and then the feelings start. The murderer has a feeling that makes him kill. The drug addict has a feeling that makes him/her take. All addicts have a feeling that makes them booze, kill and pill, whichever gives them a high. Different, and a thrill, and then it makes them ill. Then there is remorse, and regret, and no reason. I have a feeling right now. My eyes fill. They don't run, they just fill. In this perfect setting, I want to run up to her. I have talked myself into a feeling. My heart is rushing. I don't want a drink. I want her back. I don't want to look at the picture beside my too-small bed. I have had my legs smacked for being a bad boy. I want to leave the boy in his black jeans and grey sweatshirt here on the veranda where he can play by the sea. I want to leave that bad boy to play and learn how to play fair, and as I picture myself running up to Cheryl, all the years and feelings will drop away, and by the time I reach her, the man will arrive, hold her tight, turn her round, so that I can see the boy waving at me on the teak-decked veranda.

As all those thoughts rush through my head, the relatives are leaving the hall. My hands are clammy. I wipe them on the jeans. My mouth is dry, as now, writing this. I am transfixed to one spot on the path, covered by falling maple leaves. All shapes and sizes leave the hall. Mums, dads, sisters, brothers, nanas and grand-dads. They seem to be walking so slowly. They must be holding Cheryl up. Or she must be late, because she is talking to Charlotte, or killing her. I don't care as long as she's here.

She's not.

My legs are like lead as I descend the veranda. My eyes fill again. I must be in the nicest-set nightmare ever staged. I walk past the reception. She might be there. I can't believe the ups and downs of my life at this moment. I walk and walk and walk, but she isn't playing hide and seek with me. No one's come to play with me. I return to the boy. Feel sorry for him. His eyes fill, and I actually cry. All I had to do was ask. When will I ever learn? No pain, no gain.

I go to the store and buy some more paper to write on. They still haven't got any whisky in. I don't need it anyway.

I buy Cheryl four cards with various messages on, all with some sort of sorry in them.

I take them to my room and change my clothes.

SCORE TODAY:
Trip to Aberdeen methodist church: 10
Not seeing Cheryl: 0
Not being selfish: 10

I pat myself on the back and play volleyball. We lose. So what? Onwards.

Evening Meet

Chong, it seems, has turned up to see Cheech, or it's the Cuban advance. If war has been declared, the West is well down at the moment.

I pass Chong (his real name is Steve), as I arrive late at the NA. You start to get fearful of missing anything here, such is the addictive nature.

So I pass Chong, and Paul the Policeman is talking to him.

'What's your problem?'

'I ain't staying in there!'

He's just arrived!

'I am an atheist, and I ain't part of all that.'

'All that being one prayer, at the beginning and end.'

Paul fixes a stare, 'Well it's over, so go back in.'

Someone the size of addict Chong does not argue with Paul, he gives in.

So do I.

Inside the meet, Jim (Cheech) shows how together he is. He sits to my right, 'Hey, you're English, I understand.'

'Yes.'

'How are the Beatles doing?'

'That was thirty years ago.'

'Yeah, how are they?'

'Just how long have you been stoned?'

'Oh, I just wondered how they were.'

This guy must be related to Rene.

'Do you know John Lennon is dead?'

'Really, which album is that on?'

At this point, I have to join the others reeling on the floor!

Hank, tonight's speaker, is a Dustin Hoffman type. He precedes every sentence with 'you know'. Curiously, it's very endearing.

Yet another sad story, not so long. He says, 'Tell a lie long enough, they will believe it.'

So do the same with the truth, I tell myself. But where does that leave me? Hoffman says he came home one day to find the wife crying, the kids on his back, trouble at work. He rang his sponsor (a person who is there to share their addictive experience, and to help). He tells him he's in a state. His sponsor replies 'So what? The whole world is in a state.'

They talk for however long, and he gets over it.

He then says, 'That's the way it is for the average person.'

Where does that put me? Or am I being selfish, thinking I'm not the average man? It most definitely is a question.

Lewis has done a classic again. He's jumped in on question time.

'I don't have a question, I just wanna hug another buddy!'

He hugs Hoffman.

Hoffman gives an Oscar-winning performance.

Only Hoffman can portray struck dumb like this.

The scene gives a warm glow to the faces all around, and some glowing words from Howard. 'Dumb Dick.'

Late in the Evening

Policeman Paul comes in to check out the Animal House, and gives us an animal story. His own is bad enough, but the story of his dog George is so far one of the most moving I've heard.

Paul was stoned one night, as usual, when the police, whom he knew very well, informed him that George had been found in a dumpster with his throat cut. Paul's stare intensifies. I thought I loved dogs but this man had a love affair with his. George was his drinking buddy. He was known by everyone in the town; every bar knew George. They would put a stool at the bar for him, set George's drinking bowl down, and pour in a measure of Kahlúa (a Mexican coffee liqueur). George, a kyote/labrador mix, would drink all night and get stoned. He was up to eight or nine drinks. But George would get nasty with a drink, and start getting snappy, and try to bite whoever patted him. Many times Paul would be rung by one of the bars to come and take him home for being a nuisance. He would also pass out at friend's parties, and frequently end up in the back of cars and trucks. Paul says that many times he would have to travel miles to get him back. At home he had his own room and bed, where he would crash out after a drinking binge. Many was the night, Paul recalls (you can see in his face his love for this dog), many was the night he would stagger home with George slumped over his shoulders. He was buried in a wooden coffin in a proper burial place with full Mass. Paul went home, took three guns, fully loaded, walked down to the nearest park, looked up to the sky, took out the guns, and gave George a 'twenty-one gun' salute.

He was arrested.

So what?

Someone who didn't like either Paul or George or both had taken away his buddy . . . *HIS DRINKING BUDDY*.

Dale tells us a story about a friend, who was so messed up with cocaine that when he robbed the pharmacy, he couldn't get his act together to cut the eyes and mouth holes in the plastic bag to put over his head. So he just cut a large round circle. Ran into the pharmacy, with gun in hand, pointed it at the nurse and with his whole face in full view shouted, 'Give me all the drugs, bitch!'

Lights out.

STEP EIGHT

Made a list of all persons we had harmed, and became willing to make amends to them all.

CHAPTER NINE

Monday, 2 May

DAY TEN

Second Graduation Day

> Socrates was a man – I am a man – Therefore I am Socrates.
> *(Any Nut)*

Great sunrise about to come, and you are listening to N.U.T.T.Y. Radio here at Ashley.

Well, today they get to hear my story. I'm just sitting up looking through the window behind my bedstead. The orange ball is rising, saying 'This is your spotlight', to the tune of *Here Comes the Sun*.

Ray wakes and starts the day with a story of a co-pilot of his.

On a flight to Kenya, they landed, went to the hotel and the co-pilot decided to go and get himself laid with a local black whore, after first getting stoned. When he woke up, he realised what he had done, jumped out of bed, grabed his travel bag, pulled out a bottle of Listerene, poured it neat into a glass, shoved his dick into it, and shook it around violently.

Nice start to the day, Cap'n.

Up, and on to Graduation yet again. So who's going out this week?

Joe's up first. I do have a soft spot for this smoky-black-blues-singing grandad of a man. He has a special warmth. I can see why he was worth saving for his family. He does his thank you speech in rhythm. As he does it, it reminds me of the day we sat on the porch with Dale singing *Smile* and *Rambling Rose*. As we sang, all the sash windows were lifted, and our fellow inmates listened to our tunes like we had just invented music. How the simple things can please you. And the memory.

Dale is graduated, and I am dismayed. He's been a great buddy. I hope he does well. I doubt he will. But because he's been such a friend, seeking no gain for himself apart from friendship, I really hope he makes it.

Good luck, buddy.

Kelly from my group graduates.

She cries.

She's nice, and her grandmother is very proud.

Chemical Dependency

And now for your delight, Dr John Steinbeck (Neil Sedaka to you). I look at him, and just wish he would play, *Breaking Up Is Hard to Do*. We could do with a good song.

Chemical dependency is his speciality. He doesn't make the greatest start.

'How many of you know that chemical dependency is a disease?'

Everyone puts their hands up.

'Oh . . . oh really?'

You're not dealing with any ordinary fruitcakes here.

Steinbeck nil; nuts one.

Next question.

'Well, what do you do? What's your name?' He's looking at my first room mate, Dave.

'DAVID.'

'Ah yes, David.'

'I'm a bartender.'

Steinbeck zero; nuts two.

Ho, ho, ho, he falsely sighs.

'And you, Lewis?'

We all, as one, think, 'OH NO!'

'Me, sir?'

'Yes, Lewis, what do you do?'

'Alcohol.'

Three-zero. Nuts lead.

'Well, this is not going well, is it?'

No, and I thought you were going to be good. Sing the bloody song to finish.

He doesn't.

'Tony?'

'Yes?'

'What do you know about amphetamines?'

Tony knows everything. They disagree about the content of one of the drugs.

Steinbeck says, 'Well it's about a content of 97%.'

'No, it's 98.8%.'

'I think it's 97 to 98%.'

'It's exactly 98.8%.'

'Well, let's try another example.'

Four-nil.

It's over halfway through the match. He won't win and he doesn't. He's a wonderful doctor, I'm sure, and as a speaker he is still a wonderful doctor.

Ashley win four-zero.

Next round please.

He gets his point over though. Just.

Steinbeck says, 'Who is the man sitting behind Jim?'

It is actually me. Arthur to my right doesn't say anything. I say, 'Michael'.

'I was looking at the man to your right.'

'I thought you were talking to me.'

'Well, we're having a conversation, so I suppose I'm talking to you.' Nervous laugh.

I say, 'Maybe I talk too much? I'll say less.'

Arthur quietly says to me, 'You should try it sometimes.'

Well, he fell right into that one. Thank you, Arthur. I now know who complained that they thought I was here just to write a screenplay.

I don't even comment.

I thought about saying, 'Happy now that you've got that off your chest, Arthur?'

I must have learnt something. I say to myself, 'It's your problem, not mine.' Thanks, Arthur. Your paranoia helped me practise tolerance, tolerance of dickheads.

I felt bad, just for a moment.

False Start

We start another week's group counselling. I'm a little nervous; it's my turn to spill my life out on to the carpet for all to see, study, rejig, and put back. Heavy surgery, as is usual, but you can get caught out. Things can change at the last minute in group, the single most important part of the rehab game. Things do change. I have a few notes, but I think I know my life. I wait for the customary 'Michael, This Is Your Life.'

Tim says, 'Michael, this afternoon we haven't time to do your life. Tomorrow. Okay?'

'Yeah, sure.'

As I'm writing this, after the event, I wish it had been over and done with.

We say goodbye to Todd. Everyone says what they want, and he seems up before leaving. He gets to me, 'Michael, what can I say?

I've never met anyone in show business as sensitive as you. I didn't know they existed. If anything, you need to get a little thicker skin to survive.'

That was nice of him. I think he's preparing me for my debut in America.

Toughen up little boy, toughen up.

Tim says that I can call Cheryl after group. After Sara Beth's lecture.

It's the same message, different face, although we haven't hit it off exactly. I suppose it didn't help that I kept calling her Mary Beth for ten days, with Sara Beth clearly splashed over her name tag.

I think I have a Walton's hang-up. Ever since I was a child, I wanted to say goodnight to thirty people before going to bed!

I like Sara Beth. Very Sixties. Hairstyle, blonde Joan Baez.

Her message is short and clear. AA says, 'We don't care if you drink and your arsehole drops off. Just pick it up and carry it in with you!'

She's smart, and very quick. I like her very much.

We finish. I go and call Cheryl.

Cheryl's Second Call

I'm not so nervous. Apprehensive, but the shakes have gone. It's fear of what's been happening. Her voice sounds different. She says, 'You won't recognise me. I've been attending three AA meetings a day, and given up drinking.'

I'm shocked. 'You didn't have to do that.'

'I do, it makes me feel closer to you. It's like you're away at war.'

I am. I'm at war with myself.

The allotted fifteen minutes stretches to one hour and fifteen minutes. So there is a God, and the more this goes on, the more back to basics. It makes you appreciate the smallest things in life that mean so much. The voice of a loved one. A letter arriving. A Hershey bar. We talked. It was the shortest hour and fifteen minutes I have ever experienced. We were like two teenagers. I had to go. For a joke, I said, 'I've got volleyball.'

She said, 'Oh, love, I kept you from doing that, I'm sorry.'

It wasn't said sarcastically. Now that's what love is.

I descend the stairs, and see a parcel has arrived. It's for me. And it's not been checked by the policeman. I grab it, and run back to my room before being caught. Tear it open. Inside are two pairs of white socks, and a Sony Dictaphone for my birthday. And more cards. No chocolate bars. I manage to get away with an unopened parcel, and there's no chocolate!!!

I'll have to increase my charges in cash loans. I've lent forty dollars so far, at 5% interest. Very fair, I thought. Who knows when this conflict is going to end?

Geoff the bobby sees me at dinner.

'Oh, Michael, there's a parcel for you.'

'I've got it.'

His mouth drops.

'I have to check it.'

'Well, it's down in my room.'

'Oh . . . I have to check it.'

'Well trust me, Geoff, there's no chocolate in there. Socks and a Dictaphone.' I'm reminded of the old joke, 'Do you need a Dictaphone? No, I'll use my finger.'

Geoff believes me.

Time to move on to another video. Different, but still another video. A different approach, though. It's like the shopping channel. Fully made-up, Saks Fifth Avenue female presenter. It's a story about three young people called Tom, Dick, and Mary, who are best mates. It charts their drinking careers. Eventually the presenter says, 'Tom doesn't like booze any more. Dick is getting deeper into the bottle. And Mary (photo of her sprawled on the floor, legs open, a bottle lying between them), regularly ties one on.'

All the men, predictably, laugh.

At volleyball, our group won the slug-of-the-week award for most recreation.

I've just checked the outside AA meeting list, which I'm on for the first time. Great, I'm going AWOL!

We are loaded on to a small van. I sit at the back, between black Keith and Skip. It's a full van. If you get a nice driver, the radio is on. The radio *is* on, full up, blasting out some rock number. It's a real treat, even if you can't stand the tune. We pull into the back of the drugstore, thoughts of raiding it as we sit waiting for the driver. To our left, a four-year-old girl sits in a car, drinking a can of Coca Cola, full of sugar. Skip and I discuss the idea of doing a coke raid. We'll run up to the car, waving shotguns, rip open the door, and shout, 'Okay, the mother and father hit the deck! Freeze, kid, and hand over the tin of coke.'

When we get to the meet, it's in a community hall, like a downtown nursery. That strip light depresses you. It's the type which, no matter what you do to make yourself look good, you don't. Everyone in this light looks the same, and we are. We are the same addicts. The same message is given, the same message, same problem. It's all the same, except the faces and the body language. Addicts have a body language of their own. Come to Ashley for training, and you will be qualified to recognise an addict immediately. Just watch the hands and the eyes. It says it all. There's no one nicer than an addict . . . when they're sober!

On our return to Ashley, we sing, and I wonder what I am doing here. I also wonder why we get a strange look from every car that passes. Skip tells me that this is the same-shaped van that they transport prisoners in. Now I know why I'm here.

Guilty.

Lights out.

STEP NINE

Made direct amends to such people wherever possible, except when to do so would injure them or others.

CHAPTER TEN

Tuesday, 3 May

DAY ELEVEN
6.00 am

It's a chilly morning here at A.S.H.L.E.Y., Maryland, USA.

George Bush gives us his reflection. He uses the Woody Allen quote, 'We are split in two, the mind and the body.'

I thought he was split from his wife. I must have imagined that in a drunken stupor.

On my return to my room, I see Arthur going to Mass. He really should confess before going in a place like that. You're not to take the body of Christ before absolution. I think it's up to you, Arthur, but drink or not, you are going to hell, and you ain't coming back.

8.45 am

Father Martin lectures on how to just live each day as the day of your life. He says 'Make May third a day to remember.'

I will, Father, I will. But you can't remember 3 May, if you don't reach 4 May. And I won't remember that for any other reason than it's my forty-second birthday.

He calls for me.

'Got a few minutes, Michael?' Father says enthusiastically. I think, 'No, it's my few minutes off', but I'm sure we can deal. I wonder if he needs a loan, or a bar of chocolate.

Inside His Office

'I love England, you know?'

No, I didn't, but I know if I say 'Would you like to come on my show?' that he isn't about to say no!

We discuss my public 'coming out'. I think, 'I wonder how far this will go?' I've got God, now I am about to get his mortgage repayments. Still, he will be a great guest, and it will suit both of us. I also get the police off my back. All's fair in hug and war. There's no room for the usual loving here. Just the hugging.

10.15 am

The spilling of my guts is today at the group meeting. I have to tell them all about myself, who I am, and how I ended up here.

I begin.

I was born Michael Kieran Parker in 1952, in a council flat in Bermondsey, England, which I have no recollection of at all. I was born in the corner room of the flat. I was delivered by a midwife. You can tell because my belly button sticks out. It's a rough knot. I don't know why I wasn't born in the hospital.

I'm the youngest of three. There's an eight-year gap between me and my sister, and ten years between me and my brother. My earliest recollection of being alive is when I was four years old. It seems like someone dropped me at four into the world. I have no recollection before that. I had an Arran jumper on, and there was a Fifties-style dining table set in the front room of the flat. The thing about those flats is that when you're four years old, you fit. Animals adjust to their surroundings. We don't. We grow up. So the cage gets smaller and smaller.

I opened my eyes, and looked across the table. I was about as high as the Pledge polish on the table. I could see a woman in front of me with dark hair. It was my Aunt Kath. I always liked my Aunt Kath, and she always liked me. She used to give me five pounds for my birthday, which was a fortune. She was my mum's sister. There were no relatives of my dad. I never saw any. Not a grandparent, not an uncle, nothing. Nobody knows what his background was. He never spoke about it. It was all guesswork as to where he came from. My mother said, among other guesses, he was Armenian! He had that Eastern bloc habit of only bringing a bag of food home instead of money. He was a cable-layer in the army during the war. He never kept a job very long. We never really knew what he did for a living. He very rarely came home. When he did come in, he was drunk.

My earliest recollection was when I was four years old, and I felt different. I knew there was something not quite right then, but I didn't know what it was. To get attention, I would get up on the chair. I don't really remember what I did, I just did things to make people smile. Make them laugh. I can't to this day tell you whether I sang or whether I told jokes, I just got up and did things. Silly moves. Anything to entertain the aunties when they came round. I would never do it for the family. It had to be somebody different.

At school, I was taught by nuns. They were strict. I remember not wanting to go there. I screamed my head off as I was dragged in by my mother. I settled down after a while. I don't know what I was scared of. It was probably those nuns. They were frightening-looking with those black habits, and very severe. The school was only over the road. If you didn't stand straight in line, they would smack you on the back of the legs. It really hurt. I'm sure they got all their sexual frustration off on kids.

Sister Vianni, or as we knew her, 'Biryani with a Popadom on Top', used to say to the girls, 'Now, boys may be trying to kiss you, and do things that may seem strange to you. If this happens, and a boy wants to sit on your lap, carry around with you a brown sheet of paper, and put it down first before the boy sits down.' She never explained to them or us, why the brown sheet of paper! Gift-wrapped dick, I suppose.

Right from an early age, I had to work everything out for myself. No one ever explained anything. What was right and what was wrong. What was moral or immoral.

I always felt different. I felt removed from everyone else. When you live in flats, and are surrounded by so many families, you hear everyone else's arguments and rows, conversation, every squeak of every bed. Every pan on every stove. A mass of noise. Mrs Ludgrove lived next door. She only ever wore one shoe. And there was nothing wrong with her other foot! She wore a beret like Frank Spencer. I can still smell the lard from her kitchen.

I never had an opinion about quite what I was, I just felt different. I suppose I had an addictive nature from an early age. Everybody else seemed to have dads. Even if they were rotten dads, they were there. At least they brought their wages home, however small.

About seven or eight is my earliest recollection of upset in the family. My father coming home stoned out of his brains all the time, and gambling all the money. He was a compulsive gambler. Every time he lost, he would get stoned, come home, then, when he was asked by my mother where the money was, his reply was to smack her straight in the face. Charming man. He never seemed to be aware that I was there. He was aware of my mother, my brother, my sister. Never me. I used to be looking on at it all the time, like I was watching this sad film in front of me, with no gap between me and the screen. I used to run out of the flat, go to the stairway, and, when the noise got too much, sit on the concrete stairs with my hands over my ears. Johnny, a big docker who lived at the far end, used to pick me up, take me to his flat until the police were called and had sorted it all out. He was nice.

The only love I recall my father showing was when he put me on his lap once, and let me rub his whiskers. He made me laugh. Once. He never hit me. He hit my mother, my brother, not my sister. She wasn't there for a long time, she had polio. He never laid a finger on me. But he frightened me. I never worked out why he differentiated between myself and my brother.

At school I used to say things like, 'My dad's a long-distance lorry driver,' so that they didn't ask me questions. The comedy started then, because I found that if I made people laugh, the result was no questions. So it was used as a defence mechanism. And it worked.

There were other signs of our lack of wealth. My school friend Bernard said to me, 'Did you see that play on BBC 2?'

I thought, 'What's he talking about?' The telly would be in and out on rental. It was the first thing that had to go back if there was a question of having food. And when we did have the telly, it had ITV and BBC 1. What the hell was BBC 2?

Our family never hugged. Nobody ever showed any love to one another. They were too busy being protective of themselves. My mother gave me a smack now and then. Nothing untoward. We were there as a unit, but with individual lives. I felt separated then. I used to feel that this was where I lived. I'd got it as long as I put up with it. I had to find a way out. How long could this keep going on?

One day my father came in, picked up a dining chair, one of those Fifties' chairs with a brown vinyl top. He laid it straight across her head. It didn't break like a film one does. It went straight through her scalp. The blood spurted out everywhere. I thought, 'enough's enough'. My mother cowering in the corner, my brother trying to pull him off. Then the screaming started. He chased us into the bedroom, his arm was pinned round the door like something from a Jack Nicholson horror film. He was screaming to get in. The police would only come when they were called by the neighbours. Just another domestic. It was live and let row. Things got progressively worse. We would dread seeing him staggering back. He was always smart, with shining shoes, well groomed hair, always kept himself looking immaculate. He came home less and less. I got to like it. I created my own little world.

I did a paper round in the mornings and evenings. I cleaned cars on a Saturday. I earned my own money. If I had mates round on a Saturday night, I'd make sandwiches and sell them to them. They'd say, 'We don't charge you for sandwiches at our house.'

'Well, you've got a dad, I haven't, so you have to pay.'

I liked earning money. I'd give some to my mum for housekeeping, some I saved for school holidays. With anything spare I used to take my mates to Battersea funfair. It was my treat. I suppose it was my way of buying friendship.

School holidays I spent in Ireland. At eleven years old, I'd take the train to Holyhead, go across on the boat to Dunleary by myself. Then get a train to Balanah on the west coast, be picked up by my uncle, and spend my school holidays there with my grandmother. It was beautiful. They had a little bit of money from the farm. It seemed wildly more extravagant than the background I had come from. My grandmother was nutty as a fruitcake. She called us 'English pigs'. If I was playing up, she'd go up to the bureau, pick up a cane, and start beating it around to knock shit out of me and my cousins. I would run outside. It was a great sport, winding her up. She was a bit doddery on her legs. She died aged 103. She never moved away. She only ever went to the church once a week, and never ever left that spot in 103 years.

I didn't miss home. Why would I? There was nothing to miss.

I had a knack of getting people to like me. I liked making them laugh. I didn't do, 'Have you heard this joke?' I just made them laugh. I was always creating situations, to get a reaction out of the ordinary.

At eleven, I went to secondary school. St Michael's. Taught by priests. My dad left home about this time. The final blow came when, hearing him bang at the door, we wouldn't let him in. He had a double-barrelled shotgun which he poked through the letter box. I don't know where he got it from. Pawn shop, probably. It was late at night. I climbed into the bed with my mother. I was lying there beside her, the door was open, light coming through the gap. All I could see was the end of the gun, waving across in front of my eyes, an inch from my nose, then across to my mother, back to me. Over and over. It has always stuck in my mind, along with the thought, 'Why isn't she rolling over? Why isn't she rolling over on top of me?' Perhaps she was frozen with terror. I don't know what stopped him from pulling the trigger. He was mumbling, this low mumble the whole time. I think I knew then that I was going to lead a solo life. For some reason he just walked away. He shut the front door and went. Like the sheriff had told him to leave town. He lowered his gun and walked away. We literally locked him out. He lived in the Salvation Army Hostel. I didn't want to see him any more, and nobody else did. My sister hung on a bit, typical of a lot of girls — whatever happens, her father's all right. My mother started going out on Saturday nights, dancing, and I used to judge anybody who came back by how big a car they had.

I used to say, 'Marry him.'

She replied, 'You have to love someone.'

I was very matter of fact. 'Don't worry about that, just marry him.'

I lived my own life. I looked after myself. I was never made to sit in. I used my time in an enterprising way, making money. I had a jar of sweets at the end of the landing. I sold them at a penny each. They didn't go very well, as they all stuck together. I started to get a lot more streetwise. I was going to need it.

At school, I had one of my worst childhood experiences. A priest, tall and thin, with glasses, paid me attention in class. It was nice that someone older was paying me attention. He had a green Ford Poplar. He lived in the priest's house, beside the dock. He gained my confidence. I thought, 'He's nice, I think I'll become a priest.' So I decided, at twelve, to start my training for Pope. I had no feeling of God, I just thought it would be a good business to get into. I went round to the priest's house for lessons in his study. I remember the house seemed enormous. They had three housekeepers, really posh polished floors, and that smell, that Pledge smell again. That's twice I've done a pledge! Once at forty-two, and as a kid! He would talk to me. I'd listen intently. Then he'd sit me on his lap. And I remember thinking 'I don't think this is the way to get into the priesthood. Maybe he knows something I don't.'

He said, 'I'd like you to meet my relations, and then perhaps we'll take a ride in the country.'

I'd never been to the countryside. It sounded adventurous. If you've been brought up in a city, you'll know what I mean. If not, imagine living in a maze, and taking eight years to find the exit. The thought of having a ride in a car was too tempting. My love for cars was there at an early age, even a Ford Pop. He picked me up, took me to the beautiful countryside. I was transfixed, riding in the car. One person had a car in the whole ninety flats in our place. We drove into a forest. I can't remember where it was. I don't know which direction we were going. Grass. Trees. New sounds. That wasn't what I was used to at all. We only drove a little way. Everything seems miles away when you're a kid. The roads were narrower, older roads. They were only just putting traffic lights in. The sun was shining. We pulled up in a clearing in the forest. I started to feel uneasy. In front of us was a huge drop, all forestry, masses of forestry. He put his arm round me. I started crying.

'There's no need to cry.'

I didn't say anything. I thought, 'I've got to get out of here.' We were in the middle of nowhere. I stared straight ahead as he said, 'Do you know what people do when they love each other?'

'No, I don't.'

'Well, they kiss.'

I thought, 'Do they?' Nobody in our family had ever done that. This was alien to me. Somebody putting their arm round me was totally alien. I wouldn't have thought anything if it had not been alien. I grabbed the handle on the car, pushed it open to free myself. I ran across the dirt track, and dropped like a stone through bushes. It was like a scene from *Deliverance*. I just ran and ran, the thorns and bushes were whacking either side of me. I just ran. The woods got deeper, deeper and deeper. He was running behind me, tearing down the hill after me. I couldn't go any further. He grabbed me. I thought, 'This is it, I'm finished.' I was sobbing.

He said, 'No, it's going to be all right. Stop crying. Stop crying. Come back to the car.'

I couldn't go forward, there were bushes to the right, bushes to the left, trees and bushes. I went back. I was shaken. But I got my composure back. How was I going to get out of this? I knew there was something wrong.

'Would you like to drive the car?'

'I'm twelve years old,' I said.

'Yes.'

I thought, 'I'll get in the car. I don't have a clue how to drive it. I can run him over and go.' He got in the car, I didn't have a clue how the gears worked. He said, 'You can sit on my lap and drive the car.'

I did. If I didn't go along with this, I wasn't going to get out of here. I could see sweat pouring down his brow. In sheer terror, I held on to the steering wheel. My inclination was to turn it, turn the car over.

I don't know how old he was. When you're twelve, everybody seems old. I said, 'I've had enough of this now.'

He said, 'We'll go and visit my sisters.'

It was a posh house. When we got there, he carried on as if nothing had happened. I was numb. For the first time in my life, I wanted to get back to Bermondsey. Another first. The place where I felt I was having the worst upbringing, and I was trying to get back to it! Proves there's always something worse. However you feel, there's always something worse.

He pulled up a little way from the flats.

'Now you won't say anything about this to anybody.'

The usual line.

I said, 'No.'

From that day to this, I have never told anyone. I always kept my word. It won't affect him now. He's probably dead. I don't feel anything, no disgust or hatred. But I grew up in that short time. I'd survived the situation. I'd managed to take control. If I was in control, and gave my word, my word was my bond. So at twelve years old, I decided to take over my life. As it was me who was having to run it. Whatever the rub. I jumped from twelve years old mentally, to being an adult. There it was. Another kid might have ended up making it worse. Stories you've heard over the years, of them being found dead somewhere. The difference between the ones who survive, and the ones that die. I wonder how many have gone through it, and survived. I can't honestly say I sit and think about it.

So that was the end of me deciding, 'I wanna become a priest.' The experience in the countryside put me off that career choice. I just carried on with my life. I wasn't about to let anything interfere. But I wonder if it's there sometimes, and I just mentally block the whole thing out.

I did school plays, to get me out of classes. I hated school. I don't know why they put me in the 'A' stream. I never did much. They put on my reports, 'If he paid as much attention to his Science lessons, English, History etc, as he does to his stage work, he would be brilliant.'

School plays, amongst other things, consisted of me doing a pastiche of 'Top of the Pops'. I'd make out I was Dave of *The Dave Clark Five*, and do 'I'm In Pieces, Bits and Pieces', with my legs going all over the place.

Sixth form were doing Shakespeare's *Romeo and Juliet*. The sixth former who was playing Friar Lawrence freaked out about how many lines he had to learn. I was a third former.

I went to the teacher and asked, 'Can I do it?'

'You're too young.'

'Well, you've got nobody else, and you've only got two weeks left.'

I learnt the lines, they greyed my hair with white flour, and I played the Friar. That was the first time I'd gained real attention. Miss Bond, my very unfavourite English teacher, suddenly said, 'Oh, Parker, I didn't realise you had it in you.'

I turned a non-believer into a fan. My first.

My father was still missing in Acton. His name came up now and again. I can hear my mother saying, '*I wish he was just an alcoholic.*' At least that way he'd come home with some money. With booze he would have keeled over, and there would be something left. With gambling, there's never anything. That was her thinking and logic, so in my mind it was bad to gamble. Okay to drink. I didn't know as a kid that it was the drink that was making him violent. How would I have known that? Had I learnt then about drinking's failings, I would never have had a drink, even though I was born an addict.

I left school at fifteen years of age. I didn't get one 'O' level. All I wanted was to leave school, and get started on my career. They never really encouraged me. Father Salmon was the only one who sang my tune. Thankfully not the one who sang 'If you go down to the woods today, you're sure of a big surprise'. I did amateur dramatics with the Feltham Players. It was the hall that belonged to the church. Catholic-orientated. They used to say, 'Ian Hendry was part of this group, you know.'

I said, 'I'll be as big as him, one day.'

Some of them thought I needed my enthusiasm dampened down. Don't fill yourself with too much ambition. I had the 'I'll show you' attitude. They used to look at me and laugh when I said, 'I'm going to be a star.'

But they encouraged me as well. Not all of them laughed. I must have been fairly good, or I wouldn't have got any parts. I was the youngest in the group. I loved it. But I got a bit too cocky. Bluffed my way into everything. If they said, 'Is it possible for a man to swim up a river, burning like a log?', I'd say, 'Yes!', then worry about how to do it. Street mentality, I suppose.

An encounter with girls came next. A mate, myself, and two willing opposites. We picked a number. If your number matched with theirs, that was the one you shagged. I used to fix the numbers. I didn't want to shag the ugly one. I never fell in love, though.

Pauline Hart was the one I loved in school, but she went out with the best fighter, Johnny Allen. I didn't get a look-in. She made contact with me years later. She never married Johnny.

I didn't ever really love anybody. I liked them.

I remember one strange experience. It was in Earl's Court. I don't know what I was doing there. It was one of those places where a load of people share the flat. There was this tall, skinny bird with short hair, quite freckled, sort of pixie-type face. I ended up in the bedroom with her. She wanted me to do her against the door. She was older than me, quite a bit older. She must have fancied teenagers. It was a dreadful place, no handle on the door, just a gap where the handle should have been. I was standing up, her back was against the door. I thought, 'I don't know what this is supposed to feel like, but it feels very dry.' I'm banging away, making a noise, she's screaming, I'm thinking I'm giving her pleasure. I was nowhere near. I had my dick in the gap in the door. That's what was dry. I never saw her again.

*

My Careers' teacher said, 'What are you going to do for a living?'

I should have said carpentry. 'I'm going to go on the stage.'

He said, 'No, what are you going to do for a living?'

'Oh, I don't know, hairdressing.'

'You wanna be a hairdresser? Can we think of something better than that?'

'No, that's what I want to do.'

I just said it out of the blue. Then I thought about it. 'I can meet the stars that way.' I'd read about this guy called Vidal Sassoon, who was becoming quite famous. I found out that all these stars had their hair cut at his place. I had no intention of becoming a hairdresser. But I thought, 'I'll go there, meet the stars, and that's how I'll get to the stage.' I had no theatrical background whatsoever. I got the job. I used to earn good money on tips. It subsidised my £3.50 a week. It was hard work. Everyone at Vidal's thought I was strange. At the time they were all into long haircuts. I had a crew cut. They thought I was odd. I came from the docklands. When I got off the bus every night back home, my mates would shout, 'Oh here's the poof, he's back.'

I stuck with it. I was assigned to the stylist, Ricci Burns. Very flamboyant. He had navy blazers with real gold buttons on. I was only into the stars who came in. People like Candice Bergen, Lulu, Shirley Bassey, Dusty Springfield. It blew my mind completely. I had my own style of washing, 'Would you like a cold rinse? It really shines the hair.'

I only did it to make them jump. The routine went, 'Ready?'

'Yes.'

'Hold on tight to your towel.'

Then I'd turn it from baking hot to freezing cold.

'Whaaaa haaaaa!'

'Now, now, be quiet. This is good for you. You'll feel the benefit of this.'

I never got much repeat business.

Halfway through their haircut, Ricci would say, 'He does a great Shirley Bassey. Do your Shirley Bassey.'

I'd stand there in front of a client, while he'd got her freezing head bent over, going, 'The minute you walked in the joint . . .'

A fifteen-year-old junior with a crew cut, singing 'Big Spender', while they're having their hair tugged by Ricci, sticking pins in their head, then charging them fifty quid for the pleasure.

I used to have to sweep the hair up. Katie Boyle used to bring in two little Yorkies. She laid them on the floor. I swept them up. She freaked out. She didn't tip me that day.

I lasted about six months at Vidal's.

I remember Dora Ravis coming in. She was a couturier. She made posh dresses. She knew Bertie Green who owned the Astor Club. 'I'll get you an audition with him.'

She had this magnificent flat in Argyle Street. I thought, 'This is living. This is what it's all about.' It gave me something to work for. I sat in the corner and did Shirley Bassey. I was never born with logic. A fifteen-year-old kid, for Bertie Green, for the Astor Club. The villains that used to go in the Astor Club, for God's sake! He gave me heaps of encouragement. He said, 'He looks a bit like Frank Sinatra when he was young.'

That was the last I heard of it.

I got a job in the docks as a wages clerk. Whatever, I've never not had a job. I've always had money in my pocket. I had millions of jobs. Then I joined a rock band. The only reason I got in was because I had a double deck keyboard. I had some lessons. Most of the blokes in the group lived in Peckham. They used to play at a local club.

I said, 'Do you want a keyboard player?'

'Have you got a keyboard?'

'Yeah.'

'Can you play it?'

'Er . . . yeah.'

I fumbled my way through.

Next stop, Germany.

I thought it would all be experience for me on the stage. We had a good sound. Johnny the drummer was the singer. Two sax players, bass, lead guitar, myself on keyboards, and a roadie. We had a six-wheeled transit with aeroplane seats. We went off to make our fortune in a place called Sweinigan. A month there, then Frankfurt, the K.52 Club. We lived on eggs and bacon the whole time. It was the only thing we knew how to order. We lived in one room in Penny Lane, with six bunk beds, and a bathroom with no water. Tasteful. If you wanted to shag one of the groupies, you had to hang a blanket down from the top bunk.

Every night after the gig, about two o'clock, someone would go down to the station and get some chocolate. We had very little money. I remember I had this groupie in the bed. Alan was at the other end, shouting out instructions.

'I know how to shag, thanks. I don't need you telling me what to do.'

The bunk bed was going to and fro, to and fro. I heard Johnny say, 'I'm going down to the station, anybody want anything?'

I stopped rocking to and fro, lifted the sheet up, and said, 'Get us a bar of chocolate will you, John?', and carried on. They just fell about laughing.

I used to wear crushed-velvet trousers, bell bottoms, platform shoes, a trench coat. I wore my hair very long. Part of the act included standing on my head on the keyboard. It covered for my terrible playing. We did five one-hour sessions.

There was no drinking or smoking then. I wasn't really interested in marijuana, it did nothing for me. They called me the Pill Tester. I used to try stuff out first, it could have killed me for all I knew!

They were closing the K52 club down, turning it into a strip joint. Everybody started wrecking the place. Smashing the cigarette machine. We were loading, getting all our gear out, to move on to Switzerland. The manager of the place was about to pay us. He paid us very nicely, he phoned the police, and said that we were the ones that smashed the club. The police came, all our gear was halfway on the pavement. They grabbed us, slung us in the back of a paddy wagon. Next, I'm in a German jail looking at light coming through the bars. We were jailed for a week, not knowing when we were going to get out.

An interpreter realised that we were telling the truth. Eventually we were released, and told not to come back to Germany.

We played in Switzerland. I loved it.

Everything struck me. The West End had struck me, the countryside had struck me. Another life had struck me. I realised there was a reason that you were put on this earth. Each stage of my life gave me encouragement to go on to the next. I knew I wasn't going to stay with the group. I was just using it as experience to go out on my own, to be on stage. Fifteen/sixteen is young for a comic, too young for a comedian.

I was about seventeen when the band split up.

I did an interview for Butlins, to become a Redcoat. I was a year younger than I should have been, but I managed to get in. I had my red and whites which were too big. I did the Redcoat show every fortnight. Hated it. But I stuck with it because I thought, if I can't last the seventeen weeks, at £7.50 a week, I ain't going to last in show business. I made myself stick to it. I used to do the bingo calling. Lugging bingo machines round wasn't my idea of show business.

I always wanted to be in the theatre, even if it was standing there watching the resident artistes do their shows. I remember seeing Billy Dainty, Sandy Powell with his vent doll, and Reg Dixon on the Sunday concerts. I loved it. Even though my legs were buckling underneath from standing all the time. I stared mesmerised at the show. Mike Reid did his first audition for a talent competition there. The Patton Brothers were the resident comedians.

When I was still at school, with the money I earned from cleaning cars, I'd dress myself up to look as old as possible, book a ticket for the 'Talk of the Town', and sit right up in the gods, watching Dave Allen and Bruce Forsyth. Afterwards, I would go to the stage door, stand at the end of the street, watch them come out and get into their cars. I just stared at them. Saw how stars walked. What mannerisms they had off stage. But I never went anywhere near them.

A Redcoat at Butlins, called Barry, ended up being best man at my wedding. He tried to encourage me to go on stage. He was very good, but I never paid any attention. He tried to get me to do impressions. In talent competitions. I did Malcolm Muggeridge, Tommy Cooper, Frankie Howerd, David Frost, and Alan Whicker, standing on my head.

But I wasn't developing. Barry helped me by writing it all out, rehearsing me. I would never stick to anything. No confidence. Playing at it. I felt very sorry for him. I obviously wasn't ready. I was just sodding around.

So that people could understand me, I went for speech-training lessons at night school in Bermondsey. Not that many people in Bermondsey go for speech-training lessons. I was the only one there, taught by Michael Bangerta, at the time a resting actor. I used to stand against the wall going, 'Wah ooh, ooh, nooow.'

I wanted to be a comedy actor. I applied to the London Academy of Music and Dramatic Art. For my audition, I did Pip from *Chips with Everything*, and Malvolio from *Twelfth Night*. Michael trained me. There were 2000 applicants. I passed and was due to go there in the October.

In the period before, I went in for a talent competition at a local pub in front of all my mates. And I won. The only reason I think I did, was because the judges were petrified they wouldn't get out of the pub without getting beaten up! The prize was a contract to do the northern clubs.

I wrote to LAMDA telling them I wasn't coming. I was going into the other side of the business called light entertainment. I never had a reply.

I was paid off every night of the week for six weeks on the trot. I regretted my letter to LAMDA. I remember saying to a club owner one night, 'Well, this is the twelfth time I've been paid off in the last fortnight. What do you think I should do?'

'You should have gone to LAMDA.'

I knew I'd hear that for the rest of my life.

'*You should have gone to LAMDA.*'

I didn't think to write to the Principal and say, 'Can I come now?' I felt too embarrassed. I'd made this horrendous mistake.

I was paid off, booed. I performed in a place in Doncaster called the Kiki Club. There were sixteen people in the audience. A woman took notes during my act. Not one titter. I came off. The manager asked to see me. 'That impression you did of Bernie Winters . . .' he said.

'I don't do Bernie Winters.'

'Well, that impression you did of Steptoe . . .'

'I don't do Steptoe.'

'Well, you're crap anyway.'

He gave me a fiver and paid me off. I went round to the bar and the compere was somewhat softer, 'That's a shame about tonight.'

'Yeah, I've just been paid off.'

'Oh, have you?'

'They weren't very good tonight.'

'Don't worry. Those sixteen people who were in were a circus from Belgium.'

I went back to the club owner, 'It's okay,' I said. 'You can have me back tomorrow, those sixteen people who were in were a circus from Belgium. That's why they didn't laugh.'

'I don't care what country they're from. You're crap.'

I went to my digs and cried my eyes out. But I thought, 'I'd better carry on, otherwise all anybody's going to say to me for the rest of my life is, "You should have gone to LAMDA." '

You wonder why people carry on in our business. I had no choice really.

The first time I had a whisky and coke, I think I had two. I remember falling flat out on a bench in the pub. That's all I remember, just passing out. It wasn't really for me. I didn't like the taste. If it was a spirit, I'd put a soda in, or a coke, to take the taste away. It wasn't something I ever enjoyed.

I became a mini-cab driver. I worked for a firm called Speedy Cars. I managed to get enough money together to get an Austin Cambridge automatic. It was okay for mini-cabbing. I worked Friday, Saturday and Sunday solid, no time off whatsoever. No sleep, nothing. Finish in the early hours of Monday morning, then sleep through Tuesday. That left me the rest of the week off so I could go to auditions.

I applied to be Holiday Camp Entertainments Manager in Dartmouth, Devon. I auditioned for Trevor and Billie George, in

Torquay. The pay was £35 for a seven-day week. I had to entertain the kids for an hour. The rest of the evening, I compered.

Billie said, 'You're a bit young for the job.'

'I can make myself look older.'

'How much do you want a week?'

'As long as I get the job and enough to send home, I don't really care.'

That's what got me the job. Not my talent, but saying, 'As long as I've got enough to send home.'

I lived in Devon for a couple of years with Trevor and Billie. I got twelve pounds a show. Well, I thought I did, until I overheard a conversation between Trevor and Billie.

'BILLIE!'

'Yes, Trevor . . . darling!'

'I'm just doing BARRY-MORE's contract, my dear.'

'What is your enquiry, Trevor?'

'Can you tell me . . .'

'Yes, dear?'

'Should his contract read, "Twelve shows a week for one hundred and ten pounds", or "One hundred and ten shows a week for twelve pounds"?'

Billie gave me the name Barrymore. She came up with that one. She said, 'I've got it . . . Barrymore.'

I said, 'Who's that?'

'Don't you know the Barrymores – the Royal Family of the theatre?'

'Who?'

She gave me a book about the American Barrymores. Up until then, I'd never even heard of them.

'It's a bit theatrical.'

'Oh, no, that'll be lovely.'

I thought, 'Oh well, any name'll do.'

I became Michael Barrymore.

They gave me a start; nobody else did. I worked all the time. I was a star. I was made, this was it, I'd made the big time. I was doing what I wanted to do.

I went out with their daughter for a while. When they had an extension built upstairs, Trevor and I were putting the carpet in. I was mucking about with her.

'BARRY-MORE?'

'Yes, Trevor?'

'You're supposed to be laying the carpet, not my daughter!'

'Sorry, Trevor.'

I had no intention of getting married, coming from my background. It wasn't in my thinking. I was too tunnel-visioned about my work. There was only one thing I was in love with, and that was my career.

Her name was Melina, she traded as 'The Magical Melina'. I got on fine with her. It was all the props I couldn't handle. I had to help her lug them in and out of venues. I was terrified of knocking the tricks over; there was a constant danger of a massive flower explosion. I drew the line when she decided to add ventriloquism to the act. In her efforts for originality, she had a vent doll made. It was a five-foot-high rabbit, with enormous ears. I used to listen as she practised with the rabbit in her bedroom. I was never sure who was talking.

All I could hear was, 'Oiiii!'

'Yes, bunny?'

'Oim over heere.'

'Who's that?'

'Ik's me!'

'I'm sorry, I've got a frog in my throat.'

'Vell get 'im aert, and I'll jump in.'

'Oh bunny, really!'

My best mate was Jack Lilley. I used to drive him around. He was a big, fat, older comic, whom I loved. He used to tell me stories about the business. I'd sit with him in the daytime, run him to the gigs at night. I used to compere. We went round like a little troupe. It was all experience, and I was getting better and better. I started to put together some semblance of an act.

People found me hard to describe. They used to say, 'What's he like?'

Anybody who'd seen me would say, 'Well, I can't describe him. You'll have to go and see him.'

A TV talent programme called 'New Faces' was holding auditions in the local working men's club. There were acts everywhere. They let an audience in to watch, which was unusual. The place was heaving. I took Jack to it. I wasn't going to audition myself.

'I'll take you, Jack. But don't involve me, I don't want to go on that programme.'

I had my own little world. I felt sure that being slagged off by the panel would set me back ten paces. I didn't want to know.

Jack and I sat together. A man came around with forms to fill in. I said, 'No, I don't want to, I'm just here with my mate.'

'Well, you might as well have one.'

I looked at the form. 'I'll tell you what, Jack, I'll put down somebody else's name, somebody else's address, and somebody else's phone number, and that way they won't know who I am!'

I put another comic's name down, somebody else's address, and I made up a phone number. They shouted my false name. I didn't react to start with.

'That's you!'

I stood there and screamed, 'Hello, are you there, Australia?', and stood on my head!

Followed by, 'And now the news.'

I put a cardboard cut-out box on my head.

It wasn't all that great. I got no reaction.

On my way home, I said, 'Never put me through that again, Jack. It was embarrassing. It's one of the worst experiences I've ever had.'

I got back to my digs. My landlady Trish said, 'ATV have been on the phone for you.'

'Who?'

'ATV.'

'What do they want?'

'I don't know, some woman asking for you. I can't remember her name. She wants you to ring her back.'

I phoned. A researcher said, 'Hello, Tony.'

'My name's not Tony, it's Michael.'

'You're very difficult to track down. I've had to go through one address to get another address. Same with the telephone number. *And* you have a different name.'

'What do you want?'

'We'd like you on the show in two weeks.'

'No, I don't want to do it.'

'What?'

'I don't want to do it.'

'What do you mean, you don't want to do it? Why did you audition?'

'Because I was there. I don't think it's for me.'

'Well, we liked it, we thought you were really good. Different, original. We liked the standing on the head.'

'Oh, did you? What do you think I should do? I'm worried about going on it.'

'How old are you?'

'Twenty-one.'

'What have you got to lose?'

'I suppose you're right.'

A fortnight later I did the show. On the panel was Jack Parnell, Mickey Most, Arthur Askey. I got 95 out of 100. And I won the viewers' vote.

Out of that, a guy called Jack Fallon saw me, and a year later gave me six months' residency at a club called Showboat in the Strand. He had a small show going in there. I had to do twelve minutes. Jack saw something in me. He had me in every Wednesday, going over the act.

Soon after we'd opened, I met Cheryl. She was brought in as the singer. She owed him. She was due to be there a year before, and had gone to America instead. She came, watched the show, and saw me.

She had the number-two dressing room, and I was in the basement. It wasn't exactly a dressing room, it was where all the pipes ran underneath, and there was a cracked mirror in the corner. But I was happy.

I was working in the West End.

I had a dreadful checked suit. It was awful, and my teeth were crooked. Ideal for a career in showbusiness.

Bernard Delfont came to see the show with a journalist called James Green. He wrote for the *Evening News*, and gave me a good write-up.

After the show, Delfont asked to see me, 'Hello boy, who's your agent?'

'My agent's in Torquay.'

'What're you doing all the way down there?'

'It's the only place I could get a start.'

I never heard from him again.

Cheryl was the first one who took any interest in me. I thought she was Italian. I kept saying, 'Woood you ly-ke a cup of teee?'

She looked Italian. Tanned, and red hair. She spoke very well, so it didn't sound like an accent I knew. Her mum was with her. I thought she looked Italian, too.

Not realising she was a fully trained dancer, I said, 'Would you like me to show you the steps?'

Me, know-nothing from Bermondsey, was about to show *her* the steps.

She said, 'No, I think I can cope with those.'

She had a great smile. I really liked her. We became good mates. Same sense of humour. She liked me just for me, paid me the sort of attention no one else had paid me in my life before. She didn't like getting up there and doing it, she never liked that side of the business. We agreed that she would manage me instead.

She was living at home with her mum and dad. She'd been divorced about two or three years. I often wonder what she saw in me. My mates used to say, 'How did you find a girl like that?'

She made great salads. I'd never seen anyone put crisps on a salad before. Like in posh hotels.

We were sitting on the couch, about two o'clock in the morning, 'Do ya wanna get married?' I said.

'Yes!'

I didn't even think about it. I hadn't pre-planned that I was going to say it.

We were still at the Showboat. While I was there, I opened a stationer's/newsagent, in Bermondsey. It was called Parker Brothers. I'd saved the money from what I was earning at the time. The rent was £800 a year. I got overdraft facilities from the bank. I did the interior myself, got goods from the cash and carry. In its first week it took £1200. I put my brother in to run it. His family lived upstairs.

The shop really took off. It was a goldmine. I thought it would be security for me if show business didn't work out.

Cheryl and I got married at Epping Registry Office, Epping Forest on 10 June 1976. I don't know what she thought she was marrying. I wasn't exactly a catch. I had one set of clothes. We didn't have a honeymoon.

The day after we were married, I started rehearsals for *The Black and White Minstrel Show* in Torquay. I was bottom of the bill.

Eddie let me have his old car. We ended up with no money at the end of the season. He seemed to be subsidising us all the time.

I went back to the shop. My brother had a Cortina when I left at the beginning of the season. When I returned, he had a 3.5 Rover. I knew something was up. I called for an audit. He hadn't paid the bills. We had £47,000 worth of debts, and he'd gone off to Ireland with his family for an elongated holiday. They hadn't closed up, but left my mother to run things. It was a nightmare. There was £800 owed to Cadbury's, two grand to W.D. & H.O. Will's, £800 owing to the newspaper people.

Cheryl and I went in to run the shop, to try and save it. You can imagine Cheryl fully made up, sorting the day's papers, at five o'clock in the morning. Well, you can't, she loved it! It was one of the happiest times of our lives! She broke up all the 'overs' that he'd bought, all the Chocolate Easter Eggs, and sold them off individually. He'd over-ordered everything. There was masses of Turkish Delight, which we broke up into individual pieces and sold at a penny a time. It was the only newsagent/sweet shop I've ever seen to have a Sale! Cheryl reduced everything. The place was packed out. But, as quickly as we were taking it in, we were paying it out to clear the debts. Events overtook us. It broke the family apart. They should have told me what was going on.

The inevitable phone call came through. Cheryl took it, 'It's the official receiver,' she said.

I'd never heard of the official receiver. It sounded like the name of a rock band.

'Oh, is it?'

They made me personally bankrupt at twenty-four for £47,000. They took everything, including the car that Eddie had given me. Everything but our wedding rings, and £10. It was a fine start to a marriage. Judge Parbury asked in the summing up, how I could have been party to it when I was away in summer season at the time? He said the only mistake I'd made was to trust my brother. He gave me five years undischarged, and he gave my brother ten. We were both made bankrupt. I had to start again from scratch.

Cheryl worked in her mum and dad's shop. Selling clothes. We lived in a council flat. We had a bean bag for a sofa, floor tiles doubled as the kitchen worktop, a bed, and that was it. I had to have some form of income. I got a job at Selfridges, selling Playmobil, for which I got £40 a week. It didn't stretch very far, since I had to pay £11 in train fares, and £14 a week rent.

Cheryl phoned around all the agents, trying to get me work. Nobody wanted to know. I was seriously thinking of going to get a job in music publishing. A friend of Cheryl's from her singing years (Roger Greenaway), offered to help.

*

I came home one night.

'I've got a job for you,' she said.

'Oh, great!'

'It's twenty-five quid.'

'I only get forty quid *a week!* Great!'

'It's all men, that's the only thing.'

I'd never been to a stag show. Didn't even know what they were all about. I was always green about things. As a kid I never even went to a pantomime.

They were short of a comic that night. A place called the Room At The Top, in Ilford. I went up there with my bag, and my suit.

'Can you tell me where the dressing room is, please?'

'What?'

'The dressing room.'

'They're over there in the ladies' toilet'

I walked to the toilet apprehensively. Strippers and comics changed together. I opened the door. There were two girls with their legs up in front of mirrors, no drawers on, one sticking tassels on her snatch. Another, putting tassels on her tits.

' 'Ello darlin', 'ow're you? You're a new boy, aren't you?'

'Yeah.'

I got into my working suit like a sheepish little kid.

The compere was called Ronnie Twist. He was nice. 'Hello son, 'ow are you? You've never done this before, have you?'

'Nah.'

'I'll put you on early, give you a chance.'

Just before I went out, I thought, 'I'm twenty-four, I've been made bankrupt. Just got married. I'm in Ilford, at the top of the building, in a ladies' toilet with two strippers. I've got nothing to lose.'

I went out there, and I was different. All that experience had changed me. I'd grown up. I started to win.

They liked me.

They hadn't seen anyone who didn't just do gags before.

After the show, Ronnie encouraged me, 'There's something about you, you wanna stick at it. Have you done much?'

'No, not really.'

'Well, I get loads of work. Anything that comes my way that I can't do, I'll pass it over to you.'

I asked my friend Barry if he would come back and join us now that things were starting to improve.

'I've got a good job,' he said, 'reading gas meters. It's job-and-finish, so it gives me lots of free time. I don't want to take a chance that you may or may not make it.'

Bye, Barry.

One particular stripper sticks out in my mind. She was the traditional Gypsy Rose Lee style. She was fifty-odd. Still stripping. She talked like a stripper version of Irene Handl. We always changed together. On one occasion, she opened a broom cupboard in these offices where we were doing a show, took out half a packet of Flash, and half a tin of Vim, and put them in her bag.

'What're you doing?'

'Well, it all 'elps, dun it!'

She would sit there, lost in her own world.

'Ya see these shoes? I got 'em darn the Port-a-bella Road market. Owny a paand.'

They were the worst shoes. You wouldn't put them on a dog. But I encouraged her, I loved to hear her talk.

'How do you get around, your car's never working?'

'Ah, it don't matter. I'm a member of the are-ay-cee relay, and the ay-ay relay, and the are-ay-cee recovery. So when I get a gig, I ring up the RAC recovery and tell 'em me car's brerken darn, and it's outside me front door, and they come and pick it up, and I say I live wherever the show is. Then they drop me off there, and I say "Ta", and they go off thinkin' that's me 'ome. I go in and do the gig, and when I've finished strippin' and showin' the geezers me snatch I ring up the AA relay and say I've brerken darn, and they come and pick me up and I sit in the front with the bloke, and they take me 'ome.'

I learned in three or four years what it would have taken ten years to learn.

I had to drive like a maniac to get from one gig to the other, change, and go on. You didn't have time to think whether you'd died a death or not. You didn't care. It was great experience. And I used to get the cabarets out of it because I was considered clean in comparison with everyone else. Even though I put the odd word in here and there. I used to get Saturday shows for a bit more money, and I think that's how I started getting a mixture of men and women. And the men were going home saying, 'You wanna see this bloke.'

I started getting a small cult following. It was nothing to do with the world I had left down in Devon, where it was all family entertainment. I didn't know *this* world at all.

I was drinking on and off all around this period. Not much. I never remember having that much. But I don't have a very high tolerance. I might 'go' a bit, after a few at a party. That was about the extent of it. I had money in my pocket for once in my life. I did every gig there was going. I was out most nights.

Eddie started looking after my accounts then. A few bob was coming in. He looked after my money. Kept an eye on it, so I didn't end up in the same situation as I had before. Life seemed to have some normality. Even my drinking didn't seem out of the ordinary.

When I was struggling for anything, I was fine. The minute I achieved it, the problems started. When I'm struggling with things I never have any problem, when I'm after something, all the world's at one. I don't know why that is. When I achieve it, I self-destruct.

You know when someone has a glass of wine, and they go, 'Ooh, that's lovely'?

It didn't do anything for me. I don't remember it making me go doolally.

Cheryl and I were like any young couple. We were still in the early part of marriage. It was all, 'Let's have fun, life's all fun, isn't it.'

I liked feeling the high. How I got the high was of no interest to me. It didn't bother me. If someone said, 'You feel good if you have a couple of these,' I wouldn't query whether I liked the taste. It was only the high.

*

Cheryl took over the management full time. Billie wrote to me and said, 'I don't think you can have an agent and a manager,' and released me from my contract. She wrote, 'We can handle him, but we can't handle that wife!'

Cheryl put me with Norman Murray and Anne Chudleigh. She'd known Norman years before.

He didn't give me much at the beginning, but he gave me what he could. I started getting bottom of the bill on summer shows. He handled people like Dickie Henderson, Les Dawson, Little and Large, Hinge and Bracket. Particularly comics. He would get me whatever work he could in those big shows. Trying to break in a *new* comic in that world is, like, forget it.

Norman would ring up every so often, and say, 'I've got somebody I'd like to see him.'

We'd try and arrange a half-decent show. I managed to get a cabaret, as opposed to a stag, in a dustmen's club in Leytonstone, with strip lights hanging down, and a half-concocted stage up in the corner. Anne and Norman and this American agent arrived. I was changing in the kitchen. Cheryl asked them what they wanted to drink. There was no champagne, just pomagne. They only had pint glasses. The American guy asked for a whisky, and they put this single whisky in a pint glass. They came in and sat, and I did my act. I didn't hear any more, so I presumed he didn't like the whisky, or he didn't think I was any good.

I did loads of warm-ups. Norman said I wasn't going to get noticed doing football clubs and stags; you needed to be in the corridors of power.

I got thrown off a few of them. When the floor manager asked me to stop, I would carry on until I'd finished. The audiences started paying more attention to me than what was going on on the studio floor, which wasn't liked very much. I did warm-ups for Mike Yarwood, Kelly Monteith, Les Dawson, Little and Large, Marti Caine; 'Are you being Served?', 'Citizen Smith', and 'The Generation Game'.

I'd be booked for three, and I'd do one. They wouldn't ask me back for the other two.

One time, Felix Bowness said to me, ' 'Ere, you wanna watch it.'

'Why?'

'Well, you won't get asked to do many more of these warm-ups, you know, if you carry on like this. I'm just warning you, 'cause Billy Cotton Jr's in tonight. If you wanna get the work in, you've got to play ball a bit more.'

My intention wasn't to make a living from warm-ups. I was there to get noticed.

Cheryl used to come. She would sit at the back.

I was doing warm-ups for Little and Large. We even wrote a sketch for them. Gave it to the producer, and he gave it to one of the writers to rewrite. But it was already written up. We got paid fifty quid, but there was no credit. Cheryl said, 'Where's our credit on the roller?'

'I'm not giving you a credit,' he replied.

'We should have a credit, we did that routine.'

'You're not getting a credit, the writers get the credit, I've paid you for it.'

'That isn't the point. I want a credit on the roller.'

He just went berserk. Cheryl wouldn't take no for an answer. He stood up, then tore down the stairs with his head in his hands screaming, 'Get that woman out of this studio, now!'

Two security guys came along, and slung her out into the car park.

I started to get the odd spot here and there. I was one of the 'Junior Celebrities' on a pilot for a show called 'Punchlines'. When the actual show was made, I wasn't on it.

Norman Murray rang the producer, 'What's wrong with Michael Barrymore? Why aren't you using him on the actual show? Any schmuck can sit there and do that show.'

'Yes, Mr Murray, but any schmuck doesn't sit there with the disdain that Michael Barrymore had on his face.'

They wanted us to jump around and wave our arms in the air. I wouldn't do it. I felt a prat. I just sat there with a straight face.

I did a summer season with Little and Large in Bournemouth. One of my agents, Anne Chudleigh, persuaded the head of the company, David Bell, to come and see me. He rang her back, 'I don't know what he does, darling, but I'll give him a spot on Russ Abbott.' John Kaye Cooper was directing. They booked me as one of the team. It was my first real big telly break.

David Bell was to figure very highly in most of my early TV appearances. He died in 1990. He is a sad loss to the industry, and to me personally.

Eddie started our company. He gave up the rag trade to run the financial side of my business. I had a cult following. I was working on my stage act all the time.

Eddie was the father I never had. I was the son he always wanted. He would do anything for me. It wasn't 'his daughter and her husband'. He wouldn't put Cheryl before me, we were equal. And I trusted him with my life. You could never shock him. Whatever you thought was the worst thing in the world, he'd been there, seen it, done it, read it, made the film. He became a very big influence in everything I did, and how I did it.

Around about that time, I was drinking a bit. I never had a drop when I worked. You can't. Well, I can't. If you take a mood changer, you can't be anything but somebody else. It's impossible to be yourself. If you aren't yourself on stage you've got trouble.

I did two seasons of the 'Madhouse', two specials, then I left to do my first series for Thames Television. David Clark had seen me on the 'Madhouse'. He'd also used me as a warm-up man on 'Give Us A Clue'. I did God knows how many warm-ups for the BBC, and got bugger all out of it; I did one for Thames and David went out on a limb for me. I ended up with a series called the 'Michael Barrymore Show'. We tried different things. Up until then, people hadn't gone into studio audiences.

My first TV write-up came from Maureen Paton of the *Express*. One of her quotes read, 'I wouldn't like to meet this man up a dark alley.'

I saw her picture. I thought, 'I wouldn't like to meet you up a bright alley!'

I was considered 'alternative' at the time. Doing off-the-wall things.

After my first series aired, Norman said, 'If you carry on with that series, you'll be dead within twenty months, and you won't be seen again.'

I knew he was right.

'Unless they give you Studio One, a whole set of writers, and everything you need, I'd walk away from the contract.'

He'd seen this happen before, where everyone gets carried away with an artist, then the series doesn't work.

I said to Norman, 'What are you saying? Don't forget, there's twenty thousand pounds involved in the next two series.'

'I'm saying that you turn round and say you're refusing to do it.'

I've just started. I've got my first break, my first TV show, and I'm about to turn around and tell Thames Television, the biggest independent at the time, that I'm not doing the other two series they've signed me for.

I pulled out of the contract. So I had no series, no other offers. I'd got nothing. I was left wanting again.

After a short spell in the wilderness, I was offered a show for the BBC, called 'Get Set Go'. It lasted one series. Michael Grade cancelled it straight away. Bye bye BBC!

So I'd been chucked out of the BBC, I'd left Thames, my telly career had started and ended. One producer kept the faith. Despite widespread indifference, John Fisher gave me a star guest spot with Joan Rivers. It worked.

Because of the impact of that show, the phones rang again. Norman managed to get me a spot on the Royal Variety.

The Royal Variety changed everything.

I was asked to have a look at a tape of another game show. I thought, 'I've just bombed with one!' It was an American show called 'Strike It Rich'. I looked at it, Cheryl looked at it. We thought, 'It's all right . . .'

We both decided that if they let me have free rein in putting it together, we might be able to make something of it. It was renamed 'Strike It Lucky'. It started to take off. The team gelled. It was a different ball game. I had the right people round me, who believed in me. It gave me confidence. With that confidence, I started to get successful.

And I started to drink.

I would get a bit wild after a few glasses, nothing more than high jinks. I wasn't aware of any real problems. Singalongs would be the order of the day when the show was over. I often wonder if, at that time in my life, I got carried away with it all. I had Eddie, the dad I'd never had, I had Cheryl and Kit, I had a family, and success. With all that around me, I was getting the attention I'd struggled for. It started to get to me.

As much as you wish for stardom, it's never in your thinking that the bright lights will shine on you. When it becomes fact, and suddenly everyone in the street is recognising you, it's a weird feeling, and hard to handle.

There are very agreeable aspects of success. It's like winning the football pools several times over. So it always sounds ungrateful when you say it's hard.

I remember being very happy around that period, in the early days of 'Strike It Lucky'. My drinking was getting heavy for a while with the early success. The success was making me feel claustrophobic. And I relied on booze to release me from my self-inflicted solitary confinement. I think Cheryl wanted to control my drinking, and make sure it didn't go the wrong way. Where my addiction was starting to become Jack Daniels, her addiction was me.

Today, success no longer holds any fear for me. I'm fine, it sits on my shoulders comfortably. But at that time whenever I had a break from work, I tried to match the adrenaline and the way I felt when I was doing a show. I drank whisky to make me feel different. The drop in adrenaline when you stop working is extraordinary. For different pressures pour different measures.

I knew I had to stop. I did. For four years. I started drinking again at thirty-eight, the night Eddie died. But I started hiding it. From everyone, including Cheryl.

That's when the insanity began.

Cheryl never really pushed me. She'd catch me on the booze a couple of times, then there'd be guilt and remorse. I had promised that I wouldn't drink again.

Pressure from the press wasn't helping. That was the year that they implied I had AIDS. It was just too much for me to stand: coming out of Miami airport with sixty journalists in front of us. Being followed down to Key West, journalists underneath our room, above it, to the side of it, out on the beach, security having to take me everywhere.

There was absolutely no story.

It all started outside London Weekend Television. We were recording 'Barrymore'. When I came out, a journalist shouted, 'Feeling well, are you, Michael?'

'Fine.'

I was getting thin through all the worry, I was like a rake. But, then again, I was always thin. He said, 'Have you had a blood test?'

'What's that got to do with how I feel? What do you think I am, a vampire?'

That was it, I got in the car. The campaign started. They were following me everywhere. They went through my dustbins at home. Another nightmare.

There were problems on the first series of 'Barrymore'. I was very unhappy. I lost a lot of weight. Eddie had died.

Cheryl said, 'We need a holiday.'

We were due to do 'Strike It Lucky' mid-January. Maurice, my producer, put it back. I needed the break. Cheryl and I went to Key West. Maurice had a call from the press, 'We hear that Michael

Barrymore is so ill he can't continue. He's had to cancel "Strike It Lucky".'

'You want the story? The story is that we have postponed it for two weeks because the studio is not available and he wants a holiday. He's not ill at all.'

The *Star* newspaper broke it. Then every paper picked it up. The campaign began.

The headlines were unbelievable!

It was the first time I was aware of so much attention. I don't know why they took to me like that. I found that an extra pressure in some ways. The press didn't stop following me. They had this obsession. They followed me in my car, pretended they were the police, made up all sorts of cock-and-bull stories.

During this period, one person after another joined the queue to talk to the papers: Trevor and Billie George and their daughter Melina; my brother, sister, the best man at my wedding, Barry; many others, and my mother. To some degree I can understand non-family members feeling they have something to say. It's par for the course. You can't spend years seeking recognition, and then complain when you get it. Everyone has a point of view. In a society of free speech, it has to be so. Good or bad, correct or not. It's the business I'm in. But with my family, it was different. For years, I gave to my mother, and via her, to my family. It was as if I owed the whole family a living. Obviously I couldn't give as much as Fleet Street. There was one price for fame. There was another price for my family. That upset me. They never asked about me, never asked me how I was.

'How do you feel?'

Worse.

It all preyed on my mind. The press, my family, fame, the attention. I think the warmth of the public helped me through a lot of it. Because they're so nice with me, and everyone's so protective towards me. It's one of the few pressures I can cope with.

*

As I said, on the first series of 'Barrymore' there were problems. There always are. But I started to kick up about it. The same thing was happening as happened at the beginning of 'Strike It Lucky', where people were trying to format me. The reason I'd got as far as I had was because of not doing things conventionally.

I was now the head of the family. I had responsibility. But I felt lost without Eddie. My security had gone. I never had to worry before. Eddie would sort it out. That crutch was taken away from me.

I didn't grieve for Eddie for a long time.

Even when I went to places like Grosvenor House, to awards ceremonies, I'd sit there with a juice or coke. I considered it work. When I meet the public, I won't put myself in a situation where I can't cope. But I couldn't handle being at home. The pressure the press put on me, and the restrictions they put on what I could do, made me say to myself, 'I'll do what I want. I'll go where I want to go. Nobody's going to tell me where to go.'

Of course, you can't just do what you want. You learn that you can't. That's the price of fame.

In the mornings, I would wake up, and say to myself, 'I wonder what happened last night.' Somebody could have a quite lucid conversation with me, but it wasn't me. I had a conversation with Maurice, which went, 'Do you know, there's a world at the bottom of that pond!'

'Yeah, well, there's newts and tadpoles and things like that.'

'They've got cities and roads, there's a complete world. Traffic lights, buildings . . .'

Shelly Winters said, 'The insane are the only sane people.' I rest my case.

I was giving Cheryl such a hard time. I spent so long giving out to everyone else, I would take it out on her, to get rid of my anger.

I stopped enjoying work.

Maurice would try and make me feel better.

'You look very cheerless. Look at *me*. Zilch talent. You have all this wonderful talent, all the recognition. You're not enjoying it. It's such a terrible waste. Why are you doing it all, why? You put a lot into your work, you're a very conscientious person, you rehearse yourself to death with dance routines, you care very deeply about your work. You do it very well. That's why it succeeds. You can't achieve the success you've had without knowing what you're doing. But you seem to be going through a black period. I hope to Christ it doesn't last. You're not getting any pleasure out of it at all.'

Everything seemed pointless to me. And then, during a season in Bournemouth, I cracked. I came off stage one night. I couldn't hack it any more. There were 3000 people out there who were all having fun. And I wasn't. Everything that I'd worked for didn't mean a thing.

My mother had sent me a letter. It said, 'Your dad died in 1987.'

My life as a kid flashed back.

Maybe that had been the part of the jigsaw that was missing.

I was carted off to Marchwood Priory. I met Austin Tate, who became my psychiatrist. It was all put down to stress. I was only there three days. But I was on my own for the first time in my life. I needed to get away from everyone. I started talking for the first time, like I am now. I wasn't frightened any more to say it how it was. If somebody doesn't like it that way then it's their problem. I had to learn to like myself.

During my stay at Marchwood, I went fishing. Down by the lake, I got a call on the mobile phone. I couldn't return to the clinic. The place was surrounded by press. I had to go home that night. I tried to carry on. I don't like to let people down. I kept making promises that I'd get it together, saying it and not doing it.

I went back to work on the following Tuesday.

On 'Barrymore' series three, I started to lose control. I was becoming powerless. I had bottles of booze in the back of the car. I would go out of the flat in Knightsbridge, into the lift, down four flights to the basement, run round to the car, press the button, open the boot, take a swig, run up, through the lobby, across Brompton Road, into the newsagent's, grab as many magazines as I could, pay for them, run back over the road, through the lobby, down the stairs, round to the car, have another swig, suck a peppermint, go back up the four flights, walk in, say, 'Are there any magazines you want?'

And Cheryl would say, '*Tatler*.'

So I'd go back into the lift, down to the bottom and the routine would start again. In the end, it was costing me more in magazines than it was in booze. I had car magazines, boating magazines, flying magazines, all the women's magazines, men's magazines, *Fishing Monthly*, *Fishing Weekly*, *Exchange & Mart*.

Just to have a swig.

Another blow came when I was watching a TV show. My brother appeared in an advert for the *Sunday Mirror*. I looked at the television in disbelief. He turned to camera, and said, 'I'm Michael Barrymore's brother. I'll tell you the whole story about him in the *Sunday Mirror* tomorrow.' My mother also appeared, this time looking like I'd never seen her before. The hair. Her make-up. The whole look. Manufactured by publicists.

I couldn't stop crying. It wasn't their place to be there.

Later another front-page edition of the *Mirror* read, 'Barrymore's new sorrow. *Daily Mirror* finds his long-lost father in pauper's grave.'

My brother, suitably sorrowful, was pictured looking into camera, beside an overgrown headstone.

It was one of the sickest feelings ever.

My behaviour changed. I would suddenly disappear. For two or three minutes. And then reappear.

Addicts think that nobody else knows.

To me, everything was quite normal.

But it wasn't sane behaviour. It's not sane behaviour to have bottles on the top of kitchen units, grab one when somebody goes out of the kitchen, take a swig, and then sling it back up again. It's not sane behaviour, running up and down four flights of stairs to have a swig in the boot of a car. If you say 'take it or leave it' to an addict, they can't.

Cheryl and I went to Palm Beach at the end of the series, which was winning award after award.

In Palm Beach, I always fish from the jetty at the edge of the house. We were there two days and the front doorbell went. The *People* newspaper wanted to do an interview. We said, 'No, go away.'

Next thing, two other newspapers at home published pictures of me fishing. They'd been out in a boat, and taken the shot from the water. I went completely mad. The last memory I have before arriving at Ashley, is sitting on the deck, looking out to sea, with a guy called Bob Beckett talking to me. Cheryl had been moved out to a hotel. At about half past four in the morning, I turned around to Bob and said, 'So what's the bottom line then, of what you're saying?'

'I want you to go to Ashley.'

'Right, I'll go.'

Next morning, we went to have something to eat with Cheryl. We were all talking sanely then, instead of screaming and shouting at each other. I started shaking – at the thought of leaving I suppose. She thought she'd have to get me to hospital. By 3.30 pm I was on a plane to Baltimore.

Tim asks the group for their reactions, after thanking me for the way I told the story, as me, and not the stage Michael. I thought they were the same, but he's not to know yet. He's kind. He says, 'It must have taken a lot of courage to tell a story that back home could be sold for thousands.'

I am proud that I opened up. There is a sense of relief. To my right, Chong is crying his eyes out. Mr Atheist has been cracked. There must be some recognition in something I said.

Skip says, 'It seems to me that you're not happy when you

achieve things. When you're struggling, everything's fine. When you get what you're going for, the bad side starts.'

Tim comments on my story, and concludes that I fear the unknown, and that there is a piece of the jigsaw missing. They are all kind, and understanding, and give me total support. I have a feeling of elation, of weight being taken off. My natural instinct takes over. Here comes the bull. There are his horns. I grab both of them, but this time I take the whole bull. It's a moment for me, at this moment I am at one with myself. It's a great buzz, without a drop of booze – I thank you.

It's lunch again. Chong is still crying his eyes out. I had him down for comedy. He can hardly speak. The 'I hate God' voice, gone. His brick wall smashed around him. He just says, 'I'm sorry, man. But when you put your hands to your head, and over your ears to explain how you couldn't stand the rowing and noise as a kid, I just saw my little girl. I feel so bad for putting her through all that.'

Well, thank God we have a place like this to sort it out. If there were places like this thirty-odd years ago, I could have had a dad.

I leave him. He's going through enough pain. Only one day and he's broken in. But I'm sure, as all of us are, that there's a long way to go. This disease is curable, but it's for the rest of your life. I have just made the first step of my new life on the anniversary of my birthday. It's one of the best presents I've ever had. The first step reads: 'We admitted we were powerless over alcohol, that our lives had become unmanageable.'

At this rate, I'll get a BA (Bachelor of Alcohol)!

Howard's been to see the psychiatrist. He asked Dale, after the event, 'What is it they look for?'

'Your train of thought,' Dale says.

'Oh really, I thought they looked at your eyes, 'cause he said to me, "When did you first fuck up?" I said, "I've never fucked up. You and I were born at the same time. You're fucked up. I'm fucked up. We're both fucked up." I wondered why he was looking at me strange.'

'No,' said Dale, 'it's your train of thought.'

'Oh, shit! Three times in the middle of a sentence I said, "Where the fuck am I?" '

I must ask Austin Tate what heading Howard's train of thought comes under.

Another boring AA meet. Hope they're better than this on the outside. It brightens up at the end, but not because of the speakers. Skip hands me a piece of paper, neatly folded.

'Happy Birthday, buddy.'

'It's not until tomorrow, Skip.'

'So it's the first one.'

I thank him, and ask if I can open it tomorrow.

'Sure.'

Baywatch is walking towards me, with what looks like an abstract painting. It is not hard to recognise, as he's been driving me mad saying we're fellow artists. Well, he's right. We are fellow piss-artists! But that thing in his hand has nothing to do with my art. Now, I'm no judge, but how can I put this without being cruel? The truth is I can't. It is awful. But this is only my opinion.

He says, 'Will you hang this up in your home back in England?'

I pause.

If you know me well, the pause is enough. Only someone completely stoned could have painted this. It's under my bed at the moment, and I can still describe it. I can describe it artistically. It's shit. Coloured shit, but shit. But I *am* going to put it up, although not in the house. I have a summer house at the bottom of the garden. It's going in there. Any time I feel the urge to drink, I will go and look. That's all I have to do. So everyone is happy. I'm sure he will put in his CV that I have one. I hope he does!

Dale looks dumbfounded as he leaves. The silence is enough.

'We've got another new guy in today,' Dale says. 'He asked me who you are. Are you the Englishman? And what do you do? He heard it was something to do with television.'

Dale told him that, in fact, I was a porn star.

'Oh really?'

'Yeah. And he's got a dick,' Dale opened his hands to about a foot-and-a-half, 'this big.'

'You're kidding me.'

'No.'

After Dale tells me, I limp around for a while. The guy gives a look of unease. He must learn to lighten up in here.

Lights out.

STEP TEN

Continued to take personal inventory and when we were wrong promptly admitted it.

CHAPTER ELEVEN

Wednesday, 4 May

DAY TWELVE
6.00 am – It's My Party and I'll Cry if I Want to

The earliest up for my birthday. It's overcast outside. We have a rule in our home – you're not allowed to cry on your birthday. But I'm not in our home. I'm being reborn. Before I go to the hall for breakfast I will look at Skip's home-made card. It's one of the nicest I've ever had. It reads:

> *Michael,*
> *You have no idea how much you helped my sanity the first few days here. Happy Birthday. This is an IOU, if you ever need anything, anything at all, just call or write, and I will do anything in my power. Hoping this birthday is the beginning of many in sobriety.*
> *I am your friend.*
>
> *Skip*

I see Skip first thing that morning.

'Happy Birthday.'

Howard, Penny, Tony all do the same. It's nice they remember, very nice.

Gerry the Policeman does the thought for the day. Theme: 'I must train my mind to do what I think.'

'Catch a stick, back flips through a blazing hoop,' he says.

What the hell is he talking about?

When he was drinking, he thought he was above everyone else. Now he's different because of God.

Are you, Gerry, are you really?

8.45 am

Father Martin braves the rain. I try not to bump into him. Can't have the troops thinking I'm being favoured. Half of them already think that, so I should care. We bump.

'Nice brolly, Father Martin.'

'Michael. Wa'd'ya say, me boy?'

They are obviously not called brollies!

'The umbrella!'

'Yes, it's a Brigg. One hundred and fifty bucks, ya know.'

I do. I say to myself. I've got two at home. They're made in England. I humour him.

'How did you get yours? Is it nicked?'

'What? Oh yes, nicked. It's an English expression,' he explains to anyone near. 'Yes, Benny Hill used the word "nicked" in a sketch he did about losing a trophy, remember?'

I nod, 'Yes', not having a clue.

Father Martin goes over the hill.

'Who's nicked the trophy?'

He's had too much communal wine, I think.

He isn't bad, this morning. Jokewise, he starts off with 'Going to bed when you get older gets to be a chore, it's a removal of parts.' He demonstrates, removing his earplugs, glasses, teeth. Today he's on about humility, interspersed with 'When a big star is on the 'Johnny Carson Show', and says, "Don't put the camera on my left side, it's my worst," Johnny should look at her and say, "My God, you're right!" '

This would have had more impact if someone had told him Johnny retired five years ago.

He's going on about the first three steps. I sing to myself, 'There are only three steps to heaven'. *He's* off to Detroit. The

Vatican exchange, probably. He tells us step five is the hardest, because of the line, 'admit to God'. Well, I could, he confesses, and still be on course. The rest of the line says, 'to ourselves and to another'. 'Then only one other human knows the real me.'

Mmm . . . This needs translating. Where is Rene when you need him?

During the break, Ray wishes me happy birthday. Says he's got a letter from his airline group. Part of it reads. 'You are a young man, feeling better, and just starting life.'

Ray responds, as only Ray can, 'Fuck you. You don't wake up with a fifty-five-year-old body.'

10.15 am

Sal gives me a card he's got from the store. He's been at table thirty for a week now. He really is a nice man. He seems to have more intelligence than your average intelligent alcoholic. I can't think who he looks like, it's an actor. It will come to me. Sal writes a message. It says:

> Dear Mike,
>   Just a little note to wish you well on your birthday,
> and a happy sober year ahead. Thank you for getting me
> through the rough spots of the first week. You, and
> table thirty, have been very helpful.

The card reads:

> 'Wishing you a most magical birthday.'

Underneath he's written,

This card reminds me of Blanche in Streetcar,
'I don't want realism, I want magic'

Peace and love,
Sal

It's a very camp card for in here, even more so when I find out Sal loves Sondheim, and we sing 'Broadway Baby' for the tenth time.

Next we meet Counsellor Dale Edwards. The subject, 'feelings' (another tune). This place is full of songs and sobriety. He uses humour to put his subject over.

On the board he's written:

'C.M. ducks M.8 ducks O.S.M.R. C.M. tails L.I.B. ducks.'

He reads, 'See them ducks, them ain't ducks, oh yes them are. See them tails, well, I'll be, ducks.'

A titter ensues. Not a great start, Dale, try again. He's nervous, very nervous. He says he hasn't done this for a while. I would have bluffed it. My God, they are honest in here.

He says that addicts all have feelings that make them do what they do, i.e. good feeling – DRINK, bad feeling – DRINK.

How to heal yourself: get rid of taboos. Hear, hear.

Addicts, he says, suffer from reverse paranoia. 'Instead of thinking someone is following you, you think you are following them.'

He asks us to grade ourselves. Little ol' wine-drinking Roger says he's a 'B'. Mr Atheist says that he's a 'B+'.

Dale hits straight back, 'You must be an alcoholic.'

'You bet,' he yells with pride.

Only an alcoholic would make himself a 'B+'. Nothing is ever straightforward in their lives, for some, even when sober. I am an 'A'. I think that only two days ago, I would have been a 'B'. Things, for me at least, seem to be moving (a day at a time).

Dale, I find out, is Arthur's counsellor, so *he* must have passed on the complaint. Trap number two, but I'll let him off. I like him. Nerves and all. Sorry, Arthur, you're still in jankers.

Baywatch says he gets stoned at the opening of his art shows. I feel better every day.

Counsellor Dale, looking straight at me, says, 'We need to find ourselves, not what we are and what we do. You mustn't bring what you do into here.'

So if I make someone laugh by what I do, or what I say, then how do I deal with that? It's my business to make people like me. Dale is struggling here, not just with me.

Michael (Norman Bates) is challenging him on self-esteem and self-confidence, and how they go together. Bates says he feels bad. Oh shit, Dale. There is, for some reason, a strange atmosphere. Dale loses it. I hope he learns from it and goes on.

We finish twenty minutes early.

In silence.

Lunch

We collect our food. The dessert looks like an ice cream birthday cake. It has been cut into pieces.

'You can have cake or grapes,' bellows Grandma Clampitt. I take grapes, and change my mind twice.

'Make your mind up, fellah.'

'Can I have both?'

'Nowp.'

Behind me I hear, 'It's his birthday.'

She bellows on, 'I don't give a shit what day it is. Grapes or cake.'

I take the grapes.

Ray comes over to my table carrying a helium balloon, with 'Happy Birthday' on it, and a card. They all sing 'Happy Birthday'. I am suitably embarrassed. My messages on the card read:

'Forty-two is the old age of youth. Fifty-two is the youth of old age.'

'All the best, Geoff the bobby.'

'One more year full of love. Good health, faith, hope, cheers.'

'Thanks, Michael, thanks for all the laughs so far. Hope to see you on the telly.'

'Happy Birthday to the most interesting "normal" person in this place.'

'Have fun, happy birthday, mother fucker one.'

'Good luck, love yourself, you're a treasure.'

'All the best to a fun guy, from Batman. Happy Birthday, what's up with the Beatles, Robin?'

'Thanks for making me laugh, Amy.'

'Have a happy fucking birthday you ol' mother fucker.'

So on and so on (and I left Howard to the end).

1.00 pm

Group goodbyes to Sarah and Kelly. Before the group starts, Kelly cries. She gets round to telling us that the reason is she's pregnant. It never rains but it pours, for an addict at least. We go round saying what we like, good or bad, to send them on their way. They, in turn, release their parting shot on each of us. Sarah is still fixated on her little boy (and she is pregnant as well). Jesus, how does that happen? It must be divine intervention, a spiritual screwing. Three girls in my group, two up the duff. Nice start to their new life.

Sarah says 'thank you' to me for making her laugh, and to look after myself, and that she will pray for me.

Kelly, likewise; her tears have receded for a second. She smiles. She has a great face, and looks like she means it when she says, 'You can come back anytime. You know you have a family here.'

It's a comforting thought.

I just hope that if I come back, two kids don't run up to me and shout, 'Daddy'! If they do, I will know that this wasn't a dream, for some.

We also say 'hello' to a new lad – Brian. He's stocky. His dad, whom he works for, sent him here. His breathing sounds panicky. He's to my right. And on the right hand of God, stood Brian. Where is Monty Python when I need him? I am, after all, playing a major role in the life of Brian. Over the next few days, we may discover what. Loosen up Brian, loosen up.

2.30 pm – Jack Touché (alias Fred Flintstone)

Very touchy today. If any of us rubbed up the ladies as much as he does, we would be out on our arses. On the outside, he would be arrested for sexual harassment. But he's here. He's still here. He's wearing a bright pink cardigan. With his weight, he looks like a giant strawberry yoghurt. There is enough to feed the entire community, but the thought of licking Touché to death is more than any could bear.

In fairness to Jack, he must believe it's the way to relax people. To make them feel that they're wanted. It might be just my Englishness that makes me so cynical about this approach. Hug, hug. Kiss, kiss. Touchy, touchy.

'I ♡ a Touch-é.'

Yoghurt says, 'Depressed people live in yesterday. Hyper people live for tomorrow. Happy people live for today.'

And yoghurts live in plastic cartons.

Frances is sitting beside Jack. She's getting extra hand rubs, which we can all see. Is this supposed to get us going, Yoghurt Face? Because it's failing. She gives him a very secretarial look. The few of us that know what's going on are stifling our laughter. He's working his way up to her neck. He's like a blind ventriloquist looking for the hole in the dummy's back. Frances is not best pleased. She's tries to shrug him off. The hole he's interested in is not in her back.

He tells us about 'one person groups'. An alcoholic in Alaska will talk over the radio to one in the North Pole. It doesn't seem fair. Each of them live in a place with not another soul around, and they are potential pissheads. Life's a bitch.

A highlight is when the Russians speak for the first time, via Alexi their interpreter. I hope it's easier than this if my show is ever aired in their country. Jack tries to look really interested, nodding as if he knows what they are saying. With my limited knowledge of the Russian language, I think one of them has just asked, 'Have you always had a prick for a face?' I can't stay to hear the outcome, I have to leave early to phone my psychiatrist in England. Bye, Yoghurt Face!

Phone Call

I tell Austin that this isn't the easiest, most enjoyable event of my life. He's pleased. He would be worried if I said it was. I convince myself, before someone says it, 'no pain, no gain'.

He seems surprised by some of their methods, but the methods seems to work. Well, I'm here, I'm still here – just.

I try to hurry him along. I realise I've been left alone in my counsellor's office, alone on a phone, so I just hope Cheryl is at home in Palm Beach.

'Hello.'

She lets out a sound that girls do when they get their first Barbie doll. We talk and talk, and scheme how to do this again. Her voice sounds better. We are both under a great strain. She has a new counsellor. Got through one already. That's Cheryl. She says, 'This one is great, she's just like me.'

Oh, they will be pleased back home. There are now two Cheryls walking around.

I really am lucky. Women are the only reason I survive this world. They understand me for some reason, and we don't have to get in bed together to make it work. Cheryl takes care of me, and I for the most part take care of her. Behind every great man is a woman. If it were possible to have two or three more, believe me, you could conquer everything. I feel I can conquer this disease. She finishes.

Geoff the bobby has caught me. He seems to believe I'm still talking to England. Cheryl finished by telling me that the last show of the season is in all the papers, because it smashed the opposition – 'The Eurovision Song Contest', a big worldwide show. It makes me feel good. Any ego rub is appreciated in this place.

As I walk to dinner, maple seeds are dropping from the sky like rescue helicopters.

Your mission, should you wish to accept, is to go to rehab, and save all the lost souls. Some of them will self- destruct in five seconds.

One of the guys who sat on my table the first day, is on the outside. Reports are coming in that he is attending AA meetings every night. Good. He has a drink before he goes, every night. Not so good.

At the dinner, a very prim, nose-in-the-air lady is having a hard time dealing with the situation. She turns the corner. Howard is trying to bring himself round with a glass of water. He screams, 'Yuck!', straight into her face.

The sound and sight of Howard is too much for her. Eyelids fluttering, she collapses to the floor.

He steps over her, and mumbles. 'Stupid bitch.'

At the evening AA meet, we have a new guy, Mike, who sits behind me. He seems to know the ropes. He loved it so much, it's his second visit. The guy behind the lectern tells us his friend hasn't turned up, but he got lucky. God helped him. On his way here, he pulled up at a set of lights, and an alcoholic was in the car beside him. 'Come to Ashley, I need you.'

The alcoholic gets up. Within fifteen minutes, he has repeated himself five times. He grinds to a halt. From experience, drying up on stage is, or can be, one of the worst nightmares imaginable. Adam, a freckle-faced relapse, puts his hand up to suggest questions and answers. If he hadn't this meeting would have put Mike back inside a whisky glass. The meeting is crap. No one's fault. Just crap. I am becoming one of the seniors here, so I am looking forward to some new interns.

Lights out.

STEP ELEVEN

———•———

Sought through prayer and meditation to improve our conscious contact with God as we understood Him, praying only for knowledge of His will for us and the power to carry that out.

CHAPTER TWELVE

Thursday, 5 May

DAY THIRTEEN

6.00 am

'Time to get up, guys,' says Gerry. Cue music (song, 'Hello
Marylou').

> *I said, hello Maryland*
> *Early start*
> *Sweet Maryland, I'm so in love with you*
> *I knew Maryland*
> *You stole my heart*
> *So let go Maryland*
> *Brand new start.*

The Reverend Ray enters the shower room, singing Bob Dylan's
It Ain't Me Babe. It must be the chart show today. Mike is in my
shower. Well, not mine, but the one I use. Great, I'll have to use
the other one. Why does it take an intervention to see there's
another way? We are very territorial here.

7.00 am

George Bush tells us Terry; our recreation counsellor is getting
married. Good luck to him. I haven't heard his tragic story yet.
George Bush tells us that here you can get weller-than-well.
Perhaps, I think, we can get betterer-than-better. I must say he

dresses very well. Great suit. I wonder if my company have sold all my suits. His look very familiar. If they are, there's a small bottle of whisky in the inside pocket.

Sasha, one of the Russians, gives me a present for my birthday. A day late, but who cares. It's a picture he's drawn, in pen, of a man standing beside a table, with a large glass of booze on it. I lick the paper. He laughs. Well, they do have a sense of humour. I think that if ever they do attack, I'll do the licking-the-picture routine. Headline: 'Russian front dies laughing'. We have a conversation. Well, we nod a lot, with that inane grin people all over the world have that says, 'I haven't got a clue what you are saying, but I'll pretend.' Know what I mean, schmuck.

Baywatch interrupts. For once his timing is good. For all I know I could have agreed that the Russians can have Europe, as long as we get to keep the McDonald's franchise.

'Yes, what do you want?'

He wants my home address.

'I'll get it to you.'

God, how long can I keep lying? As long as it takes to get him off my back.

8.45 am

Policeman Gerry tells us there is recreation at the bar. He falls over his words. 'I mean the barber and beauty salon.'

Proves that booze may be out of your system, but never out of your mind. 'Came to realise this disease is a cunning one.' You're cured, but never free of it.

HIV is on the menu today, a subject guaranteed to get anyone's attention, no matter how hardened you think you are.

May, an HIV rep, tells us all about the subject. It's everything you've heard, plus an update on new theories. Still a minefield, still a nightmare, still on offer for $85. For just one week, folks!

I can't believe it, we have just had a forty-five minute advert based on AIDS, so that we can purchase, at a bargain price, a certificate and ticket to meet the powerful one! And have a tour of heaven. The tour for the rest of time.

Oh, by the way, in this country, tuberculosis is on the increase. A test is given free with every HIV check.

May tells us even alcoholics can get HIV, because they don't know what happens during their blackout period. Scary or what? No what, just scary!

Howard asks how long the virus can live in the air, because he has had so many tattoos.

She says less than a second.

Just make sure you don't go to the fastest tattooist in the west!

Heterosexual women are the most at risk, oral sex is also a problem.

She sums up that abstinence is the best.

I sum up that, for some, creative masturbation is the only answer.

Maybe I could start my own organisation, MA . . . Masturbators Anonymous.

Cutting an orange in half, and making a hole in the middle, is highly recommended. Full of vitamin C.

May tells of a man who gave a woman the virus. She took him to court. He was tried and convicted of assault with a deadly weapon. No comment! There is a theory that the virus originated from Africa, from apes. Howard appraises the theory: 'So some dickhead banged a monkey and left all of us to pay the price – arsehole.' Maybe that would have been safer.

The only people who take an HIV test are those who are worried. About the need.

I try to grab some air before the day gathers more pace. A 747 is preparing for landing at a testing ground nearby. Ray is standing by me. 'That's Air Force One.'

So the President has decided to bring his plane to see me. I wonder if Hilary is having a drink on board.

Ray tells me all about the plane. What it's got, which is everything. Full computer centre, side-winding missile, bomb proof.

'You name it, it has it.'

'Rehab Centre?' I ask.

'Who knows?' says Ray. He turns, Jack Benny style. 'And who fucking cares?'

10.15 am – Group

I ask Skip what his surname is. It goes on forever. He is a Polack. That's why I like him. I knew there was something. For all the jokes, they really are a nice race of people. My make-up lady is Polish.

Chong, the atheist, has gone into, 'I really love this place.' But he is still giving a scientific answer to everything. I can't understand one word he says, they are all so long.

Brian, the new boy, is getting a migraine trying to decipher Chong. He leans across every time Chong finishes talking, 'W'ad 'e say?'

'I'll tell you after,' – not having a clue what he said either. We want to look intelligent. But this man is beyond intelligent. For all that, he still fucked up his social life and family. So much for intellect.

Brian has a panic attack. It is going to be tough for this lad. He is choking, that sick feeling in the throat, heart pumping, guts spinning. Because Judgement Day is upon him – he's been asked to tell us his story of how he got here. Tim wants it ready by Tuesday, just a few days away.

I don't know what is screwing him up. I know he's thinking, 'Stuff this. I'll have a drink.'

But traitors run away.

I hope he has the courage to go over the top and fight the problem, head on. We shall see.

Tim asks to see me after lunch.

Lunch

At lunch I meet Jeff, he looks like a young James Caan. He wears full denim and a baseball cap. He is a friend of Howard's, they did time in the Penn together, so we have another real inmate on table thirty. He's got a great smile, nice manner. Nothing like getting your head blown away by a man with a smile.

Tim asks me how I am doing, says he's very impressed with me, and any time the pressure is on, I am more than welcome to return for a few days, for a refresher course. And here's me thinking, probably hoping, that I can get thrown out. I say all the right things – unwittingly – so the change, at least for the moment, seems to be happening.

I remind him that if Cheryl and I aren't going to meet this Sunday, for our great escape, I need a slip allowing me to call her. He obliges – just.

As I leave his office, having earned 200 air miles, black Keith is singing 'Under the Boardwalk'. I join in the chorus.

Kay, a 'Golden Girls' throw-out with a very expensive face, is taking over from Tim until next Wednesday. She gets a brief history from everyone in our group. She strains to understand what I am saying, so I slow down my speech, but there is really no need. She strains to understand her fellow Americans.

Kay will take over our group on Friday. I wish her good luck.

When the cat's away these mice will surely play. Especially C57 BL mice (see page 89). We shall see.

Volleyball

This is one of my new discoveries. I can play it, which helps, but like everything with me it's all or nothing. At today's match I break Sal and Lew's thumbs, in an effort to get the ball over the net. What's a couple of thumbs when you win the point and, in their case, it will help keep them sober. It's one less tool to pick up a glass with.

Jeff (James Caan) asks about me, gets to see if he likes me or not. I've learnt that that's up to him. We seem to get along well, although it's early days yet. He used to date a girl called Annabel, from England. The way she said 'Tuesday' fascinated him. 'I guess I shoulda married her.'

Howard tells me that Jeff took $900 worth of heroin last night before coming here. I will watch his progress with interest. His being so high might explain his fascination with English girls who say, 'Tuesday'.

The speaker at the evening bash is Paul, our senior PSA (Policeman). He's straight out of a Cops and Robbers film. He's the community 'Terminator'. He tells his story. Think of how much anyone can drink, take drugs, rob, fight, shout and have heart attacks, then double it; that is Paul. And he still looks like a movie star. He certainly has the attention of all the ladies, of whatever age. He's got jet-black Indian hair, chiselled features and now spends his life righting his years of addiction as a young adoptee.

One of his harrowing stories is of the time he spent in Los Angeles.

He found houses that were owned and not occupied, and he lived in one of them for quite some time. Over the months he made repairs and decorated. But, one day, he came home to find the cops waiting for him. They had him on a ton of charges. But they couldn't make breaking and entering stick. The owners would not prosecute because he had done the place up so well. In fact they wanted to thank him!

I see him afterwards. He has a parcel for me. Some white socks and a new pair of shoes. Cheryl must know someone really well at the Red Cross. He asks me if there is any chocolate?

'You have already checked it, Paul.'

'I know, but you English won the war and nobody knows how, so I'm just checking.'

'If I had some, you would get them anyway.'

He senses a bribe. 'It won't do any good!'

I up the ante. 'What if the chocolates are Belgian?'

'OK,' says Paul.

I think of Eddie every time. Bribe the guards, bribe them, all's fair.

Frances is leaving tomorrow. She wants to see my new shoes. 'You must try them on.'

I forget for a moment just what excitement even a new pair of shoes can create, anything to take your mind off the real problem. It will be sad to see Frances go. She's assumed the role of mother for a few of us, and she has been writing everything down. Who knows what will happen to her? It seems to be all or nothing with this disease. You can't *half* get well. Frances, for all the attention she has paid to the lectures, should sail through to her old age. But I have a feeling as soon as lover boy returns, all her scribing, all her intense attention will be filed away. In the bin.

When your happy, bins are full of food. When you're not, there is always a space to trash a memory.

Jeff sits to have a coffee. He says he may or may not be around tomorrow. It depends on how well the drugs wear off.

'What's the longest you've ever been off drugs?'

'Only seven days at a time.'

If he makes it, this stint will seem like years.

He says he knows Nuche (Nuche came in the same time as Baywatch. He's an Italian seaman, big, very big).

'What does Nuche do for a living?'

'He punches people to death.'

'That's handy.'

News has just come in that Nuche is very upset with Baywatch because he's stuck his finger in his ear. Nuche tells everyone that if it wasn't for the fact that he would be thrown out, he would deal with him.

I, and most, if not all the community, would cover for Nuche. Please, Nuche, smash his brains in, it will only take a second.

I am, at this moment, experiencing incredible tiredness. It's like a drug in itself and it hurts, it really hurts. I look at Cheryl and Candy's picture. My eyes are heavy, I love you both.

Lights out.

STEP TWELVE

* • *

Having had a spiritual awakening as the result of these steps, we tried to carry this message to alcoholics and to practise these principles in all our affairs.

CHAPTER THIRTEEN

Friday, 6 May

DAY FOURTEEN

6.00 am

My second anniversary of sobriety. Two weeks. I look out of my picture window.

The whole world is spinning, the two small islets seem to be moving to my left and out of sight. I have landed in hell. Perhaps they drug you halfway through, so you have to stay!

When my eyes open fully I see that it's two very low, very long cargo boats leaving Baltimore. My heart slows, I slow, and let out a heavy breath.

7.43 am

Mary O'Docherty speaks. She comes from Ireland, is now an American citizen, and works for TWA. She is in charge of their medical operation, and so is Ray's leader at the moment.

The accent is still there after twenty-three years. She is a recovering alcoholic and has turned her downfall to good. She holds the purse strings on the airline's medical funds, so is courted by George Bush for their business. Every pilot in here adds another dollar on the 15 million gross!

Not done bad, eh, Mary?

Ray has to get past her today, to secure his freedom and regain his position. He is very nervous.

Mary finishes her talk with, 'We are all the reflections from a mirror ball, thrown out from our safe home.'

Ray introduces me to Mary. She say's, 'Hello, I'm Mother.'

I thought 'The Avengers' had dealt with Mother. Steed would have a great time in here, with all his gadgets.

Ray says he's having lunch with the Pope. He's very hyper.

8.45 am

Another new face. His name is Fred. (Very elderly Fred MacMurry). They say that memory loss is one of the results of drinking or drugs. Fred has been sober for years. I'm not sure he knows where he is today. Not very helpful for a speaker.

Fred tells us that he has been a university lecturer, a Jesuit priest, and an alcoholic.

'I FORGIVE!!!'

He cures himself.

He has a great drawl and is here to talk about Guilt.

He calls it 'Guilt the Destroyer'.

He says, 'Oh, by the way.'

I don't know why. He hasn't said much to suddenly go, 'By the way.'

Dead Fred continues.

'I bet you, if I gave each and every one of you a thousand bucks, you wouldn't be able to guess where I'm going tomorrow?'

Okay, Fred, give us a thousand bucks and I'm sure we can come up with it eventually.

'Well?'

He starts that 'I've got ya' grin. 'I'm goin' to "Goose Bay", Labrador!!! God willin', save the creek don't rise . . .'

Pause.

Is this supposed to be funny, Fred?

'Hell, I don't even know where Labrador is!'

In that case, Fred, may we suggest you start finding out, time is of the essence. To this man there is no sense in essence.

He tells us he is thoroughly German.

I had him down as thoroughly nuts. (*Thought*: 'Why are so many nuts teaching Nuts?')

His German ancestry is part of the problem. He was brought up not on milk but German beer. No wonder they work so hard, it's all that gas propelling them around. Anyway he carried on the usual route, and I have been here long enough to know the final outcome. Let me guess, Fred, you were saved?

'I was saved.'

Told you.

Eventually his drinking got really bad. On a visit to Baltimore, to bury his much loved grandma, he found himself at the station, at 6.30 in the morning, drinking whisky to kick-start his engine for the day ahead. He started to lose his sight, and went into a coma, which was followed by a heart attack. His life was over, he was shot to ribbons.

He was rested for two months with his German Shepherd. There's those dogs again. He got better, went back to work. This time in Las Vegas. Started drinking Jack Daniels. Went from bad to worse, and ended up back in hospital with the DT's.

A Psychiatrist had him taken away in a straitjacket.

He was asked, after being in a straitjacket for nine days, if he thought he had a drinking problem. He says, 'I would have said, "No! I always walk round like this, it stops my hands from hurling themselves at people's faces." You are in that bad a way and some dickhead asks such a stupid question. With your arms strapped round your shoulders, you do have a problem, you can't hold a glass!'

In his day, alcoholism wasn't considered a disease; you were just a drunken bum.

'So believe me,' Fred says, 'there have been some really classy bums around. You can sit up all night with a Jack Daniels. But when your mind makes a decision – DRINK ME – then comes guilt.'

GUILT –
Is the mental operation of judging and condemning one's thoughts, words and actions, i.e. once you pull the trigger, you can't put the bullet back in the barrel.

FEAR. ANXIETY –
Just leave me alone.

SHAME –
Not being up to the expectations I have of myself, or that others have of me.

IMPULSES. SUICIDE –
Return to drinking. That's why movie stars die in motels.

We can become ashamed and guilty – about feeling guilty. 'I still have guilt feelings,' Fred says.

Followed by, 'You *should* be ashamed of yourself.'

Long pause.

He has our attention.

'GUILT TRIP!!'

Two of the women jump.

'You become alone in any situation, and become isolated.'

How to deal with it.

'Put yourself in a court room. Imagine you have three masks in front of you. Pick up the first one, study yourself, then pick up the second and become the lawyer. Condemn yourself. Pick up the third, as the judge – GUILTY AS CHARGED.'

Then the guilt trip is over. Your own ego trip, (or 'Ago' as he calls it).

'Psychopaths don't have guilt trips.'

After this, he becomes preacher-like.

'Forgive yourself from the bottom of your heart. Let the judgement be NOT GUILTY, by reason of insanity. Trust in God, be grateful for what you are, and what you have! Why is this the thing that destroys me?'

Fred is on his own guilt trip, all through this. Although I haven't said, during his speech he keeps forgetting where he is . . .

First mask, second mask, and the third mask . . .

'Did I tell you what the second was?'

Yes, Fred.

'What was it?'

The Lawyer.

'Oh yes. Did I tell you about Labrador?'

He really is gaga at this point. Nice fellow, though, and I see the point he's making. But I doubt if he'll ever remember he was talking to us today.

Have a nice time in Labrador, Fred.

10.15 am Morning Group

Kay is in charge today. We also have a new member, TC. He launches straight in, banging his chair. 'I am from a preaching family. I know all about this God SHIT!! I've sung Hallelujah. I've spoken to the masses . . .'

He goes on and on and finishes with a resounding, 'I've saved more souls than you know how to fuck with.'

He's the same as Chong the Atheist was.

Skip jumps in first. 'I don't think you've got a cat in hell's chance of surviving this. You're blaming everyone except your-self.'

Kay is impressed with all this. It saves her having to jolly it all along.

I ask him if he bought the thirty days here from a Cook's holiday brochure.

Come and spend a fabulous month here at Ashley. Find yourself again. Leave all your family at home. Forget the job, it doesn't matter. Here at Ashley you can find out what a real arsehole you've been. And for the month of May an unbelievable price of only fifteen thousand dollars! Yes, you heard *right, just $15,000. Enjoy your drink and freedom while you're reading our brochure . . . "IT'S GOING TO BE YOUR LAST!"*

TC thinks he has joined the Moonies. He had his speech all worked out, just like a good American TV preacher should. Except he's got the wrong congregation.

Chong lays into him.

He is bamboozled by Chong. We all are, but we're not going to tell TC that.

Chong, in frustration, walks out to have a cigarette.

Kay resumes control. She has enjoyed it all. Every time we say something she agrees with, she gives an aside, thumbs up, winks, smiles and goes into a coughing fit that lasts five minutes at a time. She really needs help. Every time she asks a question, she forgets, after being given the answer, what the question was.

She is a nice old lady and TC has gone into rigor mortis from the attack. In between all this, there is a lot of laughter.

Nice first group, Kay. Have a ciggy.

After lunch

How many lectures does it take to cure an addict? Who knows? But here's another – Richard. He takes a large group. There are a lot of new people in today. Richard tells us about himself. He is a good speaker, although I'm not so sure I like him.

His subject today is stress.

Richard says, '*This* is your life, it's not a fucking dress rehearsal for the *rest* of your life.'

He loved bars, the smell, the low lights, the clink of glasses, the people, the shit talk, the back-stabbing. Just like 'Cheers'.

He thought the whole world was like that. He looks like a civil servant, beard and tie, a thin Richard Dreyfuss. He loves the *Grateful Dead*. Just as well, he's talking to them.

He doesn't look the type, but then none of us do until we drink, and then we can be any type you want.

Rose is still nodding approvingly, in another 'I Love Lucy' outfit. Nodding, always nodding, the ever nodding head. I bet, if she gives it, it must be the fastest blow job in the West!

Richard says he's never been to a rehab before. 'I never had the guts. I admire you.'

Oh, thanks Richard, our egos need a little rub! I obviously missed the sign as I came in here: 'Please dump all egos in the skip provided!'

He tells us, 'I was looking at a picture of myself as a three-year-old and wondered what happened. Alcoholism . . .'

We have all got the same picture, Richard, but what happened was the little boy or girl grew up. No one told us that being grown-up can suck. It's a sure bet, if you ain't got addiction, the Higher Power has a whole host of phobias and fears for sale.

One is too many, and a thousand is never enough.

Frances left today. We sing her out with, 'Well meet again'.

It's not too popular with our drinking peers.

Remember, that's their problem.

Time for more food. You watch people getting bigger and bigger. It must be why the drive is so wide.

Jeff (James Caan) is missing. He's not enjoying his withdrawal from heroin. It's painful. The only withdrawal I've ever had has been in attempting safe sex. Not guaranteed. But not painful.

There is a note on table thirty. It reads:

I know my stay at Ashley was relatively short, but in that time I got to meet a lot of good, honest, fun-loving people. The conversations at table thirty made for a relaxing enjoyable atmosphere here at Ashley. I want to thank you for that. I wish

everybody well in their future endeavours. Maybe I'll run into some of
you guys down the road sometime.

Hopefully it'll be a healthy and clean experience.

God speed,

Adios, Jim

We are sad to lose 'Cheech'. We agree he is in a bar somewhere at this very moment. It's a shame.

It's table thirty's first AWOL.

It must be a bad-result day. Ray's not very happy and that's putting it mildly. The Captain is down, I don't want the plane to follow!

I keep quiet, and let him get it out of his system. They have told Ray he has to attend special meetings for nine months. Then they suggested he could train as a counsellor for executives, because of his background. Basically he won't be flying again. I can't say that this is the best place to find out that your career is over. It is supposed to be recovery. I can sense he doesn't think much of his Higher Power at this moment. Because of his inbuilt ability, his training, he will brave it out. Last to leave the sinking ship!

It really doesn't apply to a diving plane, Ray.

He says he's going to retire. 'Fuck 'em.'

I suggest to him that if they are using their money, take it as long as it's on offer. Then tell them to fuck it!

He goes for a walk around the greens, staring into the open sea. He has as much water in his eyes as there is in the ocean. But no one sees it. Now is not a time to talk.

I get a message that Cheryl wants to speak to me about business. I hope not, unless it is really serious. I think she has used it so we get an extra call in. Clever girl, very clever.

Baywatch leaves. He comes to say goodbye, and asks if he can have an address? Yes, anything, but just go. What a worry.

5.30 pm

I go to dinner. Howard's not here, nor Jeff. These serious addicts really go through hell coming down. Cramps in the legs, cramps in the stomach, worst flu feeling ever. If you haven't had the experience, your reaction might be 'serve them right'. Remember they are trying to correct the past, not training for round two or three, or death.

The phone call does turn out to be a ruse. We beat the system, to our benefit. It may seem like nothing, but it literally is a lifeline

She tells me my new contract is going to make me the highest-paid entertainer in Great Britain. It's a great feeling. But useless, unless I get my real act together, and my life. I will.

After the call I check how Ray is. He has taken to his bed. I hope he doesn't go into depression. When he wants to talk, I'm here, I'm still here. There is a bright side. It means I get to keep the same roommate for my stay. It's great being co-pilot to a clinically depressive airline captain. And I mean that.

My seat in the lecture hall is now flanked, on my left by Duane, a quiet lad, and on my right by TC. Next round coming up.

For the rest of the evening, I experience tiredness like I've never known.

Lights out.

———————— • ————————

Dear Michael,

Hi!!! We have been thinking about you a lot. Hope that everything is going well in your new life!!!

I heard a great saying in an AA meeting Thursday night that struck me as the truth and I thought I would pass it on:

'Winners do what they have to. Losers do what they want to.'

Pretty profound, isn't it?

We miss you, keep you in our prayers. Please write and keep in touch.

Lovingly, Alice and Lew

CHAPTER FOURTEEN

Saturday, 7 May

DAY FIFTEEN

6.00 am

It's Saturday, I think I'll have a lie in.

6.05 am

I'm up, a great sunrise. Ray is up early. His mind is really going. Paul, the big cop, shouted for me to wake up. I thought I was dreaming. I want to dream so much. It's bothering me, and I don't know why.

At breakfast, Paul quotes Will Rogers, saying, 'Don't be so ashamed that you won't sell your parrot to the town gossip.'

I love Will Rogers, I've done enough songs from the stage show about his life. Strange, that a man from so many years ago means so much to a man from 6000 miles away. Someone is looking after me.

9.00 am – Charlotte – Part 3

She's back! Melodramatic chord . . . Da da da da daaaaaaaah!!!!!

Ray is perking up. He's written a suicide letter to his girlfriend. Then ripped it up, and sent a sober one.

Charlotte's subject:

SURRENDER VS COMPLIANCE

The Russians look shocked. Surrender is not a word they have in their vocabulary. They came here to dry out and have to hand over their guns. This might just force them back on the vodka.

Charlotte tells us of an American lady sentenced to eighty lashes in Iran for drinking. Don't tell me that on top of all her other vices, she's into bondage!

I can't handle all this addiction, I don't like unnecessary pain. And I don't like Charlotte. The thought of her dressed in black leather and full of Scotch is very sobering. Something must be working.

We have a deaf mute in the rear of the room, with a friend interpreting. You will have to use your imagination, but with the Russians, it is very comical. Very.

At lunch Jeff has still not appeared.

Howard tells me that the reason Ann has been limping since coming here is not because she has a permanent leg injury. It happened whilst trying to keep her drinking hidden from her family. She hid her bottle in the bushes, in the garden. All of the family were in the house the night before she was brought here. To avoid passing them, to get to the booze, she went up to the roof and jumped, missed the bush, and despite her injury, still crawled towards the bottle for a swig. Her entire family looking on.

I think anyone would conclude that this fifty-five-year-old, very middle-class lady, has a problem. If I had got to that point in my drinking, I like to think that I would have had the sense to get a bungie rope.

That way you get at least three hits at the whisky!

It's recreation day. Nice of it to rain, just what we all need.

One of the men isn't too happy. His son is waving to him from his boat. On board are several of his son's friends. I thought that was a nice gesture, but they were all stoned! I wouldn't like to be that boy when his dad gets out.

I have to get some sleep. I go to my room to relax. Ray is walking around looking for a good hanging tree. It's a chance to look at the cards Cheryl has sent me, and some of the messages I've sent to her.

Cheryl's Cards to Me

Jessie come home there's a hole in the bed.
My love now and always, C

I need you so much to start a new life.
With you again.
No more secrets any more.
Ever my love, C

You rang today, it felt like my birthday.
And you and I have a lot of birthdays in us yet.
Love you, C

The song says,
No one knows the pain of living with a name.
That's not your own.
Mr & Mrs Barrymore can be Mr & Mrs Parker just fine.
My love forever, C

I'll be seeing you in all the old familiar places.
That this heart of mine embraces. All day through.

I'll find you in the morning sun and when the night is new.
I'll be looking at the moon, but I'll be seeing you, C

We are strong, you and I.
We can take on the world after this.
Love you so, C

Mine to Cheryl

There will be an eclipse here soon.
I will dedicate it to you because you eclipse anything around you.
Love you for ever, M

I miss you so much.
I could take a drink and pour it down the sink! M

Give my regards to 'Broadway'
And tell them I'm ready for them now!
Love you more than you know, Mikey.

I heard you on the phone the other day.
My name is Michael.
I'm a drug-taking, dope-smoking, coke-sniffing, free-basing,
    hip-smacking, thirst-quenching alcoholic.
Would you like to meet me? M

My eyes go heavy.

When I awake from my nap, one of the cleaning ladies, Judy,
has left a warning note not to smoke in the rooms, or to leave the
window open.

I see her later, and she tells me, with a smile, that it's against
the rules and Ray and I should be reported. I smile back and say,

'I'm sorry', and quickly hand her a Snickers bar. She takes the bribe.

I'm off the hook. In the main, these rules are off the wall, but the residents here are all off their heads, and I include myself.

Being a Snickers bar down, I need to restock. My new dealer, Sarah, is returning to the AA meet tonight.

At the meet, Sarah slips me an Almond Hershey. As Dale always said, you can get laid for an Almond Hershey in here. But almost all of us would rather eat the Hershey!

At the AA meet, we meet a very tall basketball player, who could charm a Jack Daniels right out of your mouth. He tells us his story. Very well off, nearly blew it all. He tells us we either progress or regress. We just don't want to 'gress'!

Dale, who is now only here on a visit, gives me a blue hospital overall, and suggests it will come in handy for raiding the drugstore. I'll keep it for such an occasion – NOT.

Considering you are not allowed anything other than basics, I could hold a great garage sale right now. I wonder who's got a garage stashed away?!

Back at the Animal House, young Darrell, a well-to-do black boy, is amazed to hear the pharmaceutical expertise of his fellow inmate. He is sobered by the thought that he is just an alcoholic. He tells us of a cousin he lost from shooting dope. In the end he was going via his penis to find a vein. This is more than I can take. I feel faint and tired, it's been a long haul to this point. I reflect on what has happened with a mix of sadness and elation. A very strange mix in the circumstances. But it's alcohol-free.

I'm sober, emotional, sad and tired, and I miss my family like hell. It's a sentence to drink by, instead, I sentence myself to sleep.

Lights out.

———— • ————

'Life is 10% what happens to you, and 90% how you react to it.'

'Attitude'
Charlie Ryan

CHAPTER FIFTEEN

Sunday, 8 May

DAY SIXTEEN

6.00 am

I wake up with Hope this morning – nice girl!

'Achtung! Achtung!' Oh no, Eva's regressed. It's 1942 again. For the first time since I've been here, the tannoy is blaring an incoherent message. As my eyes and ears open, I haven't a clue what they are saying. Maybe the Russians have decided to go for it. Perhaps they have struck a deal with Eva.

No one's rushing, except those whom the message is for. Here at *Groundhog Day* any change to the routine is welcome. Even an advancing army.

The sun has just shown its face. God must be moody, and kicked the big red ball. It's way up in the sky, where Ray would like to be. I can hear Chong the Atheist, he's singing an old Chuck Berry number. *I haven't seen my wife in three years, I'm a happy, happy man.*

7.00 am

Breakfast is pretty dull this morning, but the table brightens up with the arrival of Jeff. Fresh from Toxic Waste. He tells us he's got to get his act together. 'Apart from coming down and the feeling you have to endure, my habit to date was costing five hundred dollars a day.'

I reply, 'That takes a lot of subsidising.'

Between cornflakes, without looking up, Jeff says, 'No, that takes a lot of moving around!'

Judy, from Guatemala, has her family here. Her two children and mafioso-looking boyfriend. They look very Latin hierarchy, grandly sitting at one of the family tables. Designer headcases, whatever next?!!.

Her young son looks like an heir to something, could be a drugs ring. Why do I have the feeling that it won't be long before this boy is admitted. They must have some influence, no one else has family on Saturdays. I could push it, but making waves, for my own purpose, is not the idea. Obviously, Judy feels that she must have some separation from all this commonness. And maybe I should just get on with *my* life. Maybe, deep down, Judy is just being herself. Who knows, who cares? Outwardly, we are a family. Inside, we want to be left alone. If we had been left alone in the first place, we wouldn't be here – typical addicts' way of thinking.

Things are getting slow. So slow, that I've just realized it's Sunday, not Saturday. Oh well, heads you win, tails you are misquoted. Sorry, Judy.

Thought for the day,

'Doanes' Pills for that morning stiffness.'

Most addicted men can't remember morning stiffness. It's one of the new delights of sobriety.

Although I have ordered a paper each Sunday, the *New York Times*, this is the first one I've read. I find a picture in the magazine section, and write a caption under it. She looks in need, and would fit in well here.

*

Charlotte again, in her Sunday check suit.

Ray has made a decision to retire. Mmmm. He's going to fly a small plane. You're clear to land, Rev Ray.

Animal House is regrouping. Duane is an airline steward. With a few sheets of metal, we could start our own airline, AA-Alcoholic Airways.

Sorry about the delay in your take-off, ladies and gentlemen, please accept our apologies. On behalf of Captain Reverend Ray we would like to offer you a drink – but he's drunk it all. Duane is your steward for first class, club class, economy or whichever passenger he bumps into. Have a nice flight, suckers!

Nuche, (the high tie) asks if the Benny Hill shows, in England, show more tits. Which reminds Chong that he's sure that in his daughter's Barbie collection, there is one where you turn her arm around and her tits get bigger. I must ask him his choice of drug.

I decide to do some ironing. Trade price: two Snickers bars. I am the only one who does it at all, including the women. Very English, they all decide.

Adam & Eve question:

Was it really the apple in the tree? Or the pair on the ground?

As I chose to ignore this question, on the grounds of diminished responsibility by the questioner, I write up my step three. We shall see if I pass.

I am carrying a disease. It's one of the few you self-cure, and the disease remains for the rest of your life. If you have cancer, the surgeon cuts it out. If you are lucky, that's it. It's over. Not with addicts. It lies dormant, to challenge you forever, a bitch of an invisible disease. Only visible when fed.

*

Charlotte reads out the Derby result. Coincidence, not a word they're fond of in here, rules. The winner was a horse called Go For the Gin. We would all have had that one. But then we would be going to Gamblers Anonymous, which some say is as bad, if not worse. My dad was one, and a drinker. A sort of win double.

She tells us no one won the Lottery.

Today she is talking about maturity. If only an addict could grow up, I think. She says we are all King Baby and Queen Baby.

Like babies, we smile because we want to.

Like babies we:

1. Are self-centred.
2. Have a high frustration level.
3. Need constant gratification.
4. Cause a tantrum if we don't get our way.

I wonder what Charlotte must have been like as a child, and when she was growing up drunk. Bette Davis, in *What Ever Happened to Baby Jane*, comes to mind. Charlotte tells us that we have a half-inch tolerance level. Pre-judgement, you always argue with yourself and then argue with the person stopping your will.

'So some of you had a lousy childhood? – So what! Some of you had a great childhood? – So what!'

Some people may not agree with you, Charlotte. So what!

She remembers one of her first dates. In his swanky flannel suit, and his dad's new car. Up at a set of lights. The lights changed, the man in front did not pull away. Her date pushed hard, frustrated, on his horn. The guy in front got out of his car, walked back to Charlotte's boyfriend, and punched him straight in the mouth. She fell about laughing. I told you she was a charming woman.

Her point on maturity is to accept life for what it is. I must say she does get her point across, and I must say, I still think she's a hard nut. She seems to be a bit too jolly today. Via whispers, we all agree that she is three-parts pissed! As with a kid, addicts don't know what *later* is. Now, right now, is part of the disease. If a kid wants an ice cream, and you say, 'later', its world is destroyed. It hasn't learned what later is. With the world destroyed it will sit through the whole meal, miserable, waiting for the ice cream. My wife is the same. Only, her cravings are shoes and bags. Like a drink, one pair is never enough, and she hides them in the cupboard! I'll have to have her weaned down to just the left shoe, and then just stockings.

Charlotte tells us of a man who had been staying at the rehab. He told his wife to pick him up at seven o'clock. She lived a long way away, and it meant driving all night on his release day. She rang Charlotte and asked if it could be delayed until 11–11.30 am. It would make life a bit easier. Charlotte said, 'Of course, he's been here a month, why the hurry for a few hours?'

But the man insisted on waiting outside at seven o'clock. At 7.05 am, when his wife hadn't turned up, he picked up his bags, left, and made his own way back home. When the wife turned up, she was devastated that the newly rehabilitated man in her life could do this to her. Charlotte said, 'That's called self-willed . . . self-centredness.'

Adam shouts out, 'That's called an arsehole!'

Hear, hear.

The Siamese twin of anger is self-pity. She grows on you. So does booze. Which one is the more dangerous?

I look around the room, Jeff is here. Three days coming down, and Charlotte looms in front of you. Not fair. Addicts are great sprinters, but lousy in a marathon.

Fire and brimstone are quelled, by what I don't know. But Charlotte is happier today. We finish with Frank Sinatra singing the alcoholics' anthem, our favourite song, 'My Way'.

Lunch

Our table is now full, with the arrival of Mark. About thirty-eight, he looks like a throw-out from the Beachboys.

Duane is talking to Charlotte, telling her he's not sure if he is an alcoholic.

Ray's reaction, 'Oh, oh! We gotta convert the kid, quick.'

At the table, Lewis asks Sal who's looking after his dog while he's away.

'Neil.'

'Oh, is he your room mate?'

'No, he's my potential intended.'

Lewis carries on eating his salad. Sal leaves for a cigarette. Lewis leans over, 'Did he say what I thought he said?'

'Yes.'

'I didn't know he was . . .' He looks around to check the coast is clear, 'y'know, funny.'

'Nor did I, Lewis. I just thought he was Sal. Do you call gay people, "funny"?'

He whispers, 'Yes. What do you call them?'

'Gay. He's just gay.'

At the video, I fall asleep. Skip nudges me awake. He tells me Geoff the bobby is coming. And more importantly, his twelve-year-old boy, the sole reason he's getting himself straight. Jeff (James Caan) says, 'I bet there's things in that video you wouldn't want your family to see.'

'I didn't see it, Jeff.'

'Oh.'

In one of the few breaks, DJ Tony tells me that his mum is coming next week. And he's just found out that the two men he shares a house with are still using drugs. So he can't go back there. Or his workplace. He's got to brush himself down, pick himself up, and start all over again.

I have over an hour's telephone call with Cheryl. It's a great conversation, relaxed. She reads out a review of my last show, by Jack Tinker. It makes me feel good. She is sending it to me. She is coming on Sunday, and will stay the rest of the week, until I get out. She is trying to get me released as early as possible. I can't wait. But I shall. I tell her I love her, and she me. As I put the phone down, I feel very good about everything. I also realise that until she mentioned the article in the paper, I hadn't thought about work once. About time.

I am very happy, so are a lot of the others. They have family all over the place. They have all got into the habit of introducing me to them. It's the novelty of being English.

Frances's daughter is here. She, and her friend, have bought me a toy car and a boat to cheer me up. I sit and have a coffee with them. I have a feeling this is puppy love. Or the dad they want. I get it every time, and it costs me nothing to go along with it. I take the toys back to my room, and give them to Ray. He is thrilled. They sit on the window sill by his bed, and I am thrilled for him! We both stand there thrilled, together.

Judy, the cleaning lady, pops her head into our room. She is thrilled for the both of us. It's a light relief for Ray after all the shit that's been dumped on him.

As I go to play volleyball, I meet Skip's son. Nice lad. Very quiet. He looks proud to have a dad back. If only there had been places like this when I was his age, I might have got my dad back. All in Animal House want to see the plastic boat and car. Simple pleasures.

At the NA meet, the speaker doesn't show. Probably stoned. Jennifer the Policewoman talks. We've heard all this, love.

'Well, first,' she says, 'what I needed was a straight man.'

I presume with a straight needle.

We all join in to fill up the time. DJ Tony is really happy to be here, and says so. Ray is definitely going to Florida, *mit plane*. And

Skip tells us that in the winter, when the whole place was covered in a foot-deep ice-sheet, he bought an old pair of golf shoes from the charity shop for $2 so he could get to the drugstore for his fix. He sold them after for $10.

Time to prepare for another gruelling week at the farm. Lights out.

•

Dear Michael,

May God bless and keep you.
With God in one hand, and AA in the other, you will make it!

Love and Prayers,
Kelly

CHAPTER SIXTEEN

Monday, 9 May

DAY SEVENTEEN

6.00 am

Fabulous sunrise. Just perfect. I must work out how to get a place to live where you can wake up to that every day. Ray awakens and tells me tomorrow is a total eclipse of the sun. The last one until 2015. Now I know why I'm here!

It's laundry day, and once more the black cat crosses my path. This is either a sign, or the cat wants me to get him laundered. They love tossing in a tumble dryer. Black cat, eclipse, what is happening?

Howard is looking forward to leaving tomorrow. He might even get out tonight. The State of Virginia may need to be warned he's coming back. Just when you thought it was safe to go out on the streets, back came Howard.

Jeff sneezes three times. Howard echoes this.

'High pollen?' I enquire.

'No,' they say, 'it's a way of telling heroin addicts. They get fits of sneezing.'

The next time the Queen sneezes, I will look at her in a totally different light. In here, nobody is affected by high pollen. They are just high. My mind wanders, thinking of home, and the Christmas Day message from Her Majesty. *My loyal subjects, this last year has had its highs and lows. On this festive day, as you sit down to a turkey, or a joint of beef, I will be doing the opposite. Having a beefy joint, and sitting on a turkey.*

Ken, who first admitted me, is fishing for business. Could I refer English people to Ashley? I can think of quite a few. But I should think kindly of my fellow beings.

8.45 am

Another graduation. A week to go, to my own. Who's out this week?

First up is Judy. Her mafioso Guatemalan boyfriend is in attendance. Miss Guatemala is called. She smiles, as if she is pleased to get through to the semi-finals, really hoping that when she wakes up, she will be crowned Miss World. And that Ashley was all a dream. It turns out her boyfriend has been here before. They must do heavy discounts for families.

Howard graduates. Short speech, as follows:

'Thanks a lot.'

Looking really normal, well, as normal as Jesus Christ the biker can. I am proud of him. Just as well. He has no one else here to support him. Nice family, I don't think.

Tammy gives a slow, read speech. She's wearing a green net-curtain dress. She says a lot of 'ye-all's'. At the end, Father Martin tells us the plural of 'ye-all' is 'all ye-all'!

Old Bud (sounds like a drink), says goodbye. Says he booked in on his birthday. He was not best pleased at this. But the next day was more important. It was the real day he was born. He calls it his lost weekend. His wife is proud, and thanks everyone, saying that, of all the seasons she has lived so far, she will take the memory of this spring with her forever.

Norman Bates, Chris, the blond prison-transfer, and Penny, all graduate.

Chris tells a story of when he was arrested for drunk driving. He pulled over, and the officer said, 'Did you see the red "stop" sign?'

He said, 'I slowed down.'

The policeman made him get out of the car, put his hands on the roof, and started beating him over the head with his truncheon, saying, 'Do you want me to stop, or slow down?'

Rose, the nodding 'I Love Lucy', is last. She reads out a very long poem, which comes with free tears. Either her eye ducts need looking at, or there is so much booze inside, it's the only place for it to drain off. If that is the case, there are a few in here who would gladly suck her eyes out.

10.15 am – Group

TC (No. 1 pilot in Evangelical Airways, the only airline that forgives those in Economy) says, 'I am an alcoholic arsehole.'

Which I can go along with, until he says, 'We are all alcoholic arseholes,' which I do not agree with. But he may be right. Every time he speaks, he stares at the ceiling. Maybe it's a hangover from his drinking days. Always speaking flat on his back, or pulling big planes into the air.

Chong the Atheist has been upset by his weekend, and is staring at the carpet the whole time. Maybe he's looking for lost acid tablets. If you find one, Chong, let us all know. Skip is pleased. He's seen his big, jolly boy, the reason he's here.

Tammy says it was okay seeing Jerry, her husband. They have not been together for six months, but it was okay. She admits to being very nervous. I will find out for myself when it's my turn, but I hope I will be a bit more enthused than okay. I tell them all about my phone call. Brian saw his dad, and it caused him to have a panic attack. He really must get something done about all this. I think he needs separate help before opening his heart, otherwise it will jump right out on its own.

Lew, a new member of the group, (Alice's husband) perches on the seat nearest the door. He daydreams throughout the whole session. Something is clearly bothering him.

The powers that be are in agreement. Mark is in the wrong group. We get Bob in exchange. Bob sits in Brian's seat. This causes him to go into a state. This boy really needs help.

The whole group is unsettled. Kay gets the blame. She seems hurt. They are all acting like a bunch of kids. Daddy Tim has gone away, so let's give Nanny Kay a real hard time. I, like the good boy I am, defend her. For once, because I believe in it, not to get myself a gold star for my homework. If only I could have been like this at school.

Lunch.

When am I powerless? When my self-will overrides sanity.

2.30 pm

Counsellor Dave: the disease of addiction.

Dave tells us that this is an arse-backwards business. Self-diagnosis, self-treatment. Sara Beth sits in, to get some ideas. Jeanette is here too. She looks better, after her heart attack. She was brought to Ashley last night, had a heart attack, and was taken back out again. It's her word against ours that she looks better. It's our word against hers that she had a heart attack.

'As the disease progresses, try to stop it,' Dave says.

1. Social drinking: Says he's never found it.
2. Occasional relief drinking: A couple now and again, for medication, 'I have had a bad day, I'll have a drink for a solution, for an answer.'
3. Constant relief drinking: On the slide. You came to believe that you could combine social drinking with occasional relief drinking.

'This shit works! It starts the progression.' Dave is getting very excited with himself.

4. Blackouts for alcoholics: Still awake, still fantasising, but not aware what is going on. Ordinary people stop drinking. A newspaper man drinking went into a blackout, got fired on a Monday, kept drinking, and popped in on Thursday to report himself sick for the Monday.

'The excitement of getting the actual bottle. Relief, then guilt, then progression starts. Every day we promise not to have a drink today. Promise. I'll never do that again. When you promise that, you believe you have control. *Learn* to control. Try harder is not the answer. Try something different.'

Dave mentions someone called Gary Driver. He sounds like he should be a sports star. It doesn't matter. As Dave says, 'Now, there is one man I hope dies drinking.'

'Secondary guilt, progress, problem, then powerlessness. Powerless is not a word used in everyday-speak, but alcoholics have to use it. The danger is when, after a period of time, you have rid yourself of problems so you tell yourself it's okay to have a drink.'

Where does that leave us, Dave? I'll find out for myself.

Volleyball

I don't know what the sudden attraction is, but we now have twelve a side. Only addicts carry on against all the odds.

The evening AA meet. I'm a few minutes late. I don't know why, but they all laugh. Terry, Head of Recreation, is our speaker tonight. He's a great story-teller, the best so far. Devil-may-care attitude. He drank for years, moved from Delaware to Florida, worked at Denney's. He would work, drink, smoke, starting at 5 am on through the night, despite a pancreas problem caused by his addiction. And despite the fact that if it burst, it could kill him in fifteen seconds. Even when admitted to hospital, with all the IV's coming out of every orifice, friends brought him pot. He would drag himself over to the window, and smoke. This happened eighteen times.

He moved back home. His favourite middle brother, Michael, was a young wrestler, who kicked his arse around as a kid. He loved him. When Terry's drinking got bad, he said he'd give AA a try, but he would have to take his moustache off first. Maybe Hitler should have tried that. Michael contracted a spinal disease, and by the time he was thirty, ended up in a wheelchair. Terry was admitted to Ashley. Michael wrote to him, despite his own terrible condition. The letter had been typed for him. It had three sentences.

> Dear Terry,
> *I know you're an alcoholic. I hope you get better real soon. If you see the family, give my love to Mum and Dad.*
> Love, Michael,

Michael's compassion gave Terry his reason to make good. Terry took his brother to a baseball game, to the wheelchair enclosure. Terry had his baseball glove to catch any foul balls that ended up in the crowd of 46,000. He promised Michael he would get him a foul ball if it was the last thing he did. The match went for eighteen innings. In a break, Mikey wanted to go to the bathroom, but didn't want to miss the match. Terry held a cup. Mikey peed. It went down Terry's legs. It didn't matter. On the eleventh innings he caught a foul ball, went to give it to Mikey, and the crowd booed. There was a little kid beside them, who also had a glove, but he'd just missed it. They gave the ball to the kid. Mikey leaned over, and said, 'You mean more to me, Terry, than all the foul balls in the world.'

Mikey went into a coma around Christmas. The only time he pulled out was on Christmas Day. Two days later, they had to make the decision to hand him over to God.

As Terry tells the story, his voice breaks. Tears run down his cheeks.

He drove home. It must have been the worst test for him, and he went to an AA meeting.

At the end he says, looking straight at me, 'Michael, would you lead us in the serenity prayer?'

I stumble. And feel part of them all. All possible miracles.

I return to my room. Ray is sat on his bed doing his rehab homework. As a relapse, he has a ton of it.

'Look at this damn stupid question. "What was the build-up to your last relapse?" Very simple.'

A la Oliver Hardy, he fills in the answer, relaying it to me.

' "There was six feet of snow around my house. I had to get to an AA meet. I started digging, to get my car out of the garage. After two hours in the freezing snow, not gaining any ground, I thought, fuck it, and had a drink." Do you think that'll do?'

'Perfect, Ray.'

Lights out.

———————— • ————————

Dear Michael,
Good day to you! I'm wondering how you are feeling now that you are entering your third week at Ashley.

So much I want to say, perhaps at a later time. It's been a long four days.

Keep the faith! Peace be with you!

My love to you,
Frances

CHAPTER SEVENTEEN

Tuesday, 10 May

DAY EIGHTEEN

6.00 am

Gerry wakes us up. 'There is an eclipse today.'

Ray reacts, 'It's at one o'clock, can we have time off group?'

'I don't know,' Gerry says, 'You're not supposed to look at it, it's bad for your eyes.'

I join in the chorus. 'You mean these things come along every twenty years and you've got a rule for it? No pairing off, no chocolate, no reading novels, no eclipsing.'

Now, that's what I call organisation. Why does he irritate me, the bolshy git? I must practise what I have learnt here. Without the Gerrys of this world, how could I possibly practise serenity?

6.45 am – Breakfast

I'm pleased I did my ironing last night, whilst Ray did his homework. I've just remembered, as Ray was telling me his snow story, I sang the song from *The Snowman*, 'There's something in the air', to which Ray added, 'Well, it sure ain't my cock, bro!'

Big Frank is new in. If his huge chest is the result of drinking, he might be worth cracking open. He has a question. 'Are there band aids for black people?'

Concentrate, Frank.

8.50 am

Father Martin is not best pleased. He says his morning lecture starts at 8.45. 'I know it's a long way across the vast tracks to Carpenter Hall.'

Sarcasm does not become you, Father.

Father Martin, with a forced smirk, tells us to be here in future at 8.40.

Please respect the star turn! This will get Gerry really jumping.

Now, because of his outburst, he begins even later.

'An alcoholic who doesn't want you to know he's drinking will go into the Empire State Building, go into the elevator, and hold his breath for eighty floors!'

'Alcoholics have a genius for playing people, like a violin.

'Most of the dividends come to an addict after treatment, whilst sober. There is no Baby left to look after.'

10.15 am – Group

A quick cigarette, before group. Lew is in full make-up. Lips a very fetching pink, not too loud, and a hint of blusher to the cheeks. No one bothers to ask why, you learn to accept in here. Ray stares at Lew, as Rose puts the finishing touches, with a light powder. Lew, as only an un-camp man can say it, asks, 'What do you think? Is it me?'

Ray, still staring, 'Oh yes, it's you all right.'

Rose glances at Ray, 'Do you want some, Ray?'

Ray squeezes his crotch, 'There is only one place I like lipstick!'

Group is uptight. Skip is uptight. Chong is uptight. All the new members are uneasy. Kay has lost it. There is total anarchy.

Brian gets upset by the whole thing. They don't seem to like the way Kay is running it. They're not giving her a chance. TC is staring at the ceiling. We spend the entire session arguing.

At the end, Kay says, 'Good group.'

Before we leave, she says to Lew, 'You're looking well today.'

Lunch

At lunch, I tell Ray our group was a mess. He blames it all on Lew sitting there in make-up. Father Martin pulls me to one side, between my main course and dessert. Now what does he want?

'Have you thought about your faith, my boy?'

'Oh, yes, Father.'

'Well?'

Now he's got me.

'I'll come and see you.'

'I'd like that. When was the last time you confessed?'

What's this, a new quiz show?

'Some time ago.'

'How long?'

'Jesus!'

'Don't blaspheme, my boy.'

'Ha, ha, ha, got me there, Father!'

'Have you thought about retaking your marriage vows?'

Have you thought that I've got five minutes left to have my lunch?

I hadn't reckoned on all these requests being part of our deal. I can afford a little lie. I can always confess.

'Yes, I have, Father. I was only discussing it with Cheryl yesterday. She thinks it would be a great idea. I'll come and see you. Must dash.'

Phew, that was close!

My ice cream has melted, but I like it like that. Thank you,

Father. It's been so long since my last confession that my ice cream's melted!

Howard glances over at Father Martin, 'What did he want?'

'My soul.'

'Well, he can't have mine, 'cause I ain't fuckin' got one.'

He gives me a cassette tape that Dale left for me, and under the table, hands me a magazine. Howard's leaving, so has no more need for it. It's called *Outlaw Biker*, February issue. On the cover is a scantily clad biker girl, with massive tits. One of the headlines reads, 'Sex and Your Bike'. I quickly glance at the Letters page. One of them reads:

> *Dear Outlaw Biker,*
>
> *I'm twenty-three and a truck driver. I just bought a new 883 Sporty, and everybody wants to crack on me about riding a bitch bike, pussy bike, and other shit like that. My bike is the first and only bike I have ever rode or owned (and I paid cash)! Driving that truck over the road I have gotten addicted to the highways, but I felt kind of pinned up in that cab. A bike seemed to be the answer (and it was, I love riding). So where's all the static about having a Sporty coming from? I thought I was doing better than most people, who start riding on used Jap crap.*
>
>

Richie M.

Inman, SC

> *Editor's note: Fuck 'em if they can't take a joke. Besides, half a Harley is better than none, right?*

I have just been talking to one of the Lord's agents, and two seconds later, Satan shoves his monthly newsletter straight into my face. Like a good Catholic boy, I roll up the mag tightly, and shove it down my trousers. As I look up, two tables away, Father Martin smiles and waves. God forgive me!

At the afternoon group, Brian once again backs away from telling his story. Skip, ever the saint, covers for him. His kindness to others humbles me. He proves nothing is over until it's over.

He tells *his* story again. Kay has no idea that we have all heard this once already. We all know the answers we're going to give. But I must give Skip his due, he did embellish it slightly with another anecdote.

He ran his father's dog over. He says he felt pretty bad about that. Doing something like that would normally bother him, but he was so stoned it meant nothing. He adds, 'I'll tell you how stoned I was. I went to a Chinese restaurant. I must have been staring at the menu for an hour when the little chinky asked me what I wanted. I said, "Sweet and Sour Cunt." '

What amazes me about Skip is that he keeps a straight face as he comes out with that classic Shakespearean line.

2.30 pm

Counsellor Greg tells us about 'Route of Administration'. It's day eighteen. Halfway through getting our lives sorted. And this guy opens with, 'How to take drugs.'

Followed by, 'Now you really find out.'

Has somebody let this guy in through the back door for a joke? He shows us slide pictures of every known drug you can buy. Illegal, and legal, and how to use them. He has everyone's undivided attention. Now I know more about drugs than ever before. How to mix them, what high you get from what, and what effect you should expect. He's talking addicts' language when he says he feels it should all be made legal. To monitor drugs and stop the fighting over them. As with prohibition.

We have a new guy with us, a pharmacist. He knows more than the counsellor, more than DJ Tony, and Skip. He should do very well in here.

Volleyball

As I am playing, I can see Ray walking with 'Lady Penelope', (my nickname for gin-soaked wood). She keeps herself to herself. She only talks and walks with Ray. All I know from Ray is that she supplies table mats for the rich. She would also, I think, like to supply something for Ray. My suspicions were aroused when, after volleyball the other day, I had a shower, went back to my room, and Ray was behind the wardrobe dusting down his balls with talcum powder. He said they got hot from the fast walk.

'Oh, Ray, oh! What's the news with the woman?'

'Oh, her. She's a social drinker. I said to her, "I'm going to have a drink." She said, "So shall I." '

At the evening AA meet, we meet a friend of Jack Touché. Barney Rubble tells us he used to steal everything, or buy street goods. He never bought anything unless it was cheap or stolen. He bought six shirts. He wasn't one for wearing proper shirts. But they were cheap. He stored them in the cupboard until he needed one for a special occasion. It was only then that he discovered why they were the price they were. They were stolen from a funeral parlour. They had no backs on them. He tells us he loves Jack (Fred Flintstone as he calls him). Touché is his sponsor. They go everywhere together. Unfortunately, they keep coming here.

I take a walk in the evening. The sky is clear, the air is good. The setting is perfect. Just perfect for walking.

To the left of Carpenter Hall, I can hear giggling, and lots of shushing. I investigate. DJ Tony, Brian, Goldie (extremely young, extremely pretty, extremely small, and an extreme waste of God's creation), Penny, and Tammy are sitting round a small radio, hand jiving! Listening like it's the first time they've heard this newfangled invention. As I sit, the giggling continues, just from the girls. I haven't said anything, so what's all the hilarity for? The girls confess they have been to an outside ladies' meet in the town of Aberdeen. The driver left them, and they all decided to do a bunk. Two blocks away, they met some boys who were smoking joints, and drinking gin. They all had some. And came back stoned.

Tony looks at them in disbelief. 'You're kidding me.'

As one, all the girls laugh. Goldie screams, 'It was great, man!'

I think to myself, 'So were you once . . .'

Tammy simplifies it, 'Fuck it!'

Lights out.

———————•———————

So if you don't lose patience
With my fumbling around
I'll come up singing for you
Even when I'm down.

'Stars'

Words and music by Janis Ian

© 1972, Mine Music Ltd, USA

Reproduced by permission of EMI Music Publishing Ltd,

London WC2H 0EA

...e picture that fell open from the 'New York Times'. I tore out the page, and wrote underneath, "Take me to Ashley"! *(Greta Pratt)*

I live my life my way. I also interview my way. When will I ever learn? *(LWT)*

A message from the Queen, 1993 Royal Variety. Four months later I had a messa a bottle. *(Doug Mackenzie)*

Moments before an ovation. It looks like I'm praying. Who knows? *(LWT/EA*

'I can get to the rehab myself, I don't need an escort!' *(LWT/EABF)*

'And so it was that on the 30th day after detox, he rose again' Critics 7:1
(Book of Thieves) *(LWT)*

The picture Cheryl sent me in rehab. I carried it with me the whole time.
(Brian Moody/Scope)

Right: Ashley. Extreme left, dining room and detox.
Centre, admin. Centre right, chapel. Extreme right,
Carpenter Hall and Animal House.
(Father Martin's Ashley)

My name is Candy, and my father is an alcoholic.
(Mark Palmer)

Back in Palm Beach. Not the best advert for a return from rehab. The cream soda looks surprisingly like a beer. But I look surprisingly like a human being again. (White line through photograph courtesy of amateur photographer) *(John Davis)*

CHAPTER EIGHTEEN

Wednesday, 11 May

DAY NINETEEN

6.00 am

Gerry shouts, 'Morning, Mike, it's going to be a great sunrise, seventy-five degrees, a little chilly!'

I'm looking at it right now, Gerry knows his sunrises. Light-blue sky, no movement on the water. My imagination runs riot. For a brief moment the orange ball pauses midway. I'm looking at the Hollywood Bowl and there, centre stage, Karen Carpenter is singing, *Don't they know it's the end of the world.*

Hollywood is miles away, and so am I. A voice whispers so I am the only one in the world who can hear, 'Good morning, Michael.'

'Good morning, sun of God.'

Went to see God this morning, he's recovering well. I thought that for such a great sunrise he needed thanking.

8.45 am

Jack Touché (the wandering hand) is back, still disguised as a yoghurt.

Policeman Gerry is on the warpath, 'Come on, get in, you're late. I'm gonna have to put you guys on report!'

We all just stare at him.

He leaves.

Jack says, 'Good morning, family.'

Sixty yoghurts, twelve full of fruit, reply, 'Morning Jack.'

He says he's nervous this morning. A nervous strawberry yoghurt. Calm down, Jack, you'll turn into cheese!

Originally he was part of the space programme. Adam throws a hand-covered aside in my direction, 'They used his waist to practise orbits.'

During his first speech he is so nervous he says he is Kak Couché!

Te He Hee. Get on with it, yoghurt.

'I'm known as Fred Flintstone.'

Yes, we know.

'My friend's called Barney.'

Know that too.

'I joined the army. That's when I started drinking.'

We're back on course. Full steam ahead.

'You know, when my wife sees me she shouts, Yabba Dabba Doo!'

Stop. Reverse engines.

'I met Pope Pius the Third, you know.'

No we didn't. Why? Was he hungry?

'He said to me, "Where are you from?" '

A supermarket shelf.

'It made me want to become a priest.'

There isn't a dog collar in the world that wide.

'Then I became a top salesman.'

For a yoghurt, he's had some life.

He got promotion, he had been dry for fifteen years, and thought he would have a drink to celebrate. 'I'll just have three drinks.'

As always, it didn't stop there. Over the next five years he lost his wife, six kids, everything except his weight!

I don't know what it is about this guy. He brings out the worst in me and most of the others. It's his eyes. They never settle. He talks to you and they are on the lookout the whole time. What happened, Jack? What really happened?

10.15 am

'It is easier to build a boy, than it is to repair a man.'
'Why would a Sunday kind of woman want an everyday guy like me?'

Counsellor Greg takes a 'twelve-on-twelve'. (Two sets of twelve people. Original, eh?!) He tells us about obstacles to recovery. Obstacles such as friends. So how do we get out of that one?

Hello, friend, I know you're my best mate, but you're an obstacle to my recovery. So shift.

He asks us to shout out what we think are obstacles to recovery. Obstacles such as using peer pressure. The shouts begin:

'Setting your mind' (Penny).
'Dreams, i.e. women and chocolate' (Skip).
'Places and events' (DJ Tony).
'Parties' (Tammy).
'Environment' (Adam).
'Advertising' (Howard).
'Rosemary, the good time' (Lewis).
What?!
'Feeling too good' (Sal).
'Flight into health for cocaine addicts' (Skip again).
'Family' (Bob).
'Arguments' (Lew).
'High expectation' (Skip again, he's on a roll).
'Isolation' (Mark).
'HALT' (Lewis).

*

Greg double-takes!

'Pardon me?'

'Hungry, Angry, Lonely, Tired.'

'Well done, Lewis.'

'Experimenting' (me).

He likes my 'experimenting' line. He says, 'Very good. Which group are you with?'

'The Moody Blues.'

He blinks. One side of his face rises. 'Oh!'

'You're going to see a great video tonight. On marijuana.'

Howard isn't too pleased. 'Not fucking *Jungle Book* again.'

Councillor Greg says, 'Booze stops the flow to the testicles.'

I only wish I knew what the question was.

He tells us that when we love things, we get drunk.

Jeanette (Shelley Winters) is looking better. Her face is still a bit heart-attackish, sky-blue pink.

Roger (he's like a Wild West cowboy, a one-line gag merchant), gets very upset, because Greg said (after Roger had spun another of his well stocked lines), 'Comedians are some of the sickest people known.'

Immediately promoting himself, Roger said, 'You mean like Steve Martin, Robin Williams, etc.'

'No, they're professional.'

'You mean I'm sick?'

He slumps his head. Another counsellor loses it.

Lunch

Tammy leaves the group. She thanks me like all the others, for making her laugh. She tells Tim that she and her husband will be driving back to Kentucky. He doesn't like flying. It will take them eighteen hours. I can't work out why she's told me she is going to New York first, and doesn't want Tim to know. Seems a strange route to Kentucky. Still, that's her business. It's nothing to do with me.

Lew, whose problem seems to be mostly sexual, with a sprinkling of cocaine, has to face up to his wife tomorrow about his affairs. Which seem to have been with anybody and anything. It's always a one-way conversation with Lew. You say to him, 'Is your problem this?' He nods and stares, and you take that as a 'yes'. If you say, 'Is your problem that?' he repeats the last procedure. You take that as a 'yes'. I'm sure you could say to Lew, 'You landed on the moon, didn't you, Lew?', and get a nod and a stare. Nice man, big problems.

Guess who's coming to dinner after group? Jack Touché, again! This guy twice in a day is too much for me. I switch off. I have two packs of tic tacs with which to kill time. In the event, I end up nearly killing myself, as I swallow six at once. Not wishing to draw attention to myself, I stifle my choking. Turn blue, eyes crossed, to the amusement of Goldie sitting opposite me. As I am about to explode, Jack looks straight at me, 'Do you want to say something, Michael?'

Skip, in an effort to save my life, thumps as hard as possible on my back. Four spearmint-flavoured bullets shower Jack. The lecture collapses into laughter. Even Jack joins in. He could grow on me.

Ray tells me that he hates Touché. I'm just starting to get to feel better about him, and my room mate hates him. You can't win 'em all, Jack!

Ray tells me he's leaving a day before me. I don't know why, but there's a bit of an atmosphere in the camp.

Volleyball

We lost.

Evening Meet

This evening, after the AA meet, we sit around. It's a warm night. It's story time. More experiences. I tell them about a drinking experience of a friend of mine. Driving home late one evening, the worse for wear, as he was on many evenings, he turned into his drive. It had been a long journey, the ground was thick with snow. So as not to wake his wife, he always turned the car engine off, and coasted up to the garage door. This particular evening, he followed the same routine, opened the door, and slid out of the car into the snow. That's the last thing he remembers doing that evening. He lay in the snow with only half of his face showing. In the early hours of the morning, his exposed left eye opened. All he could see was white. He thought, 'This is it, I'm dead.' The right-hand side of his body was numb from the snow. Somehow he managed to lift his body. Completely arched over, and with no feeling, he struggled to his front door. He could not raise his hands to ring the bell. He stepped back three or four paces, and attacked the door with his head. Reeling from the impact, he repeated this three times. His wife eventually opened the door and held a mirror to his face. The only reaction he could manage was to raise the lid of the one good eye.

'Come inside,' she said, 'go upstairs, go into the bathroom, look in the mirror, and say, "Cunt".'

I return to my room. I find Ray still trying to work his life out. I can't help you tonight, Ray, I've had two fixes of Jack Touché.

Lights out.

———————— • ————————

*'Cherish all your happy moments; they make a fine cushion
for old age.'
I'm sharing a bit of my sobriety with you.
Hang in there, 'one day at a time.'*

God Bless, Annie

CHAPTER NINETEEN

Thursday, 12 May

DAY TWENTY

6.00 am

Gerry is right on the button this morning. I have had a heavy
sleep. It seems Ray is not responding. Gerry calls louder and
louder. A note of panic. Ray's still not responding. For God's
sake, Ray, you haven't gone and died? Gerry nudges him.
Ray sits bolt upright, 'Yes, Mother Fucker One here.'

He's alive.

And another day can begin.

Ray tells me my snoring is the finest he's heard so far. He
used to bunk in a room with twenty-five others, and I am number
one so far. He thought I was going to change into a werewolf!

8.45 am

Mae's story. She's from a dysfunctional family. She looks like
Cynthia Payne, who ran the Streatham brothel. This woman has
had a tough life, and out of it, with Father Martin, she's built and
runs this place. Says it all, really.

Morning Group

Chong the Atheist tells us his story. The words he uses are even longer than ever. It's hard to comment on a story you can barely understand. It gives Brian another migraine.

Tim says he is worried about the fact that in my life so far, and the way I live it, everything is done *for* me. And how this will affect me now that I have learnt to cope by myself.

We shall see.

Lunch

Tim pulls me to one side in the dining room.

'Have you been smoking in your room?'

'Yes.'

'Well, don't do it.'

'Okay.'

So who's grassed on me? I must tell the Reverend.

I tell him.

'Well, I haven't been told.'

I've got to watch my back.

Jack Touché yet again. Do we ever get parole from this man?

'The steps will be short this afternoon, family. I am going away for the weekend and I need to get to the bank before three o'clock. So I'm sorry it won't be as long as usual.'

Please, Jack, don't worry, you go away and have a nice time. We'll be here when you get back. Make sure you lock the front door, and tell the milkman, 'no yoghurt'.

The short steps end up being the same length. He talks faster, for longer!

Jack talks about step eight.

'Made a list of all persons we had harmed and became willing to make amends to them all.'

And step nine.

'Made direct amends to such people wherever possible, except where to do so would injure them or others.'

Jack explains, 'For instance, if you've stolen money and got away with it, don't just give it back. Why upset everyone? Find a way of getting the money back. So you know you paid your debt, and step nine is automatically done. You've made amends!'

I can see the Great Train Robbers planning that one.

Okay, lads, step eight. Two men disguised as train workers slow down the train. Tell the driver that they've both got sunburn and the doctor recommended surgical stockings for the face. Two others walk by the guard van at the rear, dressed as postmen with sacks on their backs. Whistling. They tell the guard their van's broken down and that they need to get these two sacks to London. As this happens, the two stockinged robbers hit the postmen and throw the two sacks into the train. Two more shout, 'Police!'

Two robbers run, one policeman runs after them, one stays, pretends to call an ambulance, and picks up the postmen. Two men dressed as ambulance men take the postmen away. Remaining policeman walks to the front of the train and tells the railworkers the track is clear. Job done, steps eight and nine complete!

> *'If the person you love leaves you, and doesn't come back, hunt them down and kill them.'*
>
> (Addict)

Becky, (an all-American college girl), tells Jack that her parents can't come to grips with all this. For her, making amends is being here.

A giant step for mankind, the first one for an addict.

We all thought there was a magic cure, Becky. Come in, get the shit out of your system and that's it. It's not the shit in your system you have to lose, it's the shit in your life.

216

Skip is ever determined to get it right. He's getting a fixation, like Sarah was with her little boy. It's starting to worry me. Be careful what you wish for, Skip. Big Frank is the same. At this stage they are hooked on getting it so right. There has to be some balance. In fact it is the imbalance that needs working on. The imbalance of how the system here works.

Chris, the bland prison-transfer, drops a bombshell. He needs to get a nightmare offloaded.

His drinking was at its worst. He was so stoned whilst his first wife was expecting a baby, he didn't notice, or care, that she was taking vast amounts of cocaine. The child was born with a bad heart, due to the addiction. After three operations the baby died in Chris's arms.

No one reacts.

What do you say? You say, 'never again.' Never again will I have to admit, in front of a fellow human being, that I am not worthy to be called a fellow human being.

TC speaks. It is not noted. I've come to the conclusion that he is totally off his trolley. Everything he says is gobbledegook.

I have a worry about the nature of addiction. That it will be put into doing the steps, rather than our choice of drug. Like a bull in a china shop. A drunk in a liquor store.

Jack asks Chong if he would like to share.

'No, I can't share at the moment.'

'Why?'

'I'm emotionally bankrupt.'

As Chong tells us about the deficient side of his brain, he stares at the floor. Jack stares at the clock. We all stare at the exit. You can hear a pin drop. We don't, thank God. In here it would be a needle.

3.00 pm – Meeting with Tim

He's had a call from Austin, my psychiatrist. He has told Tim that someone is going to the papers with a story and it's not right to keep me unaware. I think they want to see my reaction.

How do I know until you tell me, Tim?

Among other things this story includes the fact that I dress in my wife's clothes. I react. By falling off the chair.

'That's ridiculous!'

'I agree. I've got you down for many things, but that isn't one.'

'No Tim, it's ridiculous because she is a size eight, I'm a fourteen. What are the other things?'

'Nothing to bother you.'

'Well, I think I have a right to know.'

'What does it matter what they say? They are just words. Spoken by sicker people than you.'

He is worrying me. He continues.

'I'm only interested in your welfare.'

I search for guidance. 'I suppose I should tell them to join the queue, and do their worst.'

Tim is father-like when he says, '*I don't suppose at all. I know what I see is a very nice man, who does very nice things. So very nicely, tell them to get fucked!*'

He tells me to go and play volleyball, hugs me, looks me straight in the eye, 'I've got my money on you.'

As I leave, I try to put into action what Tim has told me. Not to be frightened by what people say or think. It's one of the reasons I ended up here. I go and play volleyball. Everyone on the pitch knows something is wrong with me, my game is all over the place. Sal asks me what's up. Between points, I tell him the papers have started once more, and that it's preying on my mind. Not what they might or might not say. It's just brought everything back to me. It's like I've gone back to day one. Like all my work here in rehab has been for nothing. Sal tells me to just concentrate on my recovery. Get a grip, put it in perspective, shake it off, and play the game. I put my rehab training into gear. I'm going to beat my wandering mind.

DJ Tony serves. I win the next point. I'm back on course.

Advantage Barrymore.

6.30 pm

Mike the Chef tells us the same story as last week. Just as well his food is so good, his story is starting to repeat on us. The only reason we put up with it is because he threatens us with, 'If you don't pay attention, I'll show you twenty different ways of eating hot dogs, for two weeks!'

At the AA meet, nothing new happens. Except the speaker looks like Linda Evans.

Ray, who always sits at the front (most of the time with his eyes shut, to annoy the speaker), tells me, 'I was fantasising. I really fancied her until I found out she was a slut and a druggie. I was going to undo my flies, but I thought, fuck it, I'll ring my girlfriend instead.'

I've found a new addiction. Hot chocolate. Sugar-free hot chocolate. Mug in hand I sit in the smoking room with Lew. He's telling a new lady all about the place.

'Well, nearly all the men are bisexual.'

'Really?'

'Oh yes.'

'Where do they sleep?'

'Well, all the straight men sleep in Animal House, on the left. Straight women in Bantle Hall on the right and all the bisexuals in Noble Hall in the middle.'

I assist, 'So they get the best of both worlds.'

She takes the bait. 'That sounds neat.'

'Yes, it is.'

She's fallen for Lew. 'Where are *you*?'

'I'm in the middle. Today I'm Lew, on Thursdays I'm Ethel Merman.'

She looks at me. 'I'm Michael. On Fridays I'm Judy Garland. And DJ Tony has really come to terms with himself, he covers Monday, Tuesday and Wednesday. He's the Supremes.'

She stands to leave. 'You're all fucking nuts!'

We say in unison, 'Close!'

DJ Tony goes to help Brian with his first step. As he leaves, Tony turns to me, 'You all know I am gay, don't you?'

'No.'

Two women overhear and look at him. 'It don't mean nothing. You love another person, same as anyone else. You just sleep with someone different.'

What?

It didn't even cross my mind one way or the other, but I reckon he must feel better for saying it after all this time.

Saying you're gay is the least of your problems if you're an addict, and the most if you're not.

Swings and roundabouts. And Lew swings. Both ways?

I'm still very tired.

Lights out.

———————— • ————————

As we have so often seen, true life has a habit of interjecting itself into the dream factories, and turning wonderful hopes and aspirations into shattering disillusionment.

The Joker's Wild
The Biography of Jack Nicholson
John Parker
Published in 1991 by Anaya Publications

CHAPTER TWENTY

Friday, 13 May

DAY TWENTY-ONE

6.00 am

Gerry wakes us up and tells us, 'It's chilly out there.'

Our wonderful cruise sails onward. Where are we today? I'll just look out of my porthole. Oh look, the glazier has put a square window in, the Cayman Islands look like Baltimore, and my wife looks like a fat, drunk, ex-airline pilot. That is one dream I'm pleased to wake from. I am still thinking of the papers. Will I never learn? Ray says he is ready to attack his group. Luckily he hasn't got a machine gun. We are both moody this morning. Neither of us is of any use to the other. He wants to blame his group for his life. I can't get the poxy papers out of my mind. And last night, in the middle of the night, my strictly banned Dictaphone made a piercing sound. It woke Ray up.

'What the fuck is that?' he yelled.

I said, 'It's my Dictaphone.'

He said, 'Well Dic-ta-phone up your arse!'

Charming Ray, charming.

Just realised it's Friday the thirteenth. Could work in my favour.

George Bush tells us that a young boy called Tim who graduated recently has taken his own life. He looked at his records and there were no untoward signs that he would. It's frightening. What did I say about the thirteenth? We're one down already, and here comes another close shave. Michael (Norman

Bates) who left about twelve hours ago is back. The whole room turns to look at him. They had taken him home. Outside his house his car had been wrecked. Inside, the mess that had brought him in was still there, right down to the vomit (his own, a month old). The scene was untouched, and he remained unloved. Michael had just spent a month trying to put his life together, using every tool he had been given. He opened the fridge, took out a six pack of beer, and worked his way through, his passport back to the only home he could survive in.

Before he passed out, he rang someone to come and get him. His friend. The only one who really understood him.

He rang 'Ashley'.

He is christened 'Bates, the Fastest Relapse in the West'. We all think it is a hell of a long way to come for a volley match.

A card has been left for all of us to sign. To Rene. I write:

> *'Lucy in the sky with diamonds.' When you left us, Lucy's*
> *diamonds didn't sparkle any more. I won't sing the song till we*
> *meet again.*
>
> > *Love Michael*

Every time I think about Rene my heart slows and my face saddens. It's not love as we know it. It's like the care you would give to a sick animal, hoping that you get it right. If only they could talk, if only Rene would react. I could go and free him, sit him down facing the sea, make him smile. He would make me smile. And for that, I would make sure no one took him away shackled, as he was before.

One day, Rene. Just hold on. One day.

At Mass, Father Martin gives a sermon about Saint Augustine walking along the seashore. He sees a little boy digging a hole in the sand. He's picking up water from the sea and pouring it into the hole, repeatedly.

Augustine says, 'What are you doing, little boy?'

'I'm going to pour all of the ocean into that hole.'

'You can't do that!

'And you'll never work out the Trinity!'

8.45 am

Father Martin's second gig of the day. His agent certainly keeps him busy. He's using a cane to help him walk. He is starting to show high mileage, but Catholic priests are good runners. Especially well-lubricated ones. I didn't ask where the cane was made. I've heard enough Benny Hill stories.

He reminds us that most diaries happen after sobriety.

What? I wonder where this is going . . . I'm confused . . .

'Don't make amends until you're caught.'

Oh, that's where we're going.

'Step nine. Made direct amends to such people wherever possible except when to do so would injure them or others.'

Is it me or have we done this already?!

'Made direct amends to such people . . .'

I daren't ask, 'Is there a doctor in the house?' Half the room will stand up.

Father Martin is wandering today. Not his best performance. He says, 'Al is creeping up on me . . .'

His eyes widen, his head turns slowly. If I shove a hedgehog up his back, he could ring in the New Year.

'Al-tzheimer's!'

There is a 'thank Christ for that' nervous laugh from us all.

On today's showing I have to agree with him. He keeps wandering midway from one story to another. He has to be a one-off. I don't know too many people who can give the same speech to the same crowd, with the same gags, within a week. And still get laughs. He's rare. Very rare. In his drinking days he must have been dynamite!

10.15 am

I still can't shake off thoughts about the impending Sunday-paper story. I obviously haven't been here long enough, haven't got enough tools yet. My group know something is up. I tell them, with Tim's permission, that once again I am reported as being everything you can imagine. They don't even laugh about the cross-dressing. They think it is all sick. Which surprises me, considering what *they* have to tell. I gently pass a maple leaf between my hands as they voice their support. If only the real world could be like this. Got a problem, come and talk with us. Within a few minutes, it will be solved, and we'll tell you ours so you can wonder what you were worried about in the first place.

Tim says it's very brave to tell the group what is happening.

I never thought of it as brave, more cowardly. I can't handle it so I'll dump it in your laps. What's brave about telling people what's wrong with you? This is a new world to me. I was brought up with, 'Keep your eyes open and your mouth shut.'

Mind you, look where that's got me.

Tim writes on the board, 'I know when I'm in trouble with my recovery when . . .'

'Michael?'

'When my self-will overrides my sanity.'

'What do you mean, by that?'

'My addictive nature, when pushed, will say, "Stuff all this, I'm fed up with people telling me what to do, where I can go and what I should be doing."

'Sanity says, "Calm down, don't be so selfish."

'A drink says, "You just look after yourself, no one really understands you. You're better off with me. You and I can do what the hell we like. You're not really that nice, no one is."

'That's when I'm in trouble. Because that bastard (drink) is never there in the morning to stand beside you and say, "Well, it was *his* fault, but *I* suggested he pick up the chair and throw it, *I* was the one who told him to say such nasty things to the one he loves, *I* told him that all his hard work was a waste of time." He never speaks up. And the reason I call it "him" **is** because it is "him".

'Him is me.'

'*And I don't like him.*'

There is an eerie silence. Tim gives an 'I know what you mean' nod, and says, 'Okay, Michael. Skip, when are you in trouble?'

'I think Mike has said it all.'

Lunch

I must have said something right. Tim lets me call Cheryl. She tells me about the papers. She's known about it for quite some time, but didn't want to upset my recovery. She tells me who the culprit is. It's Ricky Greene (a 'Strike It Lucky' scriptwriter). I am a little sad. I didn't think that someone I thought of as a friend, and to whom I thought I had given some considerable help, would go to the papers. I might as well get used to how life really is before I go back and face reality. I tell Cheryl that I think it would be a good idea when I get home, to tell everyone where I have been and what happened. Then I can get on with my life whichever way the chips fall. She tells me not to rush anything, but she will support me whatever.

John Smith is dead.

Cheryl gives me an update. The Leader of the Opposition died of a heart attack. Sad news in a sad place. She tells me Don Johnson was on the Jay Leno show, talking about *his* rehab experience. She said he looked great, best she's seen him. It's not a pattern I intend to follow. He's had three goes. To date. She then reports that Sunday is Kit's birthday.

And finally she says, 'Here in Palm Beach, the pelicans have returned and are sitting on the jetty, outside the house.'

I love the pelicans. The hours I have spent fishing as they sat beside me, telling them all my troubles. They had the patience of saints and the skill of disciples, as they swallowed whole, every fish I caught.

She's told the pelicans I am coming back. The weather is a scorching 90 degrees, clear blue sky, with a light chop on the water. Sounds great. She sounds even greater, and is preparing to fly out to see me. She will be staying in the local town of Aberdeen. Should be nice for one of them!

Volleyball

The tannoy blares: 'All those leaving within the next week report to Noble Hall at this time.'

That includes Skip and me. We are waiting with about a dozen others in a room, to look at a video. It's another advert, another cause to join. The fee, a very reasonable eight dollars. Reasonable that is, if you have eight dollars.

An old guy tells us why we should join and then goes into a tirade about a conversation he overheard outside, 'One of you was complaining about paying a measly eight dollars. You should be ashamed. You didn't worry what you spent on booze and drugs!'

I look across and see Skip tense up. It was him. Skip never keeps things to himself.

'Hold on!'

'What?'

Skip is furious. 'Who are you to tell us what we should do with our money? I ain't got no eight dollars, I ain't got eight cents!'

The old boy tries to backtrack. 'Well, for those who can't afford it, it's free.'

It's too late, he's lost Skip. 'Fuck free, and fuck you!'

He leaves. We all back him and follow.

Great salesman.

Outside, everyone tries to calm Skip down. I stand to one side, looking out to sea. It worries me how quickly all the training can go. You lose everything you've learnt. What's more frightening is how a nothing comment can unnerve you. You, the addict.

Skip wanders, shoulders hunched, angry, and drags his feet on the grass.

I approach him. 'Skip.'

'Oh hi, Mikey.'

I palm him a hundred-dollar bill.

'You don't have to do this.'

'No I don't, Skip.'

'Soon as I get out of here, and get a job, I'll pay you back.'

'No you won't, Skip, I don't want it back.'

'Aw gee, thanks.'

'It's my pleasure. It's cheap for a friend like you.'

My second outside AA meet. It's good to breathe some leaded town air. Brings back that old phlegm-iliar sound.

As we arrive Jeff (James Caan) says, 'Follow me.'

He walks really fast.

'Where are we going?'

'Just follow me.'

He walks through a door and there is Aladdin's Cave. The colours, the bright lights, the perfumed smells. The scene is set.

'Oh, Uncle!'

'Bring me the lamp, boy.'

'*Oh Uncle, I never knew a drugstore could look like this. Riches beyond my wildest dreams.*'

My eyes travel the length of the store. Rows and rows of Hershey bars, M&M's, Mars.

'*My name is Charlie, I know Willy Wonka, and I am a chocoholic.*'

As I walk past the shelves, beads of sweat trickle down my

neck. My fingers are dancing on my palms. Past dental products, past household goods.

Adam has entered the cave. I hear him scream. I turn. Have we been caught by the Sultan's guards? My voice carries, 'Adam, what is it?'

'It's . . . It's . . . a . . . Machine!'

'A Time Machine, Adam?'

'It's freezing cold.'

Jeff and I hold our breath. Adam passes a secret, magic coin into an opening. Strange noises build from within. The Machine propels, at great speed, a gift to welcome us to Planet Earth.

Adam takes the gift of silver and deep blood-red, and holds it up to the light. His voice, like a meteor, speeds through the air,

'CLASSIC COKE!!!!!!!!!'

Jeff collapses to his knees.

'We're rich!'

I try to restore sanity.

'Come on, quickly. The meeting starts in five minutes, we must get back before they wonder where we are.'

We collect as much sugar-laden candy as we can, pay the Genie of the Magic Till, and walk back to the meet, like three contestants from the 'Twit of the Year Show' (Monty Python). To lighten our load, we eat as much as we can. The sugar fix is awesome and we all buzz through the meet.

On our return, I am surrounded as I dish out the haul. Within five minutes I have offloaded all the candy and sugar-full coke.

DJ Tony tells me of a night raid on three vending machines.

'When did it happen?'

'It's happening tonight.'

Two raids in one day, the excitement is mind-blowing.

TOOLS NEEDED FOR VENDING MACHINE RAID

1. Dollar bills.
2. Loose change.
3. Torch.

4. Jacket (with big pockets).
5. Guts.

As the guard changes, Tony, Brian and I slip out. Past Bantle Hall, past the Russians, down a dirt track. It's 10.30. Half an hour to lights out, we must get back before then. The blackness is so intense, Tony keeps going, 'Who's that?', and, 'What's that?'

Calm down. This is not the sort of coke you used to slip out at night for!

This is real prisoner-of-war stuff.

We follow our instincts. Harry, the lawyer, our advance scout, is the one who located the machines. We stumble and walk for miles. Then, in the distance, the machines light up. Like *Close Encounters of the Rehab Kind*.

We load up twice as much as I got from the drugstore. I have to, I've got customers back at base. I try to quicken the pace, time is running out. Tony decides that my room would be the best place to keep our contraband. Thanks, Tony. As we near home base, we decide to split up, to confuse the guards and hope that no one's grassed. We hear Gerry the Policeman. Oh shit, just my luck, of all the people! We throw ourselves into a ditch. Self-preservation time. I crawl in the direction of my room. I've got minutes before he checks it. An exterior light seems to shine brighter than ever.

As I edge my way along the veranda, behind my room, our eyes meet. There is nothing I can say. Dogs don't answer. They corner me. As they are about to bark for Gerry, I reach for a Snickers bar, break it in two and offer. They sniff. Oh, for Christ sake, you're dogs. You mean you've got taste?! They take the bait, I edge a little closer, they want more or they're telling. I backtrack, leaving a trail of candy.

I can hear Gerry coming.

I get to my door.

A hand grasps my shoulder.

'Shit!'

'Kinda nervous, ain't ya?'

It's Ray.

'Where have you been?'

'I've been feeding the dogs.'

'You English, I'll never work you out.'

I tell Ray of my exploit.

'Well, let's see the goodies.'

I reach into my pockets. One packet of M&M's.

The door opens.

I throw the M&M's out of the window.

The dogs dive for them.

I dive under my bedcover.

Gerry.

'Come on guys, time for bed.' He looks straight at me, 'Michael?'

'Yes, Gerry?'

'Take your shoes off.'

'Will do, Gerry.'

'Goodnight.'

Not really, Gerry, not really.

Lights out.

———————— • ————————

In the tumult of the last moment, the sad drunkards who carried them out of the house got the coffins mixed up and buried them in the wrong graves.

One Hundred Years of Solitude
Gabriel Garcia Marquez
Published in 1970 by Jonathan Cape

CHAPTER TWENTY-ONE

Saturday, 14 May

DAY TWENTY-TWO

6.00 am

Paul, the Chief of Police, shouted two or three times in my dream. At last, a dream! I open my eyes, and he is standing there.

When will I dream again?

I feel good today, very together. I suppose the papers are going to go to town on me yet again. But so what?! It's the eve of Cheryl's arrival. I am very excited.

Michael (Norman Bates) gives a speech at breakfast. We all agree, he is suicide material.

After Mass, Charlotte

Yes, the pain goes on. We finally manage to get rid of the yoghurt, and the milkman leaves us sour cream!

What delights do you have for us today, dear Charlotte?

'Morning, everybody.'

'Morning, Charlotte.'

Adam adds a little, 'Meeoww!'

Black Keith finds the cat noise funny.

'You finding something funny?'

'No, ma'am.'

'Good!'

She gives him a 'dumb addict' look.

'Today we are going to look at step four, and . . .'

Adam talks across her, '. . . see if it needs a polish.'

Keith goes again. 'Can we all join in?'

'I, eh . . . I, eh . . . I . . . I . . . I'm sorry!'

'Do you have any willpower?'

'Yes, ma'am.'

'Try seeing how your willpower works when you have diarrhoea!'

She's firing on all cylinders today. She's says, 'In a drunken home, you don't go out of the house and talk about it. How honest should I have been? When my husband came home from work and said, "What have you been doing all day, dear?" What should I have said? "Drinking!"? Drinking makes you honest. Someone shows you their baby and you say, "God, what an ugly baby"!'

We all laugh.

'Well, it's honest.'

She continues about how step four changes you. *Step four: make a searching and fearless moral inventory of ourselves.*

I'm making a fearless inventory of Charlotte at this moment and, for all I have said, she does grow on you. But we are human beings. Nothing grows on us. It creeps up.

I, and all the others that came in at the same time, have to go to the nursing station. To get our blood results. They took enough from us when we arrived. Nobody is rushing. It's the walk of our lives as the impending result draws near. Even getting off a Charlotte lecture doesn't seem so rewarding.

It's time to play 'Is the Price Right?' Your host for tonight's show – 'Johnny Walker'. And heeeeere's Johnny!! Okay, here's three sheets of paper, which can tell you what price your addiction, and what price carrying it on. And here with your chosen results, remember, you chose them, please welcome Nurse Devile!

She hands us our death certificates, with a smile.

Tell us what the choices are, Nursey. Well, Johnny, they can either check it themselves, or, if they go upstairs, I'll explain what the readings mean.

This has got to be one of the cruellest game shows ever.

I find a corner, as do Ray and Dave. Watch somebody reading their own 'This Is Your Life – Blood'. Watch them blink repeatedly, the pupils dilating, the brain screaming, 'I must pass, I've got a good job to go for.'

> Job description:
> *Wanted: people who want to live.*
> The job requires that you open your eyes in the morning, breathe – and last thing at night close the eyes, and keep breathing.
> It isn't that hard a job. So why are we here? Because we didn't read the bottom of the job description.
> *Addicts need not apply.*

I flip to the report on the back page. They have figures beside parts of the body I didn't know existed. The only problem I have is that I am one percent off making 'good cholesterol'. Followed by, 'Have a medical twice a year and dental check every six months.'

I've passed with flying colours.

I walk over to see how the Captain is faring. I see. Basically.

If the figures on Ray and Dave's pages were added up and changed into money, they could buy me out ten times over I'm pleased to say. I lost in this game. They definitely won the car.

Ray, an old hand, surveys my report. 'Mmm, very good my friend.'

'Wow,' says Dave, 'you're a very fit man.'

I feel a little uneasy with them either side of me. Both Jekyll and Hyde standing so close. Me with fresh liver and kidneys. Ray licks his lips. I stare at him and say, 'No.'

'Not even a sliver?'

'No.'

'Oh well, we'll survive on what little we have left.'

*

Good blood (me) skips back to his room. Average to below average blood (Ray) is also there. He was quick.

'How did you get here so fast?'

'Half my liver and kidneys have gone. I'm quicker.'

He's quite up, the results were not as bad as he thought they would be, he's still standing. He calls me to him. 'I've got something I want to show you. Come with me.'

Ray and I descend the cliff via a sandy, cobbled, steep road. We get to the bottom. The sea reaches out to our shoes, and recedes. Ray, as if showing me around his palatial home, lays his palm out and says, 'This is the last undiscovered wonder of Ashley!'

I am standing on a 'Swiss Family Robinson'-type beach. I'm drawn to water. It has the most unbelievable calming influence. Others may prefer whisky in theirs. Ray and I walk along, our minds are empty. It's like Ashley, and all our problems, are at the top of that cliff, far away. I still wonder at the power of water. Why it just stops, when it could so easily just swallow us all up when it reaches the shore. It laps. The biggest monster in the world and all it does is lap. A fish jumps high into the air and I long to reach out and catch it. In the sand I find a shiny grey stone. It reflects in the light. Ray tells me it's flint. We really are back in the Dark Ages. We hardly speak.

The 'Family Robinson' will be back to this heaven on earth very soon. So we must leave. Beached driftwood, sun-dried, potential house logs, lie strewn about. I kneel in the sand and, using the flint, carve a message into the wood:

I'M A RELAPSE. HELP. MICHAEL BARRYMORE 94.

The child in me is released, he has played his last game.

I sit him on the log and walk back to reality.

Goodbye, Master Parker.

Welcome, Mister Barrymore.

Lunch

During lunch I scribble a picture of Charlotte.

CHARLOTTE.

Nice picture that. I hate to think how it would have turned out by an amateur!

Volleyball

It's Saturday, so we get extra time to play. Great, I love this game! I have to, there's no choice. I play with real enthusiasm. I always do. This is possibly my last real chance. My time here is drawing to a close. Cheryl is coming, we have our lives to concentrate on, there won't be much room for volleyball, at least not over the next week.

I get lost in this game, find time for myself, time to play big boys' games. We're a set down. DJ Tony is opposite me, Black Keith just behind, Skip to my left. Jeff sits the next point out, and lies on the grass watching the match. Apostle Simon serves fast across the net, Sal jumps to cover the return. Keith rushes forward, returns high to the left-hand court. A light breeze lets the ball hit its mark. Simon stretches, makes the contact. High into the air. I fix the ball in my sights. It's mine. I push my whole body down to set the spring in my legs. Tony covers the net for my return. My whole body hangs in the air, outstretched. Ten players, one spectator. A blue Buick glides slowly past. My mind only sees the ball, and decides to gently tip the return into the near corner. My body turns away from the drive. I can't lose the point, my confidence is high, I am high, high in the air. The only sound is the sound of play. As I go for the ball, I hear what for me is a familiar sound. A manufactured sound, a constant whirring.

Whirr – Whirr – Click – Click. Constant.

Everything seems to go in slow motion. My feet touch the ground. I turn, Jeff turns, the players look at me. I look towards the drive. I focus on the blue Buick. It glides, four bodies inside.

Whirr – Whirr – Click – Click – Click – Click – Click.

My stare intensifies, my head pans along with the movement of the car. In the rear seat, the nearside passenger's face is covered by a large black disc. I say nothing. I hope it's not what I fear. The players sense something is up. Suddenly we're playing a very different game.

Life restarts. I look at Jeff, who was nearest the drive.

'Did you see that?'

'Yeah, it rode up to Noble Hall, turned around, came back and just drove away. Looked like a rental car.'

'Were they taking pictures?'

'I'm not sure.'

'Maybe it's just me being paranoid. Maybe they were just an addict's family taking some shots of us playing volleyball.'

Sal reminds me, 'Michael, no cameras are allowed. They are strictly banned.'

Skip shows concern, 'Don't worry, Mikey, it's probably just a group of people out for a Saturday drive, taking shots of the countryside.'

Yeah, you're probably right. *Four grown men, out for a drive, just happen to pass Ashley, saw us playing and thought, 'That looks nice, let's get out our really big lensed camera and take some pictures.' I hope you're right, Skip.*

We continue the game. I feel unsteady, dry, claustrophobic. In the middle of miles of fields.

Something is wrong.

Very wrong.

Even after a walk, I can't shake off the picture of the blue Buick, the black disc in the rear window. I lose hours. I can't tell you what happened at dinner, the AA meet, nothing. In my eyes, at this moment, Ashley is obscured behind a large blue Buick. To take my mind off the day's events, I go on another vending raid, with Tony, Brian and Adam. On our return, as we cross a small river, Adam points out giant turtles. If I had known they were there, I wouldn't have done the first raid. Knowing my luck, they're photographers disguised as Ninjas. A sort of Dona-telle-lens. I make it back with a full load of chocolate. It never occurs to me that if my worries about the press are founded, I am leaving myself wide open.

Pony Express works as well as ever here at Ashley. I sit up way past lights out. I haven't discussed the events on the volley pitch. Paul (Chief of Police) and Jennifer (Policewoman), enter Animal House. I am on the couch. Paul towers over me.

'What have you been up to?'

My first thought is, 'Who's grassed? Who's told them about the raid?'

I prepare myself to take the rap.

'Me?'

'Yeah, you.'

Lie, Barrymore, just lie.

'What do you mean?'

If he finds the chocolate wrappers, I'm finished.

'I mean, what's all this about someone taking pictures?'

Shit, that was close.

'Oh, that!'

'Yeah, that. Why didn't you say something?'

'I didn't want to bother you. I was hoping it was just my imagination.'

'They're not allowed to do that. We'd better keep an eye on you.'

That's the vending raids over.

'What if it is real? What if they come back? I know these people, they will go to extraordinary lengths. I've experienced this before.'

Paul's eyes widen. He grins. 'Yeah. But they ain't dealt with addicts before. Don't worry, get to bed. See you in the morning. Oh, I'll have to tell Leonard, and anyone who needs to know, so that they are aware of the situation. Okay?'

'Yeah. Sorry to be a nuisance.'

'No problem. Night.'

Lights out.

———————•———————

Dear Michael,

How are you doing? I miss our little talks, our Sondheim times and Volleying. You were really a great help to me, Michael, especially in the beginning of my lovely stay at Happydale! I was full of fears and quite lonely, and you aided in my 'opening up' and 'fitting in'. So I do thank you for that. How is Cheryl? Is the news nightmare over? Well I guess I'll scribble off here. Take good care of yourself. God bless, and keep you safe. And please send my very best to Sir Anthony and Emma Thompson. I do admire them so.

Peace and Love, Sal

CHAPTER TWENTY-TWO

Sunday, 15 May

DAY TWENTY-THREE

6.00 a.m.

Everyone but me is up for sunrise. Cheryl is coming today. For now, the events of yesterday take second place. The thought of seeing her after all this time outweighs anything. Absolutely anything. I've just remembered part of our last phone conversation. She asked me to pack some of my clothes so that she could get ahead. She will be proud of how tidy I've kept everything. Not too pleased with the laundry results, but I'm sure it won't be high on her list of priorities. This time, I know she's coming. She flew in last night with one of our associates, John, who has been staying with her in the Palm Beach house. Ray is pleased for me. He suggests putting up a poster. He gets some coloured pens, very rare in here, a large sheet of paper, and writes.

'Ashley welcomes Cheryl Barrymore. Love, Michael.'

Pleased with his work, he hangs it outside his window, beside the veranda. I put my best pressed clothes on. Ray and I are like the family of the bride preparing for the big day. This time, if there are going to be tears, they will be joyous ones. Like all these times, the clock goes on a work-to-rule, and drags its hands. My wrist muscles tighten from the constant time check. I know the family routine. I've lived through one, without an end result, only two Sundays before. They meet Charlotte first, are prepared, and we have to wait outside. Not tempting fate, I sit on the edge of the veranda. *Déjà vu?* Not this time. One o'clock. I am behind the exit

240

to Carpenter Hall. The families come out, all shapes and sizes. Arms outstretched to the ones they love and care for. Care for enough to leave them in a place like this. To give up their responsibility. To hand it over. Give it back to us. Their loving addicts. I smoke, and try to time the last puff. It never works. This is not a film, this is real.

You can spot cashmere a mile away. I can tell by the walk, even from behind, how she feels. My heart pumps. My shoulders ease. I descend the veranda. Solid ground feels like a tightrope.

'Cheryl.'

She turns. Her figure blurs. As she runs, her figure gets no bigger. She looks so thin. I feel so tall. And so proud. So glad. It's my turn to care for her. Her whole head buries and fits perfectly into the side of my neck. I hold her so tight my arms feel as though they are clutching air. I don't know how long we stayed like that, it was very difficult to time. My watch isn't waterproof. I haven't been on a date in eighteen years, but I now remember what it was like. All new. All undiscovered. All mine.

As I'm *in* with the Camp Commandant, I break the first rule. I take Cheryl up to the veranda which backs on to my room. Jennifer, Policewoman, tells me it's against the rules.

'Father Martin asked to see us here.'

'Oh. Oh.'

Well, that worked.

'How's things?'

'Great. But I think I've been followed. The papers haven't gone this Sunday with the Ricky Greene story. I was mugged at Baltimore airport. They've taken all my jewellery, bags, credit cards, and money. Apart from that, I am great, and I couldn't give a damn as long as I'm here, and you're looking so well. How are you?'

'Well, I'm sure that as I was playing volleyball, a photographer drove up and took some pictures. It may just be my imagination . . . And *I* may just have been followed . . .'

Father Martin, in casual dress, ascends the veranda (and on the third day he rose again). He takes up most of our allotted time, mixing advice with jokes. Cheryl and I go straight back into business mode, as if we've never been apart. We tell him it would be nice if he were a guest on my next series. That's if there is one. He seems well pleased. And gives us what little time we have left, together. It's filled by all the inmates coming over to introduce themselves. We are left with only a few minutes alone.

'I am graduating tomorrow.'

'Keep it short.'

'Yes, boss. Got any Hershey bars?'

'John's got one for you.'

'Great. What have I done, according to the Ricky Greene story?'

'Er, you're a transvestite, I'm a dyke. You knock me unconscious, go out, and dress up.'

'Oh, is that all?'

'Yes.'

And that is all we have time for.

We say goodbye just outside the car park area, watched by the guards. She walks with John back to the car. I can see she is crying. Her tears are of relief. This is the best day of my life. Daddy's home.

This evening, I can't concentrate on anything. Jennifer, Policewoman, tells me off for being, as she puts it, 'Very disruptive.'

The joy of my reunion with Cheryl, the anticipation of the coming week, the return to the real world, is too much for one day. I leave the meet halfway through, and come back to my room. I lie on my bed, and pull off my sweater. As it passes over my head, I can smell her perfume. I fold it neatly, and lay it between my face and the pillow.

Lights out for me, this day, comes early.

How I'd remind you –
You remembered,
And my fears were wrong!
Was it ever real?
Did I ever love you this much?
Did we ever feel
So happy then?

Lyric reproduction of *'Too Many Mornings'*
by Stephen Sondheim
by kind permission of Carlin Music Corp.

CHAPTER TWENTY-THREE

Monday, 16 May

DAY TWENTY-FOUR

6.00 a.m.

Some people say, 'Live each day like it's the last day of your life.' What about the last day of your career?

Paul wakes me up, 'Michael, Leonard wants to see you. Get up.'

There is something up, I know it.

'What, now?'

'Right now.'

'Is it the papers?'

'I don't know. But there's a lot of activity at the front gate. You must be pretty famous.'

I'm shown to unknown territory at Ashley. Leonard's office. Very nice, too. Just what I imagined George Bush would have. He takes on that 'you've failed to meet the requirements of the board' look.

'The newspapers know you're here. The story broke in England this morning. They have pictures. Cheryl knows all about it. She has protection at the hotel. There are sheriffs blocking the gate, and we're gonna make sure you're gonna have all the protection *you* need.'

I just stare at him. 'Your recovery is of the utmost importance. We don't want you to react and take any backward steps.'

I just stare at him.

'If needs be, I'll break the rules and let Cheryl stay here, so she is safe. There are photographers, journalists, and TV cameras outside her hotel, and outside here.'

I'm still staring.

'We have had the story faxed. Here it is.'

I am reading it, and staring. It is the first time *I* get to see it. The time is 7.30 am here, 12.30 pm in England.

Daily Mirror

Monday May 16th 1994. **HONESTY, QUALITY, EXCELLENCE.**

World Exclusive

'MY DRINK AND DRUGS HELL'
by Michael Barrymore.

I am fixed for an age on the headline. For some reason, I keep reading the small print. 'Honesty, quality, excellence.' As if it's printed ten times taller than 'drink and drugs hell'. Hell on earth. Hell in print. They have credited me with a story that I have no part in. Committed to print. The picture of me, dishevelled from playing volleyball, seems to move. Laughing at me. A picture from hell. I am not shaking, just a low body vibration.

Leonard's soft voice calms the capped volcano inside me, 'Just take your time to read it.' Like the ten commandments, the tabloid punches out my life, in five easy-to-read foldaway pages. Ever so handy to slip into anyone's top pocket, to unfold for that dinner party that needs spicing up. There are twenty-six letters in the English alphabet. I didn't realise how many combinations you could make into words you don't want to see.

booze . . . binge . . . guzzled . . . dope . . . painkillers . . . tranquillizers . . . drying out . . .

cure . . . destroyed . . . nightmare . . . secrets . . . clinic . . . struggled . . . rebuild . . . shattered life . . . haunted . . .

This is just page one.

Marijuana . . . smoked . . . painkillers . . . valium . . . drank . . . bourbon . . . battle . . . drink . . . drug . . . addiction . . . clinic . . . intensive therapy . . . endured . . . pain . . . confession . . . break . . . whiskey . . . marijuana . . . pills . . . poured . . . secrets . . . strangers . . . tears . . . long nightmare . . . brave struggle . . . rebuild . . . shattered life . . . tragic . . . mask . . . drying out . . . clinic . . . patients . . . stark . . . testimony . . . torment . . . drank . . . valium . . . painkillers . . . marijuana . . . couldn't control . . . can't handle . . . drink . . . stored booze . . . pint of bourbon . . .

. . . fool.

Why does the word 'fool' hang a moment longer? Because it's the one word that says it all. The one word that can be both your friend and your enemy. As your friend, a fool is a clown, a comic, a jester, a harlequin. As your enemy, a fool is a half-wit, idiot, moron and a sucker. All they had to do was print 'fool'.

Foolishly, or otherwise, I do not read on. I can't. After all, no one is dead, except the fool in me. I don't know how someone feels when handed a mirror to look at their face after a traumatic facial accident. I can only guess. This was no accident of mine. I didn't imagine the lens focusing on me. The shutter is flicking rapidly in my face as I hand the documentary evidence back to Leonard. So much for confidentiality. So much for trust. So much money buys body and soul. I've never felt so sorry for a human being. What can I say that will help? What is to be gained? I am frozen. Locked in time. What options do I have? Stay frozen, to be taken away, and never speak again? Or defrost, and just melt away?

Leonard breaks my ice. 'Michael . . . ? Michael!'

'Yes.'

'I'll keep you informed. You can carry on, or we'll make other arrangements. Cheryl will be here soon.'

I've spoken. I haven't frozen. And I'm here. I haven't melted. One thing I have always been able to do is think. Think before you sink. This is one battle I haven't won, but the war isn't over. I rally my troops. First a head count. One. Well, it's a start. Let battle commence.

I leave Leonard's office, and make straight for the briefing room. The chapel. I see Big Frank as I enter. I tell him. He suggests I hand over to my higher power. Frank says he will help with the earth end.

At Mass I tell God I now have no control over this. With His guidance, it will be run on instinct. It's never let me down before. I apologise for not talking to Him for so long, and get a few things straightened out.

1. They had no permission to take my photograph.

2. It is not my story, as was blazoned on the front page.

3. The confidentiality law had been broken by one of my group.

If I had wanted to publicise my whereabouts, I would have gone to the Betty Ford Clinic. These stories are hearsay. No notes are taken in group, no tape recordings. The stories are misquoted. Two of them, the snow and the car through the garage, are about someone else, not me. Some of the quotes are from old reports. This has been a total and gross invasion of my privacy.

I do not court the press. I am known for my reluctance to do unnecessary interviews. I have, to date, put up with all the invasion, the accusations, because that was my choice. The word choice has been removed from me. It is no longer in my vocabulary. It was *my* choice to tell my innermost feelings to the others here, believing I was under protection, as are they. *Stories are just stories. With a real name attached, they become someone's life. Extreme torture has been known not to be able to unlock a mind. My fellow addicts told their story, revealed all, to a few strangers who vowed to respect their confidence. I did the same. It is the first time I encounter the real meaning of the word 'Betrayal'.*

Mass over. Big Frank has been busy. The troops are gathering. So are the press. I go to my graduation. I have a speech to make. I wonder if I've got Gettysburg's address? We are now under siege. Sheriffs blocking the gate, all those entering are required to produce ID. Guards covering all entrances. The sea to one side, we should be safe there. I sit in my usual place in Carpenter Hall. The graduation is about to start. All the families are here for those who are passing out. Except Cheryl. I think I know the reason for her delay. I get constant updates. I have just under a week left. I want to try and finish the programme, believe it or not. A long, very long, white limousine with tinted windows pulls up outside, under escort. The inmates all stare out of the window, and then at me. They all smile as one.

Yes siree, that's my Cheryl arrivin'!

Two guys (out of work since *All the President's Men*), open the doors. Cheryl has been secretly taken from the Holiday Inn in Aberdeen, and steps out with two helium balloons, proclaiming 'I love you'. It makes me smile. Actually, it makes me crack up!

During all this, my mind keeps flashing back. The blue Buick, the headlines, sentences such as, 'I was sitting on the steps outside having a smoke, when I saw this really gangly guy staggering out of a car'. I didn't stagger. My breathalyser read zero.

Cheryl enters Carpenter Hall. She has to sit away from me. It's the rule. She blows a kiss, and waves. I smile back. This is the first time we have seen each other since the news broke. To anyone looking on, you would think it was just another day.

Father Martin calls me to the stage, to receive my medal. He says, 'The next one to graduate comes from England. Over the last month, he has endeared himself to us all. He has never taken the role of the big star, which he is back in his country where he is loved by millions. I have experienced that special quality, as they and you have. Michael, come on up.'

I rise with pride. The whole room cheers, and makes me feel wanted. Cheryl comes to stand beside me. I walk to the microphone. Pause. Look around at all their faces. They smile their approval.

'My fellow Americans. The reason I am here, is my flight from London was diverted from Miami to Baltimore. The airline put us up here. There is nothing wrong with me at all. It's all been a terrible mistake. I asked, "When am I likely to get a flight out of here." They said, "As soon as the crew clear detox." My first encounter was my room mate Ray,' (he smiles), 'who showed strange intelligence. Every time the tannoy blared "Anyone requiring a lift to Carpenter Hall in the buggy, meet at Bantle Hall in five minutes", he would leave our room beside Carpenter, saying "Can't stop, got to catch the buggy." He'd run the length of the complex, ride back, get off, look at me and say, "Still ain't got the idea, eh?"

'I would have booked in here for Christmas, but *you* try getting a reservation. You may have noticed the two dogs attend every meeting except Charlotte's. During the storm last night, I was lying in my bed when lightning struck. Charlotte was standing there looking like a flashing Christmas tree, screaming, "All men suck!" I would like to thank Father Martin, my counsellor Tim, all at table thirty, and Skip, Tony, Sal, Howard, Chong . . .'

One by one, I go around the room, naming, from memory, every single woman and man, and of course, Cheryl. Finishing with, 'I hope my problems with the press don't become yours.'

The warmth of their reception makes me even stronger for what is ahead. I will always thank them.

But which one went to the press?

Cheryl thanks them all. Father Martin hugs us. I have a group session to go to. I won't let anything interfere. At this point I have no idea of the story's impact. Cheryl brings me up to date.

'The reaction at home has been unbelievable.'

'What do you mean?'

'They are all praying for you, and just want you to get better. My hotel is full of press, but they don't know I am in there. We have to get rid of the stretch limo. It's a bit obvious. They have arranged for me to go back with the patients when they leave for the outside meet. We have to plan how we are going to deal with this. How are you?'

'I feel strange.'

'Please don't worry. We will sort it. I'm only concerned that you are not put back by all this.'

'If everyone is behind me, I'll fight it. If not, I have nothing to fight.'

'You have plenty to fight, and you're worth fighting for. A television journalist ended a report at home by saying, "It's raining in London. Even the angels are crying for him."'

I must use what I have learnt here. I am going to group.

Cheryl and John go to Leonard's office to lay out their plans. She looks really tired. The mixture of emotions must be mind-blowing.

At group, we discuss with Tim all that has happened. It's odds-on that Tammy is the culprit. As yet unconfirmed. Skip, and all, are very upset. I tell them I want to carry on, and I don't want it to dominate the group sessions. Tim thanks me, and adds his encouragement.

At lunch, Cheryl and I sit at the family table, barely eating a thing. The whole place is abuzz. I gain something from it. I am allowed to come and go from lectures as needs be. I won't abuse it. If I want a trial run of the real world, I am surely getting it.

It is time for Cheryl to go. The limo leaves without her. I kiss her goodbye. She is bundled into the middle of fifteen addicts, a baseball cap covering her face. As the van speeds away, a tiny hand, from within the addictive scrum, waves. Now, that's what I call style. She calls it suffocation!

The rest of the day, I discover people I never knew, who have never spoken. The head gardener, who up until now just grunted in my direction, introduces himself, 'Hi, I'm Bob. Really nice to meet you. You sure in hell is one famous guy. D'ya know Benny Hill?'

'Yes.'

'He's funny, ain't he?'

'Yes.'

'You're like a David Letterman, somebody told me.'

'Apparently.'

'They're stopping everyone at the gate.'

'So I believe.'

'I've been here years. Never seen anything like it.'

'Oh. Well, I hope it's not stopping you from doing your work.'

'No, no problem. You need anything, just let me know.'

'Some poppy seeds?'

'Pardon me?'

'Doesn't matter. Got to go. Bye.'

'Bye now.'

He waves.

At the evening meet, most of the PSA's (Policemen and Policewomen) are noticeable by their absence. Geoff the bobby's walkie-talkie keeps interrupting the speaker. It crackles, 'There's more of them down here.' He goes off. He returns. It crackles, 'Someone's trying to get in via the golf course.' He's off. He returns. This goes on all through the meet. I stare at the speaker as if it's nothing to do with me. At the end, the speaker comments,

'Before I finish, what in the hell is going on? I've been coming here for eight years, and I've never had to show my ID. I thought the second word of this fellowship says "Anonymous".'

They all laugh. And turn and look at me.

Outside, I see Geoff the bobby, breathless.

'It's lit up with TV cameras at the gate, like a Berlin Blitz. You'd better keep to your room.'

I put myself in solitary confinement. As I lie on my bed, trying to absorb the events of the day, Ray gives me some fatherly advice, 'Fuck 'em all if they can't take a joke.'

Lights out.

———————— • ————————

Drought and famine in TV land
Read the Sunday papers credit card in your hand
Sing your song of freedom just to ease your troubled mind
And save your guilty pennies for the ones you leave behind.

'It's A Long Long Way'
UB40

Words and music by Ali Campbell, Robin Campbell, Earl Falconer, Norman Hassan, Brian Travers, Michael Virture, Terrance Wilson and Jim Brown.
© 1993, reproduced by permission of Fernscan Ltd/EMI Virgin Music Ltd, London WC2H 0EA

CHAPTER TWENTY-FOUR

Tuesday, 17 May

DAY TWENTY-FIVE

6.00 am

Ray finds the whole thing a constant amusement. He's up before me for the first time. Also, for the first time, he speaks before me. 'I ain't standin' any more of this. I'm goin' to Leonard to complain. If I had known I was sharing a room with a junky, I would never have come here. I'm a decent, upstanding alcoholic. I've got a reputation to protect.'

He cheers me up with his banter. It's light relief, and a better start to the day. Cheryl is coming at eight o'clock. I need to get ready. Ready for what, at this point, I have no idea. I don't really know how I feel. I'm too busy dealing with it.

As she arrives, she tells me she's managed to elude the press, who are now increasing in numbers.

Tim said yesterday, 'Well, they have printed their story, that should be an end to it.'

Wrong!

The next instalments arrive:

'DRUNK PRIEST SAVES COMIC MIKE'

'BORN TO PLEASE, BENT ON SELF-DESTRUCTION'

'BARRYMORE IN MYSTERY CLINIC STAY'

'BARRYMORE FIGHTS A LIFE HOOKED ON DRUGS AND DRINK'

I manage to get through a group session. Tim asks me if he can have lunch with Cheryl and me.

At the lunch, Cheryl and I are tense. She hasn't slept for three nights. I feel on trial. We eat nothing. She finds it all too much. Reading the reports second-hand, like she hasn't been privy to what has been said. I feel under attack from all quarters. She runs out of the dining room, crying. I follow.

Outside Bantle, we argue openly. Not our style at all – neither is unnecessary publicity, but that choice has been taken away. In two days we have gone from happiness to misery. She feels hopeless. Millions of people are reading all this for the first time, and so is she. Selfishly I defend my situation. She doesn't know what to believe any more. The tools Ashley have given me lie broken. It's all been a waste of time. The one person I held on to, I feel is putting me on trial. How many trials can I have in one month?'

I'm going to walk out of the gate, down to the town of Aberdeen, and get pissed.

I'm shaking. She's shaking. We are left alone to deal with all this. It's the only way. The deed has been done. It splits us apart. Happiness is a thing called journalism. I can't stand seeing her cry. I don't want this. I don't believe she does. I hold her. I use what I have learnt. She needs help. I have been looked after. What has it been like for her all this time? Left alone. What happens to the one with the hole in the bed, where their loved one used to lie? What happened?

Cheryl's Story

Before we arrived in Palm Beach, one of Michael's worst nights came when his family were on the television in an advert for the *Sunday Mirror*. His mother was unrecognisable, sort of made over. He reeled, fell to the ground, then bolted out of the flat. We found him eventually.

Austin Tate spent eight hours with him the next day, going over it. We still had four shows to make, and he seemed to rally. Ironically, I think they were four of the best shows he's ever made. But he wasn't the same. I kept hoping against hope that Palm Beach would be the answer. He'd had to cope with the strain of the show, and that final humiliation from his family, the final betrayal. I hoped that if he got away and had a holiday, he'd feel better in himself, and would recover. But it was hoping against hope. When we left England, I knew we wouldn't be back for a long time. Michael had no idea. I packed enough, as I always do, to stay away a long time. And we did.

I began to think he was mentally ill. More and more, he was acting strangely. On the plane over to Palm Beach, the strain was showing quite badly. You could see it in the fishing picture of him. Then Brian Wells (a reporter from the *People* newspaper) appeared at the door. I found him intimidating. Our privacy had been invaded once again. It was supposed to be our holiday, we needed it badly.

At that time, I was incredibly thin. People were much more concerned about me than they were about Michael. I was down to six stone. It had been a very long series, and I looked like I was cracking up. I think that drew attention away from Michael. Although I was mentally all right, physically I was at the end of my tether.

In Palm Beach things went from bad to worse. Michael wasn't enjoying anything. The sun didn't make any difference, the place didn't make any difference, the water that normally makes him feel so much better, didn't. He was becoming more and more unhappy.

I wasn't aware of him drinking at this point. He didn't drink in front of me anyway. I thought he was going to have a nervous breakdown. I didn't think beyond that. I thought, 'He can't go on like this. He needs some help.' I wished we'd never come so far from home. Because there I would have got Austin. Eventually that's what I did.

Michael couldn't sleep. His life was hell. But he didn't make my life hell. Even though he was desperately unhappy, he tried very hard to appear normal and happy. As if, 'it's okay, everything's going to be all right'. It certainly wasn't.

Then he started being physically ill. It frightened me. I didn't think he was going to survive. I thought he was going to die. I know he wanted to.

In the middle of the night, I rang Maurice Leonard. I was desperate. I waited until Michael was asleep.

'I know I need help. I've got real trouble. I'm very concerned about Michael, and I don't know who to turn to, where to get help. If I just ring a hospital, it's going to be headline news.'

Maurice got me the number of the place in California where Austin was at a convention. I finally got through and woke him up. Austin's voice was like it was in the next room. It was weird.

'I think this is it, Austin, he can't go on. He's very ill. What do I do?'

I described how it had been.

'I agree with you,' he said. 'He does need help. There's a man here with me called Bob Beckett. He lives in Palm Beach. He's getting the eight o'clock plane out of here. Hold on. If you can't hold on, you must get emergency services. But if you can – do. Bob will be with you within hours.'

Bob was. I told Michael that I'd asked a man to come round to help him, but Michael wasn't really listening. He was adamant, 'I'm not going to talk to this man.'

But when Bob walked in, he did talk to him. It took a while, but eventually Michael agreed that he had to go somewhere. Life wasn't worth living, the way he felt. He couldn't go on as he was. So we arranged a place that was safe. We balked at the thought of the Betty Ford Clinic. I still thought that Michael was mentally ill. Michael did, too. Bob knew the right place. He told us about Father Martin's Ashley. The next day, Michael started shaking. There was no time to lose. I couldn't go with him. I was in too much of a state.

The tape of the final show of 'Barrymore' arrived. He had to be at the airport in forty minutes. We watched the final number, 'Never Met a Man I Didn't Like', and Michael went. It was all over so quickly. The minute he was out of the door, I thought I'd made a terrible, terrible mistake, that this was all wrong, that we could do better than this. As he went, the house was incredibly silent. I've never felt quite as bad as I did then. After about ten minutes of just sobbing, I turned on the television, just to make some noise in the place.

'Hurricane warning!'

Then the storm hit. Michael was in the air somewhere overhead, and Palm Beach was in the grip of this storm.

I fell apart. I couldn't cope at all. I had to be reminded to comb my hair, and put some clothes on. I couldn't do anything. I was paralysed.

People think that Michael and I are cosmetic. That nobody can be together all these years, morning and night like we are, and still be real. There must be more to this. I honestly think that this is why the press have homed in on us to the extent that they have. They genuinely feel that we are a business partnership. That couldn't be further from the truth. We are husband and wife first.

When Michael left for the rehab, I watched a Sid Caesar documentary. He's the only comedian I've ever been able to relate to Michael. He seems to have been genuinely real, as Michael is. He seemed so full of talent that the talent was almost destroying him. I kept looking at these similarities. He'd attended a rehab, but he didn't come out for ten years. That preyed on my mind. I honestly didn't know whether I'd get Michael back. I felt so bitter about everything, and I was worried about him to the point where I couldn't eat. My stomach churned the whole time. I couldn't forgive the people who I believed, and still do believe, had put him in there. He never got over the day of that advert. His mother and his brother. For your mother to do that is so dreadful. I've got no conception of it. I came from Kit and Ed, and I think that was part of my problem. I couldn't believe a family could do that to someone.

Michael carried on giving his mother money for many years. Constantly buying her things that she would throw back in his face. Then, she rang, and told us she wanted a new house, or she would go to the papers. It was getting out of hand. She was demanding more money than we actually had. So we said, 'Go on, then. Do what you like.'

She did.

The phone call was made at the weekend, and the article appeared on the Monday. That was it. It was the first major blow. It was all very bitter and nasty.

I can't forgive her for continually sticking the knife in. She knows that it doesn't do him any good. There's been a lot of speculation. Some journalists write that there must be something more to this. That Michael is not the man we believe him to be. In their stories, it's as if suddenly, for no reason at all, we have turned our backs on his family. I'd never have married a man who would do that without just cause. His mother and brother have never explained the real reasons. They can't, they're too implicated. They don't know anything about Michael. They haven't seen him for ten years. They write stories as if they're in contact, as if they know us. They constantly say, 'Please come home. I love you.'

It's rubbish. Absolute rubbish. Anything that they can make money out of. We're just a meal ticket, that's all we are.

Michael was on the brink. Yet again, all directly connected with them, and I was about to lose him. I can't forgive his mother for that.

Michael rang to tell me he'd arrived.

When he was off the phone, they said, 'You can ring this number, but he can't speak to you. Our rules are that until we say you can speak together, you can't. But if you want to check up for your own peace of mind, you can call here.'

So every morning and every night, I rang, and spoke to this woman called Kim, 'How is he? Can you tell me how my husband is?'

It was as if Michael was in intensive care. I imagined this straitjacket world, and a bare room. I had no sense of what Ashley was really like. My instinct was, 'I've got to get him out. It's my duty in life.'

Austin was the best thing for me. He spoke to me sanely. Ashley's attitude was, if you have a problem getting through to our people, and you're upset about your husband, get your own counsellor and let them sort it. We only look after the people inside.'

I was very much out on a limb, but life had to go on. I wasn't really getting any better, I wasn't looking after myself, or functioning very well.

Eventually, I got myself together enough to go to AA meetings, and get a counsellor. I was going into another world. I remember sitting at the back of that first AA meeting. The man said, 'Good evening.'

My eyes filled with tears.

I couldn't understand a word that man said at the beginning. He did the whole introduction, and I didn't get one word of it. I couldn't stop crying.

I started to go to Al-Anon (the support group for addicts' families). The personal warmth was wonderful. At the first Al-Anon meeting a lady called Meredith said, 'The best thirty days you're ever going to have is when he's in there. It's when he comes out you're gonna have a problem!'

I wasn't allowed to go to the first Sunday visit. I knew for sure that if I went I'd get him out. I promised Ashley, and Austin, that I wouldn't go. That Sunday was hell. I wasn't aware that Michael didn't know I was coming. When I found that out, it broke my heart. Because I'd have crawled to Baltimore.

My first conversation with Michael's counsellor was brief.

'Hi, I'm Tim, Michael's counsellor. I know a lot about you. I know that Michael's doing very well, and you're very co-dependent.'

That was it.

I didn't get much change out of any of them. I couldn't have gone through it without Austin. It was like a campaign to get a prisoner out of a camp. I thought Michael, on a couple of occasions, sounded frightened.

It turned out that he was just feeling low because he had to tell his life story. But I didn't know that then.

Al-Anon teach you to live your life without the other person. So that you're strong. I was never a really good subject for them. I didn't *want* to live without Michael. The whole thing was very scary. I counted the days until I could get to Ashley. The nights and the mornings were the worst. Every morning I woke up thinking he was in bed with me. I didn't know if Michael would ever come back. And Ashley would not commit themselves.

I sent him cards every day. Some days, five or six! I didn't have anything else to do until I flew to Baltimore.

I was very nervous. I couldn't wait to see him. I got out of the plane, and stood by the hire-car depot. Two men mugged me. They took the lot. Identification, credit cards, jewellery. They spent on the credit cards within ten minutes.

The hire car man said, 'You can't hire a car without ID.'

'You just saw the man take it!'

Eventually they let us have a car.

None of this mattered. I was going to see Michael.

That was a Saturday evening. The next morning I arrived at Ashley. The rules are, you have to watch a video first. That was the worst part. Because I just wanted to see him. I couldn't concentrate. The video was ghastly. It's terrible to make people sit there like that. I don't know what was said on the video. I know I couldn't get my breath, I wanted to be sick. It was just awful. This went on for an hour.

Eventually we filed out. I couldn't see him, and then I did. He was silhouetted by the cliff. I ran up to him, and he just picked me up in the air, like a little doll. It was like we'd never been apart. It was the best day of my life, by far. There has never been a better day.

That night when I went to bed, I'd never felt so happy. It was worth all the pain. I went to bed feeling that no matter what, to have this day was worth everything. Whatever I'd been through, and whatever I'd have to go through, it would be worth it. I closed my eyes.

The phone rang. The *Daily Mirror* had gone to press. I promptly went to the bathroom and threw up. It was a short-lived happiness.

*

Tim takes us to his office. This is his forte. He's seen this so many times. The family arrives, not knowing what Ashley is going to hand them back. Anger, the sort that only love can create. *You* come here to have your life sorted out, your family are left to sort it out for themselves. Love doesn't have a great exchange rate.

Tim understands her, me, it all. He has to negotiate for both sides in a war, knowing that all both sides want is peace. We agree that to start tearing each other apart is not to anyone's advantage. It's just extra pages for a daily newspaper.

As soon as Cheryl and I calm down, we get back to the business in hand. It is deemed necessary to call a press conference, if only to give ourselves some respite when we leave to return home. Henri Brandman, our lawyer, is monitoring events, and preparing to fly out in two days' time. It has been decided to have it here inside Ashley on Friday morning. It's not an appearance I'm relishing, but it has to be done. When the going gets tough, the tough make speeches. As Cheryl prepares to leave for the hotel, more faxes arrive:

'TOP TV STAR'S DRINK AND DRUGS NIGHTMARE'

'DRUG AND DRINK HELL BARRYMORE HID FROM HIS WIFE'

'SINK OR SWIM OFF THE BOOZE'

'BARRYMORE IN DRINK AND DRUGS CLAIM'

'TV STAR RUMOURED UNDER TREATMENT AT ASHLEY'

You build up your own immune system against germs. Or they spread and break you down. I toughen my resolve. As Cheryl leaves, she reminds my about wandering out in the open. 'Them trees have eyes!' I reroute my journey through the rehab, avoiding the open areas and driveways. I should be safe walking along the cliff edge. There's only the expanse of the Cheapspeake River, and there's only a couple of guys in a fishing boat, anchored up . . .

FLASH!! . . . FLASH!!

That's unusual, they're sending the fish a coded message!

Judy from housekeeping runs towards me, 'They're taking photographs from that boat!!'

She rugby-tackles me to the ground.

Oh great, Judy, that should look just great, 'Barrymore in drugs hell, and penalty shoot-out!'

'How long have they been there?'

'Quite some time. I hope they have my good side.'

The Ashley van is summoned. It pulls up, obscuring me from the boat. They bundle me in, and reroute me back to my room. I watch from the safety of my room as a police launch chases the photographers, disguised as fishermen.

Ray creeps up behind me. I'm lost in the disbelief of what's happening.

In his best English accent, he yells, 'Smyle, Bar-ee-more!'

I jump, my heart jumps, my sense of humour jumps! He's standing there with a long black tube made to look like a lens, erect from his flies! I laugh. He laughs. Thank God for the Rays of this world.

Ray's attitude is great. He keeps me sane through all this insanity. He's very up. The main reason being he's leaving in two days. This is a very different room mate. He's like a child at Christmas. He's going to get all his toys back, his house, his boat, his freedom. Hopefully not his whisky bottle. He seems to have accepted his situation. I'm sad he's going, he's been a key part of my recovery, whether he knows it or not. I hope he survives out there. At the moment he's just being plain stupid, singing, *'Oh, de Camptown Races sing der song, do dah, do dah . . .'*

It rubs off.

At dinner this evening, I can't take any more. During one of our breaks, another round of songs brightens up the already bright evening. We all decide to give soul music a rest. Adam, Tony, Sal,

Keith and myself sit looking out to sea, singing a medley from *The Sound of Music*. In the middle of 'Doh, a deer, a female deer', I rise, throw open my arms, look heavenward. At the top of my voice, I proclaim my guilt, that I am not who I say I am. I am, in fact, Julie Andrews.

'*Yes, cue the cameras, lights, sound, action.*'

I leap into the air, and with gay abandon, run towards the cliff edge, spinning around à la Maria, singing, 'The hills are alive with the sound of music. My heart wants to know . . .', and disappear off the end of the cliff.

The boys, on cue, in between wiping their eyes, sing, 'Nobody takes a cliff-fall like Maria!'

All they see is my head pop up in the distance. It's a real tonic. No gin, and no lemon. Nothing at this moment needs a bitter taste added.

We are locked into Animal House tonight. There have been several attempts to get to me. My fellow inmates have to put up with the confinement. I apologise. They don't care. I think they are secretly enjoying all the attention. It takes the heat off them.

I go to my room. Ray is still singing, *Zippedee Do Dah*, whilst ripping up all his notes. I lie on my bed, and look at the update.

The faxes keep on coming.

Lights out.

---●---

Even our closest friends seldom knew the details of the strife in our families.

A Life of My Own
Hazelden Meditations

CHAPTER TWENTY-FIVE

Wednesday, 18 May

DAY TWENTY-SIX

The routine changes drastically. I don't check the sunrise, I don't wonder what the day will bring. At breakfast, Howard asks me to sign his book. It's a ritual with all who leave. Usually it's just the ones who are in your group. I have a pile to sign. I spend the rest of the day, and every spare minute, book-signing. I shall miss Howard, and I shall pray he lasts out there. I'm not so sure he will.

Morning group yet again discusses my problems. Tim hands me some editorials. He thinks they will cheer me up.

Philippa Kennedy in the *Daily Express*

INTRUSION INTO A PRIVATE AGONY

'Barrymore is by far the most talented and endearing comic we have, and if the stress of producing his customary excellence has taken its toll on his health, and he now needs specialist treatment, then he should be able to get it without being publicly dissected.'

Richard Littlejohn in the *Sun*

MY YEARS OF HELL WITH THE STARS BY BOOZY THE BOTTLE

'Where would the newspapers be without My Battle With The Bottle? Barely a week passes without yet another celebrity emerging from a drying out clinic to talk about their victory over the demon drink. But there are two sides to every story. Today, in this column, The Bottle answers back.'

Jack Tinker in the *Daily Mail*

MY HEART GOES OUT TO BARRYMORE, THIS HAUNTED COMIC GENIUS

'Frankly, the news that Michael Barrymore has been fighting a losing battle with drink and drugs during the very time his career has rocketed him to the pinnacle of his profession, astounds me. It is like saying the Queen Mother is a fetishist, or the Pope an atheist. However, if it be so, then my heart goes out to both Michael and Cheryl. Theirs is a special partnership, forged by an obvious mutual affection, but also dedicated to the unique talent that is Michael Barrymore. If what I read is true, for their sake, and for the national sense of good clean fun, I pray he is soon restored to sober health and to us.'

Lynda Lee-Potter in the *Daily Mail*

THE BITTER MEMORIES THAT HAUNT BARRYMORE

'In the end, he used his own pain to enrich the lives of the rest of us. His rotten upbringing made him uncannily intuitive with other people. He's made a triumph out of despair, and is one of the few great comedians for whom people feel not only admiration, but love. The public reaction to his current problems has not been prurient interest, but sadness and compassion. Everybody is praying for him to recover, because on stage and on television, he showers his genius and talent upon us with a kind of dizzy abandon.'

It works.

Cheryl arrives at lunchtime. She is looking much better. She still hasn't been discovered at the hotel, even though she can hear the journalists in the rooms next to hers, reporting their stories back to England. We have a more businesslike day. My rehabilitation is suffering, but needs must. Thank God it happened when it did. If it had been during the first week . . . I don't even want to think about it. It's all too close for comfort.

'Have you packed any clothes yet?'

'This afternoon.'

'They haven't changed you that much!'

I need to get ahead. I have to think about the press conference. There are many ways to skin a cat. If I am one, I don't know how many lives I've got owing.

As I pack my stuff, I glance at some more of Cheryl's cards. Strange how they read, now that all this has happened.

We spoke today, darling (May 2nd). Try not to be unhappy. Grab this with both hands, so that we get this right first time. You've got the world at your feet, and me, who loves you more than words can say, and people who really care about you. Not you the star. And the best dog in the world. It's time that you were happy too, just think how it will be when we are together again. It will be okay, sweetheart, I promise. C

Remember to be careful what you wish for. I was very careful wishing for you. I love you so. C

I'm going to love you like nobody's loved you, come rain or come shine. Happy together, unhappy together, won't it be fine.

> Ray Charles soundtrack, *King of Comedy*
> My love, C

I pick up the photos of my family. As I do, I hold Eddie's picture in front of me, and think of him. How he would have dealt with all this. He would be proud. No matter what, he never found a down side to anything, only hope. He survived all, because he never had to ask himself why he existed. His words are in my mind, like he's standing beside me, saying, 'You're as good as anyone else, and better than the rest.'

I'm coming home, Ed, back from the front. I'll see you in my dreams.

My dreams as a kid included flying in a Lear jet. Cheryl phones me from the hotel. We can't take the scheduled flight back to Palm Beach. All planes are suddenly fully booked. I wonder why. It doesn't take a lot of working out. There may be just a few people who would like to join us on the journey to Florida. You know, maybe ask a few questions. Security would rather we left by private jet. They will take us as soon as the press call is over, to a private airfield. The jet will be waiting, and on our arrival in Palm Beach, the local police will escort us to the house.

'Is this all really necessary?'

'Do you have any idea what is going on?'

'No. Well, a bit. Remember, I'm not in the real world. Even seeing the continuous paper reports has an unreal feel to it.'

'Well, believe me, it's necessary.'

I've always believed her. I've said it a million times, now all this has happened, I have no wish to change my belief. Cheryl made me what I am, and she accepts the whole deal, even though the warranty ran out years ago.

Howard gives me a hug, to say goodbye. Not his style at all. He's not all heart, but what is left, he gives. He's nervous. Institutions have played a major part in his life. The look on his face reads, 'I'll be back, just popping out to show them why they need people like me. Why my sort are here. So that we all have something to balance our lives with.' I look at him as he is driven away.

> *Everyone considered him the Howard of the County.*
> *Valium, Methadone, they let him have it all.*
> *He stood tall, let his body have it all,*
> *Till it turned all pale and yellow.*
> *You could have heard a needle drop,*
> *As he turned his head and said,*
> *'Promises are done, I won't be the reformed one,*
> *I'll walk back into trouble if I can.*
> *It won't make me freak, I'll be back inside a week,*
> *You won't have to ask me where I'll be,*
> *They'll always bring me back . . . to Ashley.'*

The chance of paying any attention to lectures diminishes. I'm continuing to reroute myself. They have more or less stopped policing me. I'm on my own really. What can they do? They have to restore sanity. It's in danger of affecting the other inmates. I see Ken outside Administration. He was the first person I met on my arrival. He's very upset about all that's happened: 'We have never had this before.'

'I'm sorry.'

'We are sorry for you.'

There are a lot of sorrys in this place.

He looks suspiciously at a man who is arriving to start treatment. Ever since yesterday, when a woman spent three hours crying her eyes out about how helpless she felt over her alcoholic husband. She needed to get him to a safe haven such as Ashley, and could Ken let her know what they would do for him, and how he would be looked after. Ken did his job, showed her round the place, gave her all the details, tried to stop her crying. The whole account ended in print. She was a journalist.

Thirty-six hours to the press call. I need to get my thoughts together. I miss a lecture, and sit on the veranda beside my room, gazing out to sea. I want to empty my mind, and just restock with what is important. The evening is starting to bring its darker colours to the sky. For a moment, I trick myself into believing nothing has happened.

Lee sits down beside me. 'Mind if I join you?'

I give him a Pope-like wave. He knows it means, 'Be my guest, but keep your mouth shut.' In silence, we watch the scenery.

'How are you feeling?'

'Fine.' (Which means 'fucked up', 'insecure', and 'neurotic'.)

'What's up, Lee?'

'I've got to leave today, my insurance company won't pay.'

'Have you managed to get something from your stay?'

'I suppose.'

'Why have they stopped the payments?'

'I've used up a lot on another illness.'

Silence.

'I've got AIDS.'

I don't ask him how.

'Why are you here for a drinking problem? The last thing I would do in your situation is worry about how much I drank.'

'I have no control over AIDS. It will be what it wants to be. I can do something about drinking. Mum and Dad deserve that. I've let them down enough. My brother died. I need to control something. I haven't told my group about the AIDS. You're the only one.'

'Why have you told me?'

'I just thought it would make you feel better, knowing there's someone willing to swap.'

I don't reply. He says no more. Angels wear the most ordinary disguises to make out-of-the-ordinary people.

'Zippedee Doo Dah . . .'

Ray continues as I iron my clothes ready for the big day.

'Well, I'm gonna miss you, my friend. *Zippedee Ay!* I'm outta here in the morning. *My oh my, what a wonderful day!'*

'What do you think I should say in my speech?'

He thinks. 'Keep it very simple. When they say. "Mr Barrymore, are you an alcoholic?", say, "Yes! Are you syphilitic?" '

'Thank you, Ray!'

'My pleasure. *Zippedee Doo Dah, Zip-A-Dee Ay!'*

Lights out.

•

Our shameful acts are not unique, and this discovery is our gift when we risk exposure.

Holding Back
Marie Lindquist
Published in 1987 by Hazelden Foundation

270

CHAPTER TWENTY-SIX

Thursday, 19 May

DAY TWENTY-SEVEN

I wish it was Christmas Eve. Then tomorrow I would get to see my presents, instead of press-ants. They can carry ten times their weight, and all in the head.

Midway through breakfast, a name tag lands on table thirty. As I turn to see who placed it, Ray is walking away. He doesn't look back. 'See you around, my friend.'

'Bye, Ray.'

He's gone, swifter than Nurse Devile's needle. I should have known Ray would leave like that. No hug, no small talk, and no promise. It's another airport to him, he's flown the nest. I never got to write him a Benny Hill song. I hope he can conduct his life without it. He always told me, 'I've survived for thirty years, falling out of the sky.'

He doesn't conduct his life, he lives it. The right way. Ray's way.

All the President's Men are everywhere. Clint, chief of security, surveys the whole place. His hands draw a perfect outline as he instructs his troops on the plan for my press call. 'I want men here, and here. Cut off the route here and here. Cover these buildings here.'

This is serious stuff. He's making me smile. It took fewer men to sort out Butch Cassidy and the Sundance Kid! As I pass, Clint slowly turns, 'Where're you goin', fella?'

If he says, 'Make my day', I'm finished.

'To the gazebo.'

'Let me check it first.'

I think you'll find it's still a gazebo. Unless it does impressions. What is he going to find in a gazebo? Hanging journalists?

He calls me over, 'It's okay.'

'Yes, I'm thinking of getting one when I go home.'

'Pardon me?'

'Nothing. Thanks a lot.'

I hope he eases up by the time the press arrive.

The roof of the gazebo is crowned by the name tags of all those who have graduated. A man-made quilt of names to insulate the roof, to keep the heat on those new to here. To remind you you're not alone. I place Ray's tag among those who have fallen in previous conflicts, fallen to addiction. A hidden monument.

On my way to group, Clint is still laying his plans. A news report in an American paper is asking why they are spending so much money on police and security for the English man. I haven't a clue. That's your problem. I originally came to America for a holiday.

Cheryl gets to see me for a brief moment. So much is happening, and, with the five-hour delay between countries, she has to get back to the hotel to deal with everything. And they still haven't found her. All the papers will be covering tomorrow, as well as the TV news network. Oh, great! Todd the newscaster, who left a couple of weeks ago, can say at the end of the bulletin, 'I knew him.'

At group, Tim says, 'Michael will be leaving tomorrow after his press call. So we will say our goodbyes in the usual way. One by one, tell him how you feel, and how you'd like to see him do. Then he can reply. For myself I want to say how impressed I've been with you Michael. You've brought another flavour to the group. You've taken in what it's all about, and helped not only yourself, but the others. If you ever give up comedy, I think you'll make a great psychologist. It's been great. Thank you.'

Brian, TC, Chong and two new boys, say wonderfully encouraging things to me.

Skip is last.

'I . . . I . . . I'm . . . gonna miss you, buddy. You . . . you . . . you gave me hope . . . and friendship. With what you said . . . and how you were with me. Hell you even gave me the shirt off your back (I gave him one of my T-shirts). I know I'm gonna make it out there. I got to. And I know you will too. I'm always there for you. No matter what. Ya understand me? I mean, no matter what. I love you, buddy.'

The family have said it's time to go. I'm a month old, time to face reality. Tim, after I have thanked them all, says nothing for an age. Long enough to let all the tears and laughter of the past month parade by. To salute the new boy as he leaves to conquer.

Outside, I thank Skip personally, for being a measure for me. I won't forget him, ever. I give him my name tag, to put up in the gazebo.

'I'll put it in a special place.'

I don't want to know where he is putting it. It will be among many names, up there with the class of '94. Skip, Howard, D.J. Tony, Sal, shaky Lewis, Jeff (James Caan), Adam, Simon the Apostle, Captain Ray, Jerry the college boy, Tammy, Sarah, Kelly, Black Keith, June, Dale, TC, Brian, Chong the Atheist. Hundreds of others. Rene. And Michael P.

On the rear of the tag it is printed, 'Father Ashley'.

My pseudonym.

After collecting my money from Accounts, all the ladies who look after us in Animal House want to have a picture taken with me. A banned camera appears. My instinct is to be wary of such a thing at this time, but what am I worried about? It has to be time to stop such nonsense. I refuse to be frightened that the boogie man will get me. I resolve not to jump at shadows any more. We secretly pose on the veranda. Slips of paper are passed with addresses for the photos. More news arrives. Jacqueline Onassis is dead. I never met Jacqueline. *It may be presumptuous of me, but you will surely take most of the attention, and, as a present from me for the way you've handled your life, I give all the attention paid to me, to you. I thank you.* Well, it was worth a try. Anyone else?

Ayrton Senna killed. *Dear Ayrton. Talent and skill of your magnitude is rarely seen. Please have, with Jackie O., as much attention as you surely deserve.*

John Smith to be buried tomorrow. It'll take the heat off me.

Well there is, whatever happens, plenty of news around. As you gather, I'm not the most willing of patients. On my last night in my all-too-short bed, I pray.

> *Dear God,*
>
> *All I ask for is happiness. How and when you get me there, I'll leave in your very capable hands. I'm sorry that I haven't spoken to you for so long. I got delayed by quite a few years, while I was making a mess of myself, so that you really had a decent job to do in my refurbishment. I didn't want to bother you with the knocks I've had along the way.*
>
> *Thanks for giving me a good model body, even if it's a bit long. And the hair is on the retreat. I have shouted for you many times in the last forty-odd years. You must have been in the district a month ago, and heard me.*
>
> *Thanks for being there. Thanks for bringing me here. Thanks for all the laughs, and thank you for putting Cheryl into my life.*
>
> *See you in the morning. It's nice to have a friend like you around, even though we don't talk much.*

Lights out.

————————— • —————————

Dear Mr Barrymore

    This is suppose to be my homework. My teacher says we have to write a letter to someone we admire or our favorite person. I can't give you my address cos my dad might be mad if I get a letter.

    In the paper your dad sounds like mine a bit. My dad is always drunk and sometimes belts me. He dosnt belt my sister, but Im not bothered cos boys should be tougher anyway.

    I am pleased that you dont drink anymore. I will never drink I hate alcohol becaus it makes people do nasty things.

    People think I'm brave when I didnt cry for my mam but I still cry sometimes when Im in bed. I think its oka to cry when you're 11 dont you. My dad thinks its soft. I've never told anyone that before. Bet youve never cried before but I thinks its oka to cry for your mother.

From

Michael aged 11 + 10 days.

CHAPTER TWENTY-SEVEN

Friday, 20 May

DAY TWENTY-EIGHT

Naked as a newborn, I'm standing in front of the assembled press, white light from cameras strobing the whole effect. I can hear a piercing cry, 'Get out, get out, get away.'

'Get up. Come on, buddy, get up.' Paul looks down on me.

'I was dreaming.'

'It ain't no dream, buddy, they're on their way.'

Paul leaves me to get ready, and I console myself that at least I've started to dream again. Dream analysts would have an answer for that particular dream. I'm pleased to be out of it.

After breakfast, Leonard tells the community that the programme for today has been changed. Details are posted. And for the morning, Carpenter Hall will be off limits.

'Michael is leaving us today. We wish him well. And I would like to ask him to lead us in the serenity prayer.'

We all stand and hold hands in a huge circle. They all bow their heads. I take a moment to look at them for one last time.

> *God, grant me the serenity*
> *To accept the things I cannot change,*
> *The courage to change the things I can*
> *And the wisdom to know the difference.*
> *Keep coming back, it works if you work it.*

Our hearts are not filled with too much emotion, just smiles and lots of,

'See you, buddy.'

'Good luck, buddy.'

'Thanks, buddy.'

And lastly Skip, 'Hi, buddy!'

'Hi, Skip.'

'No.'

'I'm pleased to hear it.'

'You write me now.'

I walk back to my room. There is no time to linger. A hairdresser, manicurists, and a make-up girl have been ordered, and are waiting for me in Animal House. Back to 'work'. Is this really necessary? Only in America. Reluctantly, I strip down, lie on a portable make-up bed to be polished and given a final dusting for the press. Hands dance over my body, adding twinkle dust. Cheryl never leaves an inch for criticism.

Henri Brandman sits by me, dictating how he wants the press call to go.

'I want you to keep it very simple. There will be no questions and answers.'

I question. 'No jokes?'

'None.'

'Okay.'

Clint walks in.

'How long d'ya want these guys to have?'

He's too excited for Henri's liking.

'When I give you the nod . . .'

'I'll throw them out!'

'No, please, let's keep it calm.'

'Say twenty minutes, and that's it, out?'

'No, I must dictate how it goes. You wait for me to say it's over.'

'I'll have men standing either side of Michael.'

'I don't think that's necessary. They're journalists.'

'Pretty tricky if you ask me.'

'Well . . .' He gives him a 'go away and play with Action Man, not my client' look.

'Oh, so I'll wait for you.'

'Thank you.'

Henri's eyes roll round to me.

'So here's what we'll do . . .'

'Hi, Mikey!'

Father Martin enters. Henri jumps.

'Gettin' ye all fine and dandy I see! I'm gonna miss ya, Mikey, me boy.'

Henri has minutes to go.

'With the greatest respect, Father, I have to get prepared. We have little time. Could you give us a minute?'

'Sure.'

Cheryl enters.

'Hi.' (Cheryl)

'Hi.' (me)

'Hi!' (Henri)

'Hi!!' (Father Martin)

'Hi, hi, hi!!!' (in unison from the make-up department)

Henri tries to continue, 'So where were we?'

'Michael, I just wanna say goodbye.' Leonard enters! 'Hi, everybody!'

'Hi!' (all)

'Mae wants to say goodbye.'

Henri, wishing he had the power of a judge, 'Can I . . .'

Mae enters.

'I just wanna . . . hi, everybody!'

Clint follows.

'You want them in now?'

Henri's head is twisting almost full circle.

'No, please, everyone, I need to get this together. It's very important. I must have quiet.'

From under a towel, I hear the update.

'We all go in. I speak first. Then you. Then Father Martin. Maybe some photos, and that's it. Understood?'

'Yes.'

We go over some legal points. As Henri talks, my mind wanders.

A lawyer, a priest, my wife, the body being prepared. They didn't want to tell me. This was the best way. In my wanderings, my imagination runs riot. Father Martin looks serious, 'Please, Mikey, for the sake of all those boys, for their future, break down and cry as they take you to the chair. You've done with your life. Be an example. Show them you ain't such a hero.'

Cheryl joins the drama, 'Are you mad, my husband?'

Henri seems to be Fonda. If one of the jury has a doubt, then there just might be eleven other angry men.

The hairdresser pops his head into the scene.

'He's ready. Ready as he'll ever be.'

Clint ends the daydream. 'We're ready.'

In reality, Father Martin delays us for a second. 'Mike, my boy, I want you to have this.'

He hands me a framed picture of him meeting the Pope.

'There have been great occasions in my life. This is one of them. And meeting and knowing you is the other. God be with you always. And He will.'

You can't thank a man like this, you thank God you ever met him.

Cheryl holds my hand. Henri walks in front. We decide it's better to leave the Pope picture to one side. Cameras roll, lights flash, pens write frantically. There are no disguises, everyone is playing themselves. For some reason I feel calm. No fear. Cameramen don't push and shove each other, they go about their picture-making with dignity, waiting for the look that will match the journalist's article.

Clint's security flanks all sides of the hall. Father Martin sits to the left of the podium, the life and soul of the alcohol-free party. Cheryl is by my side. As my eyes pan round the room, I feel for the first time that I am in control. It is my life to live how I want. If I decide to close a chapter, I can. They will describe the scene how they want. After the ink has dried, it will become just another story for them. Just another part of my life for me.

Leonard and Tim are sat among them. They give me an encouraging smile. Henri rises to the lectern. The whirring and clicking of cameras increases. No blue Buick.

Henri continues,

'Ladies and Gentlemen, good afternoon. Thank you for coming. May I first introduce Michael, Cheryl, Father Martin of Ashley, Colonel Travers, and myself, Henri Brandman, Michael's lawyer and, I would like to think, a good friend. You will be hearing shortly from Michael and Father Martin. Before you hear from them, I would like to mention a few matters.

'Michael's situation became public by virtue of an article that appeared in the *Daily Mirror* in England, which is also sold in America. The article purported to be Michael's personal and authorised account of his situation. He would wish you to know legal action is contemplated in respect of that article, both in England and in America. Michael's claim in England will be based on breach of his copyright, breach of confidence, libel and passing off. But for the fact that Michael has only just finished his course at Ashley, court proceedings would already be under way. Michael will shortly be instructing American attorneys. It is also envisaged that the article may be the subject of police action against the publishers and editor of the *Daily Mirror*.

'For the total avoidance of doubt, the article is not an authorised or personal account of Michael's situation.

It is understood that the Press Complaints Commission in London are also investigating the *Daily Mirror* article.

'What, however, is the most unsatisfactory aspect is the fact that publication of the article hindered Michael's recuperation programme significantly, and Cheryl's involvement in same.

'It also hindered the recuperation of sixty other patients. You will hear more from Father Martin on this point shortly. Michael has received a number of offers from newspapers for his personalised and authorised account of his situation. He thanks the makers of those offers. He does not wish to accept any of them at present.

'What Michael and Cheryl do wish to have, and very badly require, is a week in Florida in which Michael may continue his recuperation in privacy. Particularly in the light of what I have mentioned before. I would please ask the media to respect their wish for privacy.

'Michael wishes me to indicate that he will be fit and well for his Blackpool season commencing in June.

'May I finish by mentioning that it is not envisaged that there will be a question and answer session after the words from Michael and Father Martin. Nor will there be an opportunity for members of the media to meet with Michael, Cheryl or the Father privately. There will be an opportunity for Michael to be photographed with Cheryl and Father Martin. You are please asked not to go to any other areas in the rehab.

'I now pass you to Michael.'

I rise and say nothing for seconds. Much longer than any comedian would leave between gags. Timing is the art of comedy. Silence is the art of survival. Only four days ago, I stood at this microphone at my graduation. The sound of laughter filled the room. Today no eyes will be rolled to comic effect. I just stand still for the first time in my life. I think of Eddie, and say:

'*Good morning, everyone.*

'*I speak with relief at knowing, and understanding, a disease that has been eating away at my sanity for years.*

'*I have been humbled by the experience here at Ashley, in a community of people from all walks of life. There has been little or no contact with the world outside. I had no idea how the people at home would react. They have responded with encouragement, and love, which leaves me with nothing but pride. I have never allowed my condition to affect my ability to perform, i.e. if people believe that running around the stage means that I am on something, the answer is "no".*

'*Also, never, at any time, has my marriage come into question. It is as strong now as it has ever been. Indeed, it is stronger. It is for Cheryl's sake, and my own, that I came here.*

'*I arrived here a month ago looking for something, and I found me. And it is me I give back to her, and to the people who accept me for what I am.*

'*I cannot express enough thanks and gratitude to Father Martin, the people of Ashley, and Maryland.*

'*Thank you.*'

Father Martin firstly asks the journalists assembled to search deep down to make sure they are free of addiction. It has a quietening effect.

'It has been said that Michael drank the plane dry coming over. He arrived sober, and jumped into the programme the next day with both feet.

'What we found was a man so genuine and so ordinary he won the heart of the whole community. His ego isn't bloated, what you see is what you get. I think he is a great man.

'He told me Ashley was his home. That's quite a compliment. His treatment will improve Michael's life beyond his wildest dreams. When he goes home, he will find that, as marvellous as his work has been, it will be better. The love and respect people had for him before will increase by God himself only knows how much.'

Clint takes no prisoners. 'Okay, that's it, this way.'

Henri injects, 'You may have some photos, gentlemen. Only here at the hall.'

A few of the journalists try to get an extra comment. I just smile in answer. Photos of the happy couple are taken. We are all separated. Clint's men escort the media from the premises. Henri gathers us together for a debrief. He thanks Father Martin, Leonard, Mae, Cheryl and myself. No congratulations are given, just thank you's.

Henri leaves. Leonard and Mae wish us well. The engine starting on the limousine breaks the silence as Cheryl and I say goodbye to Father Martin.

Cheryl holds his face. 'Thank you for giving me back my husband. You're a very special man.'

I stand like a schoolboy who's been found after being missing for a month.

Father Martin openly cries. 'Aren't times like this awful? You find special people in your life, you don't know where they come from, they just appear. God sends you them. When you realise they're special, it's time for them to go. Think of us, don't ever forget us. I will pray for you every day for the rest of my life.'

His scrubbed cheeks make the water from his eyes run fast. I say nothing. Cheryl comforts him. We all hug. As we part, he holds me at arm's length, 'You're a very special person, Mikey.'

'Thank you, Father.'

Paul tells us it's time to go.

We part, leaving Father Martin to ready himself for another mission.

Security lets us into the limo. Two of them are riding along on bikes beside us, a back-up car behind. All the President's Men. They will take no chances.

The limo driver turns to receive clearance to depart. She is a strapping, uniformed woman, her military-style cap slanted back like a New York cabbie. A perfect part, in a perfect setting, for Mae West,

> *I used to be ashamed of the way I lived.*
> *Did you reform?*
> *I got over being ashamed.*

(*Going To Town*)

As we pull away, a hand raps at the window. I ask the driver to stop. I lower the window. Paul looks serious, 'I just wanted to say, Good luck, buddy.'

'Thanks, Paul.'

'And by the way . . .'

'Yes?'

'If you do come back again, next time I won't let you get away with the chocolate you had stashed in your room.'

He smiles.

I smile.

The limo pulls away.

I look back at Ashley. As a final farewell, the maple leaves give one of their finest displays.

When the limo pulls up beside the Lear jet, I remember that I'm not the best of flyers. The scene before me doesn't help. I wish my imagination wasn't so vivid. I can see Buddy Holly, Will Rogers, Patsy Cline, and Glen Miller, waving to us. Two young pilots welcome us aboard. Clint is still on edge. That's where I leave him, on the edge. Within minutes of arriving, we are taxiing along the runway. The co-pilot turns to ask us to put on our safety belts. As he turns, I see Ray's face on the young man's shoulders.

'*Well, time to take off. Time to take off your shoes, hit the whisky, and let's boogie.*'

I smile. The young man looks at me inquisitively. Once in the air, he walks back. 'Would you like a drink?'

Cheryl and I look at each other. She lets me speak for myself.

'Yes, please.'

'We have whisky, gin, vodka, beer, wine. I don't really know what's what. I don't drink.'

The similarity between him and Ray evaporates.

'I'll have a coke, please.'

We land early evening in Palm Beach. Another limo. Another town. No press. No hullabaloo.

Back home, and in America, the evening news is showing my speech at the rehab.

We arrive at the house that I left a month ago. The whole place is covered in yellow ribbon. I sit on my own for a while, in exactly the same spot I remember sitting last time I was here. I sit for hours.

At night, in bed, Cheryl and I hold on like two strangers thrown together in a violent storm. Both relying on each other to survive. I look at her for as long as I can. I don't say a word. I don't have to. For now, no more speeches. Carly Simon's voice fills the room, singing, 'My Romance'.

My eyelids close, as a final curtain on the day, and a month in my life.
Lights out.
Candlelight on.

———————•———————

Dear Mike,

How are you! I'm feeling great and staying clean, and it has been so easy so far that it's scary. If that isn't a miracle, I sure as hell don't know what one is.

Please – be well and happy. You are in my prayers daily. I hope you have the soul-happiness I do, because it is simply wonderful. I'm working my programme and it seems to be working – one day at a time.

Your friend always,
Love, Skip

CHAPTER TWENTY-EIGHT

Homeward Bound

I had a week to get back into the real world – before getting back to work. The lull in proceedings was welcome. The press did leave us to have a break.

I attended my first outside AA meet. They were much more relaxed than at Ashley. Cheryl and I were getting used to being back together again. Going to the AA meets became like a drug in itself. They are very addictive. I let all that had happened take a back seat for a few days, and just played. Everything looked and felt different. It's hard to explain without sounding like a fanatical religious crusader. Believe me, everything is brighter on the other side of your mind. The unaltered side.

During the week, more news reports of my press call came in. We flew home, leaving America on Independence Day.

I walked into the Arrivals hall. The cameras flashed, yet again. We were met by Andy, who looks after our international flights at Heathrow. With his broad Scottish accent, he brought it all down to a sensible level. 'What the hell have you been up to? You said you'd by in by eleven o'clock. That was two months ago. We've been worried sick.'

The smile I gave him was the one used in the papers welcoming me back.

Mike, my driver's first words were, 'Don't tell me, I bet I can guess where you've been for your holiday! Bleedin' 'ell, for the last month, you've been on the telly and in the papers that much, it's like you never left. How are you?'

'Fine.'

'Good, fancy a drink?'

I had to get used to all the banter. It didn't worry me. It helped me get through the next hurdle. It was a few days before my opening night at the Opera House, Blackpool. My first live show for a year.

I met Alan Harding for the first time in two months.

'Oi, you.'

He has a way with words.

'I phoned to meet you in Florida. Cheryl said you were out fishing. One night, I can understand. Even a week. But two months? You okay?'

'Yes.'

'Good, let's get back to work.'

We rehearsed day and night.

The opening night, three thousand people, including the media, attended my return.

What has happened to me has made me a happier, more contented man. It doesn't stop me getting uptight, reacting to things. I used to deal with problems by having a drink; I don't now. I don't want to change things. I'm in no rush. I live a day at a time.

You can't give a pill to an addict. An addict doesn't take a pill, he takes the bottle.

There are two sides to everything, but you don't want an audience to see the other side. I don't think it's fair on them. I'm not so frightened of people's perception of me any more. I don't mind the warts and all. When all this happened at the rehab, it took a weight off me. I can cope with living with just me.

I learnt that if I make myself happy, everyone around me's happier. I've got the ability to make people around me laugh. I also have an ability to make their lives a misery. A total misery. I can switch from one to the other. Mood swings. The nature of the disease. A defence mechanism working in reverse. You know, that defence mechanism that I talked of when I was a kid, where I started. That defence mechanism where I made people laugh. I just thought, 'I'll make them cry as well.'

It was like screaming all the time. Not now.

Just talking brings up things, you suddenly get pictures in your mind, and I can see myself as a kid, and it ain't all so bad now. I survived it. There ain't a problem in the world that isn't solvable. There's a lot to live for. I like being forty-two. I've got mates. People who actually care about me.

I wouldn't do any harm to anybody. I never have done. I find no joy in being angry with anyone. That's why talking about it is so good. That's why the only cure for this disease is pouring out what you feel to someone.

After all, I've come through it. I've been there, done it. And I've exorcised the demons. I was taught at Ashley to live my life a day at a time. I learned to walk the walk, and talk the talk. They taught me to say how it is. If it ends tomorrow, this is the best day I've had in my life.

On the side of stage, as my overture played, Cheryl held me, and just said, 'I love you.'

I walked centre stage, looked up, saw Eddie's face.

The curtain rose.

The entire audience rose to their feet.

I was back in business.

---•---

One night a man had a dream. He dreamed he was walking along the beach with the Lord. Across the sky flashed scenes from his life. For each scene he noticed two sets of footprints in the sand: one belonged to him, and the other to the Lord.

When the last scene of his life flashed before him, he looked back at the footprints in the sand. He noticed that many times along the path of his life, there was only one set of footprints.

He also noticed that it happened at the very lowest and saddest times in his life.

This really bothered him, and he questioned the Lord about it. Lord, you said that once I decided to follow you, you'd walk with me all the way, But I have noticed that during the most troublesome times in my life, there is only one set of footprints. I don't understand why, when I needed you most, you would leave me.

The Lord replied. My precious precious child. I love you, and I would never leave you during your times of trial and suffering. When you see only one set of footprints, it was then that I carried you.

Footprints
Author Unknown